Married A Stripper

M. S. Parker - Cassie Wild

ISBN-13:
978-1542803144

ISBN-10:
1542803144

Table of Contents

Part One

Chapter 1

Piety

My head.

Shit…my head.

I had a concussion once, but it hadn't hurt like this. Moaning, I pulled a pillow over my head and prayed for oblivion. Or death. Right now, I was willing to take either one.

The pounding inside my skull only got worse, and as the bed shifted under me, my belly started to slosh around, making me feel nauseated too. That was just *lovely.*

The bed shifted again, and I snapped, "Would you be still?"

"Sorry," a rough voice muttered.

A rough, deep *sexy* voice.

Somehow, that fact managed to penetrate the fog of pain and exhaustion, and I tugged the pillow an inch lower. It didn't help. It actually made things worse because some moron – probably me – had forgotten to close the curtains last night and now the piercing bright light of a Las Vegas morning was trying to singe my retinas. But I needed to know why I'd just heard a *man's* voice in my room.

No, in my *bed*.

There shouldn't *be* a man's voice in my room.

Or anywhere in my vicinity.

I tugged the pillow lower.

Nope.

A little lower.

A disgruntled grumble came from my left, and I turned my head.

Blond hair, sun-streaked and rumpled, hid half his face, but there was no denying one simple fact.

There was most definitely a naked man just inches beside me.

And I sure as hell didn't know him.

Yelping, I half jumped out of the bed, but fell on my ass as the blankets refused to come with me. They were tangled around his body, hanging on him for long moments before finally coming free.

I scrambled backward and clambered to my feet just as he shoved upward onto his elbows, looking around with a surly snarl.

Oh. Wow.

He was…oh. Wow.

And naked.

Oh. Wow.

"Who the hell are you?" I blurted, my hangover momentarily forgotten as I found myself staring into a pair of beautiful, pale blue eyes.

He blinked, the irritation in his eyes fading, replaced

by the same confusion I felt. "I…" Thick lashes, black and dusted with gold on the tips, fell over those amazing eyes, but even that couldn't hide one plain and simple fact – he was checking me out the same way I'd just checked him out.

Immediately, my nipples tightened, stabbing into the sheet I held clutched to my breasts.

"Ah, the name's Kaleb," he said softly and thrust a hand through his unruly hair.

A shiver raced down my spine as he spoke. An accent. I was such a sucker for an accent. "You…" I swallowed and told myself to get a grip. "You're Australian. Sydney?"

A thick blond brow shot up. "Good ear. Most Yanks wouldn't recognize the difference between somebody from Sydney versus somebody from Perth. Spent much time there?"

"Um, no." With a weak smile, I shrugged. "My…family travels a lot. Or they used to." I shrugged, not wanting to get into any of that. Besides, I had other things on my mind. Like why he was in my room. Although *that* was obvious. He was naked. I was naked. I reached up to push my hair back. Sunlight glinted off something, and I froze.

"Oh." Swallowing nervously, I stared at the gaudy thing on my left hand. "Oh, *shit.*"

I glared at him, only to see him standing by the side of the bed, staring down at something I didn't think was his toes.

What in the hell was he doing? Admiring himself?

He reached down and understanding dawned, mostly because I saw the empty condom wrapper on the nightstand. Blood rushed to my face, and my head started to spin.

3

No. Oh, no.

"A dream," I whispered. "This is all a crazy dream."

I waited for the sexy Aussie to tell me otherwise or maybe come over and pick me up, kiss me…something that would convince me that maybe this *was* a dream. He was too busy walking toward the bathroom, treating me to an excellent view of his perfect ass – not an image I could easily look away from.

"Not happening," I said and pinched myself hard enough to hurt. Things were looking more and more insane by the minute.

In desperation, I rushed for the door that opened into the adjoining suite.

The lights were still off, and it was thankfully dim in there. Astra, my best friend, must have remembered to close the blinds, the wench.

I fumbled through the dark living room area and found my way into the bedroom. The blinds were pulled there too. I was tempted to just lay down and curl up next to her, but I needed to know what was going on.

She was snoring softly, and when I shook her, she swatted at my hand. "Not today, baby," she mumbled.

"Wake up, Astra. It's me."

She swatted at me again. "Oomph."

"Astra!" I shook her harder. When that brought no response, I went to the windows and grabbed a handful of curtains, jerking them open. She screeched behind me.

"Bitch! Close those damn curtains!"

"Wake up and talk to me," I said, ignoring her. If I could handle the marching band in my skull, she could handle the light.

She cracked an eye open, bloodshot and tired. Okay, she probably had a marching band of her own.

But unlike *me*, Astra didn't get totally wasted and

4

forget things when she got drunk. "What happened last night?" I asked, holding up my hand, wiggling my fingers to give her something to focus on.

A wide smiled curled her lips, and it even went to her eyes, bloodshot and tired as they were. "What do you mean, what happened? Forgotten already, sweetcheeks?"

"Astra," I said slowly, praying for patience. "I'm going to kill you, chop you into tiny pieces, and toss the remains out all over the desert. You'll be eaten by scavengers before your family even knows you're missing."

"Oh…savage." She looked unfazed and sat up, lazily stretching her arms over her chest. The skinny strapped silk nightshirt she wore barely managed to cover her considerable...assets.

I wouldn't have had so much trouble. But then again, her breasts were probably the only thing holding the shirt up, with its deep vee neckline and high cut sides. Astra had one hell of a body.

That nightshirt would've gaped down to my belly button. My body was strong and firm in all the right places, but an abundance of cleavage was one thing God had not blessed me with. I was smart, attractive. Confident too. I also had ridiculously wealthy parents who tried to control my life, but no excessive boobs in sight.

The man upstairs had also seen fit to give me a best friend who was ridiculously insane. She sat on the edge of the bed, grinning at me even though I suspected she was every bit as hungover as I was.

That was bad.

Very bad.

If I got too drunk, things got a bit hazy for me – okay, a *lot* hazy – but Astra could pack it away like a

5

sailor and not forget a thing.

"What are you grinning at?" I waved my hand in her face, making light flash off the cheap plastic ring with its gaudy fake diamond. "And what the hell is this?"

"Isn't it fantastic? I had to spend like five bucks getting it out of that stupid bubble gum machine after I conned some guy into selling me the quarters. I had to flash him a look down my shirt."

She leaned backed on the bed, her weight braced on her hands. I stared at her. "What are you–?"

I didn't get to finish because she blathered on. "I'll tell you what, those things are rigged. They're even worse than the slot machines. I got so many stupid tattoos. I don't know what I'm going to do with them." She shrugged. "I guess I'll give them to my cousin. Or maybe one of the kids down at the shelter back home."

I shoved my hand through my hair. "Forget the tattoos!" I waved my hand at her again, the ring flashing at me mockingly. "This! Explain."

"Wow. You really don't remember anything?" She laughed and got up. Wearing nothing but the nightshirt and a skimpy pair of low cut panties, she came over to me and looped an arm around my neck. "Sweetheart, that handsome hunk of man flesh from Down Under…"

She paused dramatically, arching her brows as she waited.

"What?" I demanded, ready to shake her.

"He's your husband." She winked at me and spun away, pausing to stretch before she picked up a robe and tossed it at me. "Here. Put this on. Toga parties are so…*college*."

The robe hit my chest and fell to the floor.

Gaping at her, I sank down on the edge of the bed while my brain struggled to process her words.

6

Husband.

That was the word she used. I'd heard her correctly, I think. But...maybe not. "Astra, what did you just say?" My voice came out in a weak whisper, not quite the calm and steady tone I'd been shooting for.

"You got married, girl!" She laughed, sounded delighted. "It's crazy, the things that can happen in Vegas. Man, I *love* this city."

This was a joke. It had to be a joke. But my heart was racing, and my face felt strangely hot. Pinpricks seemed to dance all up and down my spine, and my head was spinning, but it had nothing to do with a hangover.

"You can't be serious. You're joking, right?" I gave her a look of sheer, hopeful desperation. She had to be joking. Had to.

Astra smiled, and this time, it was a little less Mad Hatter and a bit more reassuring. "Piety, babe, it was your idea."

"No." Shaking my head emphatically, I said, "No. No, no, no...I get a little reckless, sure, but this has *Astra Traore* written all over it."

"Okay...well." She poked out her lower lip and shrugged. "Maybe you made a joke, and I thought it was funny, and we got to talking about it. But you were all in!"

"Why would I go *all in* about marrying a stranger!" I wanted to scream. Or maybe laugh hysterically. My belly revolted, and another thought occurred to me. I just might be sick. Where was the damn bathroom? I knew where it was on my side of the suite, but in here? Thinking just too damn hard right now, but I didn't want to walk back to my room.

He was in there.

That beautiful, gorgeous – what had Astra called

him? – hunk of man flesh. A beautiful piece of man flesh. Too beautiful.

Frazzled, I stared at the floor. The robe caught my eye, and I picked it up, pulling it on before twisting the sheet into a ball. Then I looked up at my best friend. "Since you seem to have a clear grasp of the situation, why don't you tell me why I supposedly married this guy?"

"There's no supposedly about it." She shrugged and sat down next to me. "You married him. We've got it on video, and we're going to upload it onto YouTube."

YouTube...

"You're nuts. You're *crazy*. My parents will freak out. Hell, this might kill my dad." Silas Van Allen just might have a heart attack. His precious daughter getting married to some stranger in Las Vegas? I laughed shakily. "Well, we *did* talk about finding a way to get him off my ass about *settling down*."

"Exactly!" Astra beamed at me.

Rising to my feet, I pointed a finger at her. "Don't give me this crap about it being my idea. Maybe I made a joke, but how drunk was I? And how drunk were you?"

Astra looked hurt. "What? Don't you think you're capable of something this dastardly and brilliant?"

"How about *insane*?" I flung a hand toward the other suite of rooms. "That's a human being over there. Apparently, we went and decided to do something just to screw with my dad, and we're dragging him into it. You know what my dad is like!"

"Oh, chill out, PS."

I made a face at the nickname. "Don't tell me to chill out. I *can't*. I'm *freaking* out." Hearing movement next door, I looked at Astra helplessly. "What do I do?" I whispered.

8

"Oh, honey." She came toward me and wrapped an arm around my shoulders. "Relax. Kaleb was all in with the idea once we explained how tight-assed your daddy is." She stood up and held out a hand. "Come on."

I stared at her waving fingers, wondering what she wanted me to do.

"What?"

"We should go talk to him." She smiled again and took my hand, trying to pull me after her.

Shaking my head, I remained where I was. "What kind of idiot Justice of the Peace would marry two people who are obviously drunk? Considering how my head feels, I must have been walking into walls."

"Not quite." She gave me a smile of sympathy. "You maintained *really* well. And as to the JP? You flashed enough money. You do that, most people will bend the rules a little bit, especially for a Congressman's daughter."

Groaning, I dropped my face into my hands. "Great. Just great." I turned into a lush after two days in Las Vegas and had also lost touch with my inner moral compass – *bribing* a Justice of the Peace? "I'm turning into my parents. Oh, shit. What if I'm turning into my *mother*?"

Chapter 2

Kaleb

"Would you be still?"

The voice was husky and soft, straight out of a porn flick, and I rolled toward it, seeking out the warmth and scent of a woman. Sexy and sweet, it went straight to my dick, which was already doing its morning salute.

"Sorry," I muttered.

I was about ready to reach for her when a high-pitched yelp had me jerking up in bed. "What's–?"

The *wrong* got caught in my throat at the sight of her. I don't think she even heard me anyway. She was too busy wrapping herself in a sheet and gaping at me. After a second, she snapped her jaw shut. I clenched mine so it wouldn't fall open.

"Who the hell are you?" She stared at me, her big, dark blue eyes wide and startled.

"Ah, the name's Kaleb."

"You…you're Australian. Sydney?"

"Good ear." *Talk. Act human. Don't stare at her damn tits.* "Most Yanks wouldn't recognize the difference between somebody from Sydney versus somebody from Perth. Spent much time there?"

"Um, no. My…family travels a lot. Or they used to."

I wasn't having much luck not staring at those perfect, perky breasts, so I climbed out of bed and looked around. My head was still cloudy, and it hurt like hell. What happened last night? What time was it?

A thousand sticky thoughts pushed through my head, but I couldn't untangle them.

I could do one thing – use the damn bathroom.

"Fuck," I muttered.

I didn't think she heard. She was swearing about something too, but I didn't think it had anything to do with the rubber that was in a rather precarious position on my semi-erect penis.

Grabbing it, I looked up and caught sight of her staring at me.

"A dream." She closed her eyes as she whispered it. "This is all a crazy dream."

Not likely. If it was a dream, I would have been balls-deep inside her, not standing there with a bloody headache and a crumpled up condom in my fist.

I stalked into the bathroom, desperate to get away from the woman for a minute. I had to think.

I just needed a minute.

Once I was in the bathroom, I shut the door and leaned back. "What the fuck happened?" I muttered.

Spying a waste bin, I tossed the rubber into it and tended to business.

The nagging sense that I'd forgotten something – something important – tugged at my brain as I moved to the sink to wash up, but my mind stayed annoyingly blank, and I finally had to admit that it wouldn't do any good to just stand in this bathroom while that raven-haired beauty stayed out there, probably getting more and more frustrated.

As I washed my hands, I stared at my reflection in the mirror. I looked hung over and pretty damn shitty. That wouldn't go over well with the new boss.

New boss.

"Fuck."

I grabbed a towel and wrapped it around my waist before leaving the room. Clock! Where was a damn clock? The woman, along with another, came through the adjoining suite's door at the same time.

I still didn't see a clock. "What time is it?" I said.

"We…um…" The girl from the bed looked at her friend, a shorter, cute thing with curls, curves and a wide smile. "We need to talk."

"I can't," I barked. "I'm going to miss my bus if I haven't already. What time is it?"

I couldn't lose this job. There was too much depending on it.

Spying my clothes in a tangle on the floor, I grabbed them and almost took them into the bathroom, but for right now, modesty be damned. Without another thought, I dropped the towel and grabbed my jeans, jabbing one foot then the other into the legs as the women gaped at me. *Yeah, commando, ladies.*

"Look, you need to slow it down," she said, giving her friend a desperate look.

"I *can't*, sweetheart." I grabbed my shirt, and something thudded onto the floor. My phone. When I grabbed it, the screen lit up, showing the time.

"Dammit! I'll barely make it."

"Wait," she cried out, cutting in front of me when I would have sat down to put my shoes on.

She looked as desperate as I felt. Maybe she had a job riding on the next few minutes too.

I had doubts about that though. The room we were in was the kind I'd expect to see given to a princess – or a queen. That was what she made me think of – royalty, even wearing that robe and a worried expression. It was in the way she carried herself, so haughty and above it all.

And I didn't have time to think about how *proper* she might be. "Anyway, I hate to dash, but I have to go." I cut around her and sat down, shoving my feet into my shoes. I grabbed my shirt and pulled it on as I stood up.

She was right there, not two inches away when my head cleared the material.

"You need to be quiet and listen." She poked me in the chest with her index finger.

A gaudy, fake ring glinted up at me.

"Nice taste in jewelry, love."

"I'm so glad you think so," she said, giving me a sarcastic smile. She held her hand up and waved it back and forth in front of my face. "It's a damn *wedding* ring."

"Wedding…" I blinked. "Fuck me, are you *married*?"

If she was, she needed a better man. One who'd put a real ring on her finger and not that horrible piece of junk.

She blinked at me, shaking her head. "You're beautiful, but maybe you're not too bright," she said slowly.

I stiffened instinctively at the insult before reminding myself it didn't matter what some prima donna American babydoll thought of me. I had enough to deal with anyway.

"Aw, my feelings are hurt," I said, forcing out a mock sigh. "Anyway, I've got to run. I've got a new job I'm starting, and if I'm late, I'm screwed. You can…look, I'm sorry. I was drunk, and I didn't know you were married. Doubt it will make much difference, but tell your husband I'm sorry."

"Fine," she said to my back. "The man I slept with last night wants me to tell you he's sorry."

I froze. One hand on the door knob, I stared at the pale, gleaming oak and tried to make sense of those words. *The man I slept with…*

Slowly, I turned around and stared at her. "Is that supposed to be a joke?"

She had crossed her arms over her chest as stood

13

there, glaring at me, her chin in the air. "Do I *look* like I'm laughing?"

No. She looked like she was torn between crying and hitting something. I could sympathize with the feeling.

"You…" I looked back at the ring, then at her. "Are you telling me…?"

Her lip curled into a snarl. "We got hitched last night, *sweetheart*."

"That's not possible," I said, shaking my head. "I don't even know your name."

"That's what I said. But my friend assures me the wedding *did* happen. She recorded it. We've got a license…somewhere. As to our names…" She came toward me, her right hand outstretched.

Good, if I had to look at the awful plastic trinket another moment…

Slowly, I took her hand, staring into those gorgeous eyes.

"I'm Piety," she murmured.

"Kaleb." Then I laughed, feeling like the entire world had flipped upside down. "Look, I'm sorry, but I…I still have to go. If I lose this job, I'm screwed."

Chapter 3

Piety

I finally convinced him that we're married, and he's worried about losing his job.

I could have rolled my eyes, but then I reminded myself I wasn't someone who'd ever had to worry about money before. When you didn't have to do that, it was easy to dismiss things that seemed relatively simple.

"We have to figure this out," I said. "I mean, your boss will understand, right?"

He gave me a tight look and shot another glance at his phone – checking the time. He swore and shoved it into his pocket. "Too late now. The bus leaves in two minutes. I'll never make it." A scowl twisted his features and he spun away, swearing under his breath.

I took a step forward, only to stop myself. I'd been about to comfort him.

I didn't even *know* this guy, and I wanted to make him feel better.

"How in the hell did this happen?" he demanded, still facing away from us.

"Well…" Astra laughed a little, as she gave him a nervous look.

I had a bad feeling we might have just messed up his life even more than mine. Judging by the look she gave me, Astra was thinking the same thing.

"It's pretty funny, really. We were all drinking. You were at the bar, and you were cute, so I dragged Piety over to sit down and talk with you. We all got to talking, and we told you about how Piety's parents are *serious* control freaks and that they're pushing her toward this guy who is *so* fucking lame. He gets excited talking about spreadsheets." She paused as the stranger – *Kaleb*, I reminded myself – turned around. "Spreadsheets!"

"I'm still waiting to hear how talking about spreadsheets got two strangers married."

"Yeah. Me too." I rubbed a hand over my belly because I was still feeling seriously nauseated and my head was spinning. Feeling his eyes on me, I glanced his way and stopped rubbing, reaching up to clutch at the neck of my robe instead. He wasn't gawking at me or anything, but there was something about the way he watched me that was unsettling at best. "Seriously, I don't get how I could have thought this was a good idea, drunk or not."

"But you *did*." Astra grabbed my shoulders and shook me a little. I groaned, batting her hands away.

"Stop it." I sat down on the edge of the couch and glanced from him to her. "Explain why I thought this was a good idea."

"I did–"

"Astra." Giving her a hard look, I waited.

"Fine." She huffed out a breath and then gave the hottie from Down Under a brilliant smile. "See, her parents are the *most* uptight people you've ever met, and they are constantly pushing her toward somebody who could be a clone of her dad. In character, not physically,

16

because that could be gross. But he is a stuffed shirt and so uptight. They keep nagging her–"

Kaleb held up a hand, and Astra went politely quiet. She beamed at him, and he returned the smile, although his was a lot less...excited. "Look, this is all fascinating, and I assume I should know something about my...wife's family. But none of this is answering anything."

"It *is*," Astra said emphatically. "Just give me a moment. "See, that's why we're here. They were driving her crazy, and after they tried to set her up on some sort of crazy couples thing with this killjoy, we knew we had to get away for a while."

"And we came here," I said, sighing. "Astra, you're not exactly explaining." I took a deep breath. "I remember going down to the bar for drinks. Then...nothing until this morning when I opened my eyes and saw this ring. So explain *this* part of things."

"You thought it would be funny." Astra sighed and moved over to sit beside me. She took my hand and then looked over to Kaleb. "You were on the stool next to us. There was a woman...she was flirting with you and pushing really hard. Piety could tell you weren't into it, so she told her to lay off."

Kaleb shook his head as if trying to shake the memory back into it. "What happened next?"

"Well, the woman got pissy and asked her what the problem was. Piety said you were her fiancé. You laughed about it. When she got up and stormed off, we asked you to join us." Astra shrugged. "We got to talking and...well, Piety said it was too bad her dad hadn't been there. If he'd heard her telling some chick that you two were engaged, even though it was just a joke, he'd have a heart attack. And I told you guys you should do it – marry him. I'd videotape it, and we could upload it to

17

YouTube."

I rubbed my forehead, feeling a pounding headache that had nothing to do with alcohol.

"Why, oh, why would I think this was a good idea?" I muttered.

"Because we were drunk and stupid, and you were pissed off." Astra looked over at Kaleb. "You were pissed off about something too. I don't know what because you wouldn't say. But you loosened up a bit, and we all got to laughing and having a good time."

Kaleb raised an eyebrow. "A good time still doesn't equal getting married."

"I..." I grimaced and then looked at Astra before meeting Kaleb's eyes again. "My dad is a senator. Silas Van Allan from Philadelphia. He's planning on running for president, and my mom...well, she's already mentally redecorating the White House. They've got ideas for how their lives will be, and they're doing everything they can to make sure *I* do everything *I* can to help expedite his career and improve his image."

"Come on, they can't be all that bad," he said, crooking a smile at me.

My belly flipped at the sight of it. A dimple, one that deepened into a wider groove as his smile grew, caused my heart to stutter a few beats. Dimples. That smile. That accent. Well, if I was going to go and marry a stranger, I sure as hell picked a hot one.

Then my brain locked in on what he said.

"Oh, they're worse." Heaving out a sigh, I looked over toward the window, not seeing anything around me but the life they were trying to force me into. "They hate my job, hate the things I enjoy. Sometimes I think they only had me because they thought about all the photo ops I'd present them with. That and everybody *knows* that a

18

family man is much more trustworthy."

Rolling my eyes, I managed to smile at him.

"And that's it. Somehow my shitty mood translated into *hey, let's do something stupid*. We're in Vegas, after all. Right, Kaleb?" I hesitated before asking, "It is Kaleb?"

He gave me a short nod, still looking distracted. He pulled out his phone again, checked it.

"Look, this job...I'll call you a cab, pay for it. We can discuss this again later?" I hated how much he was stressing over this job. And I could tell he was. He'd only checked his phone like...oh, ten times in the past five minutes.

"No such luck, Piety." His accent gave my name a sharper sound, but I liked it. His smile was sharp too, full of edges that might cut. "The bus I needed to catch was leaving the city. They're gone by now."

"Oh." My belly dropped a little more, and I rubbed my temple. "Okay, I'll find some other way to get you where you need to go. We'll rent a car or something. Just what is it you do?"

"I'm with Flames Down Under." He said it calmly, staring me straight in the face, but there was a daring glint in his eye.

I couldn't understand why. That meant nothing to me. "And just what *is* Flames Down Under?"

"Oh...*oh!*" Astra squealed and started to laugh, clapping. "This is *perfect*. Piety, it's *perfect*. Really!"

She laughed even harder, all but bent over now.

"What's so funny?" I glared at her while Kaleb moved over to the window and stared outside. Probably searching for his bus.

"Flames Down Under. Honey, he's a stripper! Flames Down Under is kinda...well, they are almost like

19

the Chippendales, but from Australia…and *way* hotter, if you ask me."

Oh, shit.

My face went hot, and I shoved upright, glaring at Astra. "You think this is funny? My dad is going to *freak*. Dammit, Astra, stop laughing! I married a stripper! My parents are going to kill me!"

Chapter 4

Piety

The second the words left my mouth, I wanted to take them back.

Appalled at myself, I looked over at him and said, "I'm so sorry. I mean, not that I really…it's just…"

"It's fine." He made an absent, clearly distracted motion with his hand, his gaze once more returning to the window, his jaw locked tight.

"I really am sorry. I imagine you work pretty damn hard and I–"

"It's *fine*," he said, his accent doing nothing to soften the word, and this time, he looked at me. His jaw was tight, but there was something about the way his eyes met mine that made me think he had other things on his mind besides my unintended insult.

"Are you…um…well…I know you're worried about the job, but I swear, I'll get you wherever you need to be."

He shook his head, his expression pinched. "I need that fucking job. I need the *money*. It's…never mind."

Something flashed in his pale eyes, a mix of fury and

helplessness, and my belly twisted into a hundred ugly little knots. Something was going on. I didn't know what it was, but I had a feeling it was bad. And I wanted to help him. Stranger, husband, it didn't matter. No one deserved to look like that.

"Hey!" Astra clapped her hands, drawing our attention to her. "I've got an idea. Kaleb, this could really help you out."

The look in her eyes was sly, and her smile had that devious slant to it that I knew all too well. Shit.

I almost told her I didn't want to hear it, but sometimes her ideas *did* have merit. Still, I was more than a little suspicious as I studied her. She was practically rubbing her hands together in glee, she looked so pleased with herself, and that was never good.

"Just what is this…idea?" I asked warily.

"Hire him." Astra moved a little closer, standing between us like a referee as she looked from me to him.

Kaleb and I stared at each other blankly.

"Hire me?"

"Hire him?"

We spoke at the same time, and the inanity of it left us both smiling awkwardly at each other. He gestured to me, and I cocked an eyebrow at my best friend. "Don't take this wrong, Astra, but I'm not exactly the sort of woman who wants her own personal exotic dancer."

"That's not what I meant." She rolled her eyes. "But for the record – you're nuts. Why *wouldn't* you want your own private exotic dancer?"

"Just because you want your own personal pool boy, your own masseuse, a personal shopper, your own driver…"

I rolled my eyes at her, although I was teasing. She had none of those things. She joked about it, but while we'd both been born with the proverbial silver spoon, neither of us liked being waited on or catered to non-stop. Each of us had a personal assistant, but that was simply because we couldn't keep things straight thanks to everything our parents were constantly expecting us to keep up with.

"Look, this has all been fun, but I need to figure out how to get to my gig," Kaleb interjected.

"We've already figured that out." Astra folded her arms across her chest, looking determined. "Just at least hear me out. If you don't want to do it, I'll rent a car and chase down the bus myself." She waggled her eyebrows. "I wouldn't mind seeing Flames Down Under all up close and personal."

"But—"

"Five minutes!" She moved, placing herself in front of the door, spreading her hands against it. She tossed in a bright smile and then looked at me. "Trust me, PS. It's *way* better than just uploading the video to YouTube. You can prove to your parents that you're done letting them dictate your life. *And* we can help Kaleb out since we went and screwed up his job."

"As fascinating as this is, whatever you're planning, I don't think you can pay me what I'd be making with Flames," Kaleb said, looking more and more pissed off by the minute. "I'm the new boy and I'm still learning, but I made fifteen hundred dollars last week – American – and that doesn't include the tips."

I didn't blame him for being pissed. Fifteen hundred dollars was a decent amount of money to a lot of people. Except I could do better. I didn't know what pushed me to say anything, but to my surprise, I was the one to speak before Astra could pipe in. "I can pay more than that."

He swung his head around, a startled expression on

his face.

"I can." I lifted a shoulder. "Granted, I don't know just what Astra has in mind, but I can pay more than fifteen hundred a week. My assistant makes almost that."

He started to say something else, but he stopped abruptly, shaking his head. "It doesn't matter how much your assistant makes, unless you plan on hiring me to take her place. Look, I really need to be going."

"Just listen." Astra placed herself between him and the door. "Just listen to me for five minutes, and within the next half hour, Piety will *pay* you fifteen hundred, *and* we'll make sure you get a ride to wherever your bus is heading if you decide you don't want to do things my way."

That caught him off guard.

Me too.

I mean, it wasn't like I couldn't afford it, but it was irritating when other people got free and loose with my money. From behind him, I gave Astra a dark look, then wiped it off my face before I moved to sit down on the couch.

"It's a fair deal," I said, keeping my voice neutral. "After all, we messed things up. We can at least rectify the situation."

"Absolutely."

Kaleb looked from me to her and then back. Then he shook his head. "The two of you are insane. You know that, right?"

Chapter 5

Kaleb

Insane.

It didn't even come close.

And I wasn't any better.

Hands braced against the shower wall, I stared down at the floor. Water dripped into my face and eyes, ran down my cheekbones and chin, then along my nose before falling to my feet.

Water pounded into me from five different angles, the pressure so high, I almost felt like I was getting a top rate massage.

There was one thing to be said for this set-up so far – the shower was top-notch.

I could stay in here for another week.

Or at least another hour or so. If I could do that, maybe things would start making sense.

Somehow between last night and now, I'd gotten married to one of the most elegant, beautiful women I'd ever met. Not to mention, she was funny and determined. And that was just from the little bit of time I'd spent with her.

And her shower…

Groaning, I angled my back so that one of the jets hit it full on, pounding away stress that felt like it had been building for years.

I needed to make some phone calls. I had to call my boss for one. Even though the bus had already left, I owed it to him – and the rest of the guys – to let them know I wouldn't be in. Not today, not any other day in the near future.

I felt like a piece of shit leaving them hanging, but even if I could get to the next tour stop, the bottom line was that Piety was offering more money. A heck of a lot more money. Once I'd heard her friend out, Piety had disappeared, and in less than twenty minutes, she'd returned with cash as promised.

But it hadn't been fifteen hundred.

It was two thousand, and she said if I helped her out, she'd pay me five *times* that.

Ten grand. The exact amount I needed.

While she was gone, I'd looked her up on my phone. It wasn't hard to find information about her. She was indeed a senator's daughter and a bit of a do-gooder. Her parents looked like they had a pair of matching sticks shoved up their asses. If they were as bad as she was letting on...

But even as doubt formed in my mind, I pushed it away. My parents were gone. It was hard to think about doing something just to piss them off although I knew I'd done it a time or two. This, well this was a bit more extreme than anything I could've thought up. Still...

Shoving away from the wall, I reached for the shampoo. I couldn't stay in here forever, as much as I was tempted. Even the toiletries smelled like money and the scent hit me hard. It reminded me of how her hair smelled.

Just that tease was enough to have my prick going hard, and I groaned, squeezing my eyes shut. I didn't need to be thinking about how damn sexy she was.

It can't hurt...you're married.

I ignored the taunting voice and focused on scrubbing my hair.

Piety and I were *not* married – not really. Whatever bogus marriage that had been performed between us was a sham, one that would be annulled once Piety had done whatever she needed to do to convince her parents to leave her alone.

Moving under the spray, I rinsed my hair, still trying to pretend I wasn't acutely aware of how it seemed like the scent of her surrounded me. She smelled so damn good.

Don't think about it.

Hard not to though. She smelled good, felt good. I bet she tasted even better.

I was already doing a cockstand, and with a vicious swear, I turned the water to cold as I finished scrubbing up. I was shivering by the time I climbed out of the shower, but at least I wasn't about to walk out of there looking like I was ready to jump...Piety.

My wife had come to mind first.

"Focus, Kaleb."

Eyes closed, I pushed aside thoughts of the tempting Piety Van Allan and thought about what I needed to get done. Get my stuff from the hotel, call my boss, check in. It didn't really seem like all that much, but I still felt like the world was spinning around me.

"One thing at a time."

Once I was dressed, I reached for my phone and leaned against the marble countertop, staring at the shower stall in front of me.

I'd call my boss – or should I say *former* boss – first.

He would be pissed off, probably argumentative. And still, it was the easier call.

Another stab of guilt rose up, but I grabbed it and throttled it, shoving it deep inside a dark closet. I excelled at that. Guilt had been my best friend for a while now – a very one-sided friendship. He visited me daily, and I ignored him, pretending the little shit didn't exist and everything was fine.

On the other side of the bathroom door, I heard a bright, happy spate of laughter. That would be Astra. It suited her, that wild laugh, the name. Piety's laugh was calmer, more subtle. No reason for such a smooth, easy sound to hit me right in the gut, but it did.

Looking around the bathroom, I figured I had as much privacy now as I was going to get, so I dialed the number and waited.

"You tell me one good reason I shouldn't fire your ass," Jim Romo snapped, his smoke-roughened voice harsher than normal. He paused, taking yet another drag of his cigarette. Cancer would bypass his mean ass, looking for more fertile ground. "Come on, I'm waiting."

"I can't," I said calmly. There was no point in beating around the bush and leaving him hanging. "Something's come up, and it will be pretty much impossible for me to keep the job."

There was a faint pause, followed by a not so faint explosion. "What in the hell do you mean you're quitting? This is the thanks I get after giving you this gig?" He paused to suck in a breath. "You ungrateful piece of shit. You had no *talent*, no *skill,* but I took you on anyway. Now you're leaving me hanging."

"I'm sorry." Reaching up, I pinched the bridge of my nose. "I can't say anything more than that. I didn't plan to leave you hanging, but there's nothing I can do. Something's come up."

I wasn't about to tell him the truth. I was already coming off like an ass. I didn't need to make it worse by telling him it'd been a bad combination of alcohol and a woman.

"Fine," he bit off. "You do whatever the hell you want, pretty boy. But don't think you can come back. I'm done with you."

The phone went dead. Lowering it, I closed my eyes. That had gone about as well as I'd expected, and I'd deserved every bit of it. Still, it was nothing compared to what I had to do next.

Eying the phone narrowly, I picked it up and swallowed the bile that had been rising up my throat ever since I woke up – and not all of it because of the hangover.

"Just get it over with," I muttered to myself.

I dialed the number and waited. One ring. Two. Three.

It went to voicemail, and I gritted my teeth, swearing silently as her voice came on the line.

"This is Camry. You know the drill!"

I didn't bother leaving a message.

She hadn't called back the last few times I'd left one, and I didn't really have anything new to say.

A wild hoot of laughter came from beyond the door, drawing my attention to the women waiting in the main part of the suite. Despite myself, I was drawn to the levity between the two of them. Drawn to *her*. I'd like to hear her laugh, and maybe see her smile again – not that caustic one that had flashed across her face when she spoke about her parents.

I wanted to see a real smile.

And damn what I would've given to have met her under different circumstances. Shoving away from the counter, I moved to the door and opened it. *Time to face the music...*

Silence fell, the conversation between them falling to a complete stop.

Two gorgeous women looked over at me, and I had another fleeting thought about how crazy my life had become. Not just in the past twelve hours, but in the past few weeks, the past few months.

A year ago, it had been almost boring. I surfed. I went swimming. I worked at the shop. A nice, boring routine.

That was it.

Now, I was staring at a woman I had somehow *married,* and I decided this was about as awkward as it had been the first time I'd gone out on stage. Well, maybe not quite that bad. But it was damn close.

"So…" I shoved my hands into the front pockets of my worn, faded jeans. "What do we do now?"

Piety got to her feet, her wide, sexy mouth curled into a smile that made me wish I could remember anything from last night. "Today, we're going to have fun."

"Fun?" I repeated. Running my tongue across my teeth, I debated whether or not I should say anything, but then I decided what the hell. "You've already paid me two thousand dollars. You're paying me another eight–"

"Actually, another ten. I said I'd give you five times that. That's ten."

She'd changed and showered, her hair a little damp. Her pale blue sundress showed off her long legs, and offered just enough cleavage to be tempting but not enough to be scandalous. She looked tired, but I'd be hard pressed to tell that she was suffering the same hangover I was. If I hadn't seen her earlier, I never would have guessed she'd been black-out drunk less than twelve hours ago.

Distracted by everything about her, it took me a moment to catch up with what she said. "Wait – what? You're paying me *twelve-thousand dollars?*"

"Yes." She lifted an eyebrow. "Is that a problem?"

"Yes!" Without realizing it, I'd half-yelled and lowered my voice. "No. It's just...why in the hell does this matter so much to you?"

"Wait until you meet my parents, and you'll get it." She glanced over at Astra before moving toward me. "Anyway, I figure you have clothes to pick up. You need to check out of your hotel, right?"

"Yes."

"Okay." She was dressed similarly to me, in jeans and a t-shirt, her amazing subtle curves making my cock take notice. "Then we'll take care of that, spend the day getting to know each other before we leave."

"We're leaving?" I rubbed my neck, the headache that had been threatening edging closer and closer. "Where are we going?"

"Philadelphia. My family reunion." She pushed her hair back from her face and shrugged. "I've already bought your plane ticket – hope you don't mind. I...um...well, I checked your wallet while you were showering and took care of the arrangements."

"Oh. Okay." Wow. She was...efficient. Efficient. Confident. Capable. Sexy. Man, was she sexy. I realized I was staring at her mouth and jerked my attention back to her eyes. "Okay, so let's go to...well, my hotel first, right?"

She nodded, and we moved to the door.

31

Behind us, Astra called out. "Have fun, you two! Don't do anything I wouldn't do, PS!"

"Yeah." Piety snorted. "That probably covers murder and dismemberment. I don't think there's much else."

I was smiling as we left. Once the door closed behind us, I looked over at her. "PS? Why'd she say that?"

"Because she's weird." Piety rolled her eyes. "My middle name is Sabine. The whole name is a mouthful – Piety Sabine Van Allan. PS. Also, I told her more than once that I think my folks had me as an afterthought to help my dad's career. Afterthought…PS."

She glanced up at me and shrugged. If I hadn't been staring at her, I probably would've missed the flash of pain that moved across her eyes, then disappeared. I didn't need to know much about her to understand what had prompted that look.

I shook my head. "I don't see how anybody could think of you as an afterthought, Piety Van Allen."

Chapter 6

Piety

Those words tugged at my heart, and as we stood out in the hall, I found myself reaching up to touch his cheek, wanting that contact. His eyes widened a little, and it was that alone that made me realize what I was doing.

I forced a smile. It was fake, but I knew from experience it would come off as real enough. One thing a politician's daughter learned how to do at a young age was how to offer a sincere-looking false smile.

"Sorry…you've just got…" I pretended to brush something off his cheek. "There. All better. Come on, let's get going."

I started down the hall, my face flaming as he caught up with me.

What had I been getting ready to do?

Oh, man.

What was I doing, *period*?

Paying him twelve thousand dollars to be my pretend husband so I could get my parents to leave me alone?

Except it's not pretend, my conscience whispered. *You* did *marry him.*

He was quiet as I pushed the elevator button, and I glanced up to find him studying me. The elevator door slid open, and we stepped inside, but my wish to have company to keep the conversation at a minimum went ungranted.

"Do you want to do this?" he asked softly. "Or did your mate talk you into it?"

I didn't blink twice at the word *mate*. I'd spent one of the best summers of my life in Sydney the year after I graduated high school. He'd dropped a lot of the terms I would have expected somebody from fresh out of Oz to use, and I found myself smiling a little at the language.

"Astra and I have been friends a long time. She can nag me into a lot of things," I admitted, "but she can't push me into doing anything I don't really want to do." I met his eyes and smiled. "This isn't a bad idea."

Oh, yes, it was.

"You don't sound too convinced of that."

I blinked, wondering if he was guessing or if I'd lost some of my skill at masking what I was thinking.

"What makes you say that?" I asked as the elevator doors slid open.

"Something in your eyes. You look…nervous." He shrugged as we came to a stop in the middle the lobby. All cream and gold, it was understated elegance in the middle of one of the glitziest cities in the world.

Not too far away lay one of the many entrances to the casino. I reached over and took his hand. "Come on."

He followed along, but when he saw where we were going, his brows went together. "If you want to gamble, I'll probably just stand at your shoulder."

"That's fine." I slanted him a glance over my shoulder. "Or you could let me spot you a hundred dollars. If you don't do much with it, fine. And if you win anything…it's yours."

"I…" He scowled even harder and I wondered if he ever let himself have a little fun. I would've thought a stripper would've been a little more daring.

"Come on." I winked at him. "It's Vegas. You gotta live a *little* bit while you're here."

"I'm living plenty, thanks." He flashed me a wry smile, one that managed to set my heart to racing. "I ended up with a beautiful bride, didn't I?"

That prompted a real smile even as I rolled my eyes at him. "I…well, I don't think that counts. We were drunk off our asses."

I continued to tug him along with me as I sought out one of the cashiers. After getting some cash, I pushed a hundred into his hand. "Know how to play Texas Hold'Em?"

"Yes." He shook his head as he gave me a wry grin. "I guess you don't know how to take no very well, do you?"

"Sure I do." I nudged him with my elbow as we made our way over to the gaming tables. "The problem is…you haven't exactly said *no*. Come on. One hand, and if you don't have fun, I'll leave you alone."

* * * * *

"One more hand."

"No." I glared at him and his ever-growing pile of chips, although I wasn't really mad. He'd taken that hundred I'd given him and somehow turned it into over seven. "If I didn't know better, I'd think you were a card

35

shark."

The dealer laughed.

So did Kaleb.

"It's just luck." He winked at me and a couple of others chuckled.

"The little lady's a sore loser," a heavyset man next to me said, leaning close enough that I could smell the remnants of his breakfast on his breath – onions and sausage.

Pleasant.

"Not really. I'm just a better winner." I gave him a bland smile and got up to take the seat that had been vacated next to Kaleb. "I'm done though. I'm going to find a slot machine and engage in something a little less strenuous on my poor little female brain."

He half-choked on the water he'd requested from the server when I fluttered my lashes at the man across from us, who blinked at me, clearly wondering if I'd somehow insulted him.

The dealer was holding back a smile.

I left her a tip and gestured to Kaleb where I'd be. He could see me from the table, and I could see him. We'd exchanged phone numbers earlier, and since he was enjoying himself – and kicking ass – I figured it was as good a time as any to move onto something I didn't totally suck at.

Plus, I could get away from sausage and onion breath.

At least that was the plan.

I'd only been at my chosen slot machine for ten minutes when the one next to me opened up. When Sausage and Onion sat down, I mentally groaned but ignored him, focusing on the machine in front of me. All the luck I was lacking in Poker today, I was making in spades on my shiny slot machine. I was up to almost twelve hundred dollars, and I'd started out with a hundred.

"Well now, looks like you found your groove, sweetheart."

I didn't respond.

Sometimes if a girl ignored the creepers, they went away.

And…sometimes they didn't. When he patted my shoulder, I glanced over as if just now noticing him. "Oh, hi. Bored with poker, I see."

"Yeah. That Australian shit is cheating or something, I kid you not." He smirked over toward the table and then smiled at me. "Maybe you and I could go hit up another game…or something."

"No, thanks." I focused back on the machine, then laughed when three *7s* lit up on the play line and music began to jingle.

"You're doing pretty well there," he said, admiration a little too thick in his voice.

I made a low noise in my throat that could have been a thanks – or anything else.

"How about I buy you a drink?"

Geez. The man wasn't getting it. Looking over at him, I said, "I've got one. I'm not interested, okay?"

"Hey, I'm just being friendly." He leaned a little closer. "Seeing as how you aren't here with anybody–"

"Piety."

Kaleb's voice was entirely too welcome. I didn't let myself smile or show any other response as I glanced over my shoulder at him. I just nodded before looking back at Sausage and Onion. "Actually, I *am* here with somebody. My husband is that Australian shit you were insulting."

Face going a florid shade of red, the man glared at me before looking over my shoulder at Kaleb. "Hey...I didn't...look, buddy, I wasn't meaning nothing. We were just talking."

"Of course you were. Now you're done." Kaleb's voice was cold.

I smiled into my coffee as the seat next to me quickly became vacant. Kaleb sat down, placing a fresh coffee down in the empty space between the machines. "Was he bothering you?"

"Yes." Looking over at him, I offered a smile of gratitude. "I was handling him, but he had a head like a rock. Getting through would probably take a sledgehammer." I paused, head cocked as I considered. "No. Just the right amount of testosterone. Some men only respond to that."

He skimmed his fingers along my shoulder. It was a light, friendly touch, almost platonic. "Makes me want to apologize for my gender as a whole."

"No need." I traded out my nearly empty coffee cup for the one he'd brought over. "Is this mine?"

"Yes. You seem to inhale it."

"It's my addiction." I sighed lustily and took a sip before focusing back on the machine. "You're a sweetheart, you know that, Kaleb?"

"A nice quality to have in a temporary husband, I suppose."

"Well, I think it's a nice quality to have, period." Before I could get too wrapped up in my pretend spouse, I pulled the lever on the machine and watched the numbers spin.

* * * * *

38

"No." I looked at the ride in front of me. The damn thing looked like it couldn't decide if it wanted to be a roller coaster or a giant see-saw. Nerves jangled in my belly, and I stared at it a minute longer before shaking my head and backing away. I ended up backing right into Kaleb and almost, *almost,* stayed there. Laughing nervously, I turned to look at him. "Sorry. And um…no. *Hell,* no."

"Oh, come on. It'll be fun." He moved in a little closer and the scent of him flooded my head.

Flooded my head and threatened my senses too. It was mid-afternoon, and with every passing hour, I had to remind myself more often that we weren't on any sort of *date.*

This was…well, it was *business.*

Kind of.

Sorta.

Business that had brought us to the infamous roller coaster located on top of one of the tallest hotels in Vegas – the one that went speeding over the edge of the hotel itself. And he looked *excited* about getting on it.

"Look, I'm all fine and dandy with *regular* roller coasters," I said. "If you want to ride Space Mountain or something like that…" Inspiration struck. "Hey, I know! We can go to Disneyland. Maybe skip my family reunion and go to Disney, and I'll send them a postcard. *Sorry we missed it. Honeymooning at Disney with my new husband.*"

He cocked an eyebrow at me. "Now you're just trying to distract me. Okay. If you really don't want to ride, do you mind if I do anyway?"

"Um…" I glanced at the ride again. "Sure."

"Awesome." He squeezed my arms and moved

around me, heading toward the ride.

He got maybe ten feet away, and I swore, telling myself that if I went plummeting off the side, I'd at least die a relatively painless death. He shot me a look when I caught up with him. "Change your mind?"

"You're up here because of me," I said sourly. "If that thing breaks down and you plunge to your death, you shouldn't do it alone."

To my surprise, he broke out into a deep, sexy laugh.

The sound of it sent shivers down my spine, my nipples tightening in response. Thoughts whirled through my brain as I tried to remember something, *anything* about last night. I was so distracted by that, I didn't realize how little of a line there was until he came to a stop just a few feet away from the gate and announced, "Looks like we'll get to be on the next one."

"Great...wait, the next one?" I looked around, panicked.

"Hey, look at me." His voice, low and cajoling, had me doing just that, and I sucked in a breath when my eyes met his. He'd dipped his head, and we were practically eye to eye. "It's just like any other roller coaster. Anchored with steel into concrete. It's safety checked just like any coaster."

"It's hundreds of feet in the air," I said weakly.

"If you don't want to ride, don't ride." He crooked a grin at me. "I won't plunge to my death, I promise. Wouldn't want to make you a widow, after all."

I almost got out of the line, but for some reason, I couldn't walk away. Not from him. "I...no, I'm riding."

"Then look at me. Don't look around you. Don't think about it being on a building." He brushed my hair back from my face and his thumb came in contact with my skin.

Rough, calloused…different from what I was used to. In my social circle, I typically only met a certain type of guy. It sort of limited my dating to *that* certain type of guy. Most of them had manicures about as often as I did.

What would it feel like to have a man with calloused hands touching me in more *intimate* places?

My breathing hitched, and I tightened my hand around his wrist. I didn't even realize I'd reached up to grab him until I felt his pulse beating against my fingers.

"You're scared," he said grimly. "Come on. Let's forget this."

"No." I startled myself with the strength of my response. "I'm…well, yes, I'm scared. But…"

"Tickets, please."

I backed away from him, swallowing nervously. What would he think if he knew the reason I'd grabbed him, that the reason I was breathing hard had nothing to do with the coaster and everything to do with him?

"We're getting out of line," Kaleb said.

But before he could take action to echo his words, I grabbed the tickets from his hand and shoved them at the ride attendant. Blindly staring at Kaleb, I said, "No, we're not. Come on, hubby. It's kind of our honeymoon, right? Let's live a little."

"But…"

I pulled his arm. "Let's do it before I lose my courage!"

He chuckled and started to walk with me. "You've got more courage than a lot of people I know."

Once we were sitting and had to deal with the restraints, I squeezed my eyes closed. He must have noticed because he took over helping me with the safety harness when I fumbled. When he took my hand in his, my heart flipped a little.

"You're going to love it, Piety."

"Yeah…right. Just like dinner with Mom and Dad," I said glibly. I opened one eye a fraction. Oh, no…

In my head, I was screaming, trying to figure out what was wrong with me. I'd hit my head and was suffering massive personality changes. I'd hit my head and was delusional. I'd hit my head and lost my free will. I was having a nightmare. *Something…*

Then he squeezed my hand. "It's almost ready to go."

No…no dream. He was rubbing his thumb up and down the inside of my wrist. It was a slow rhythm, probably meant to be soothing. But I felt each stroke in places that had nothing to do with my wrist – or my arm. My nipples had contracted to hard little points, and my pussy throbbed. If I could have moved, I might have been squirming in my seat.

What is wrong with me…?

"Here we go…"

The rest of his voice was drowned out by the shouts of others and the roar of metal on metal.

I opened my eyes. "I changed my mind! Let me off!" I shouted desperately as the lights of the city began to rush closer. We were going to fly right off this damn thing.

Then we were being pulled right back.

"Oh, shit. I don't…"

He squeezed my hand again.

We plummeted forward. The lights whirled, and Kaleb's knee pressed into mine.

Oh…

I didn't know when I started to laugh, but I was still laughing when he helped me out of the car, and I collapsed against him, feeling almost delirious from

42

adrenaline…and want.

"It looks like you had fun." He brushed my hair back. The wind had blown it all over the place.

I returned the favor, still giggling even as the feel of his soft hair sent a wave of heat through me. "I didn't. I hated it. I think it's…" Another snort of laughter escaped me. "I think it's stress giggling."

"Is that a thing?"

We started to walk, and I elbowed him in the side. "Don't make fun."

"Want to ride again?"

I shot the coaster a look. "No!" But the thought of having him holding my hand, feeling the hard length of his thigh against mine…Shit. "I don't know. There are other rides in Vegas. Or we could go get dinner."

To my surprise, he pulled me against him for a hug, and this time, *he* was the one laughing. "You did have fun, see? You almost thought about getting back on, didn't you?"

"Yeah." I blushed and caught his hand, tugging him along with me so he wouldn't notice. I wasn't quite ready to tell him the only reason I was even tempted was because *he* would be on there with me. I felt like I was in ninth grade all over again, crushing over the cute boy who had helped me with advanced algebra two.

* * * * *

"What time should I meet you in the morning?"

Kaleb had walked me back to my room, and now that he'd retrieved his bag, he looked like he was about ready

43

to take off again.

"I don't know. Where's your..." I stopped, feeling like an idiot. "Son of a bitch. You don't have a hotel now, do you?"

He rubbed the back of his neck. "Well, no. I don't see why you're calling me a SOB for it though."

"I wasn't..."

He grinned at me, and I realized he was joking. "Ha, ha." Rolling my eyes at him, I gestured at the bag. "What were you going to do? Wander the strip until you found a place? Go down to the desk and see if they had anything here?"

"The idea occurred to me." He shrugged, looking unconcerned.

"Oh, for crying out loud." I passed my key in front of the door, and as the electronic lock slid open, I said, "You can stay here. The couch has a fold-out."

My cheeks went red, but I continued talking as though we hadn't already shared a bed the night before. What we'd done while we were drunk was different. We were stone cold sober now, and while I was seriously attracted to him, we didn't know each other.

That small fact couldn't be overlooked.

"That's not necessary." He backed away a step.

I caught the handle of his duffel. "No, it's not, but it makes more sense than you trying to find a room. If it takes you an hour or so, then you might not get much sleep, and we'll have to make an extra stop on our way to the airport. Why *not* stay here? We can order up a pizza, a few beers..."

"You know how to tempt a man." He blew out a breath, staring off down the hallway. Slowly, almost reluctantly, he nodded. "I've got to make a call though."

"Sure." A giddy sort of excitement unfurled through

me as he followed me into the room. "No problem. Use the one in the bedroom suite if you want. Totally private."

He nodded and left his bag on the floor in the entryway, tucked neatly against the wall.

As he walked off, I leaned my back against the door and watched him walk away.

How crazy was it that part of me almost wished this *was* real?

I'd had more fun with him today than I'd had in a long, long time.

If only I'd...

No. Don't go thinking about kissing him, Piety. He's a stranger.

Yes, that was the voice of comment sense. I wanted to stuff a sock in its sensible mouth.

Chapter 7

Kaleb

Of course she's going to make me sleep on the couch.
Various parts of me – from my dick to my bruised ego – were arguing that I hadn't spent *last* night on the couch.

But last night we'd been drunk and stupid.

Today we were sober, but I was clearly still stupid because I still wanted to get naked with a woman I barely knew. My cock was trying to lead me around, and I couldn't let it. I had too many things going on. No, I actually only had *one* thing going on. One thing because I'd pretty much given up everything else for this. For *her*.

Camry.

She still hadn't called back.

I couldn't keep letting myself get distracted over Piety, even as…distractible as she was.

Like now. She bent over the table, putting something down, and my eyes strayed over the curve of her ass. I could see myself moving up behind her and cupping her hips, moving against her. She had a nice ass, round and tight and her legs were long, strong, and muscled. She'd mentioned a few things off and on during the day that made me think she was probably as physical active as I was – or as active as I *had* been before everything went to shit.

Brooding, I turned away and carried my duffel over to the couch, staring at it for a long moment as I thought about Camry, the money I had to make – the money Piety was going to pay me. If this didn't work…

"What do you think?"

I whipped my head around. "What?"

Piety had moved up next to me, and I hadn't even noticed. Staring down at her, I found myself wanting a taste of her mouth – one that I remembered.

All I had in my head were disconnected bits and pieces, and it wasn't nearly enough.

She grinned. "You're a little distracted there."

"Yeah. Thinking." I focused back on the bag in front of me and unzipped it, as though something in there would be terribly fascinating.

I had a feeling the woman next to me was on to me though. She knew I was preoccupying myself so I wouldn't look at the *real* thing that fascinated me – her.

"I was just wondering if you had anything specific you wanted on your pizza."

"No. I'm easy." Then I paused. "Unless you're going to get really crazy and put fish or fruit on it."

She laughed softly. "Okay. No anchovies and no pineapple. Maybe a supreme? I'm craving a big, messy pizza."

"Yeah. Fine." From the corner of my eye, I glanced at her, hoping she'd leave. Hoping.

But she still stood there.

Straightening, I met her eyes. "Did you want to go out and get it or are we ordering in?"

"Oh, ordering in. Definitely." She grimaced and

dropped down on the couch, kicking off her bright yellow sneakers. "I'm worn out, and my feet are killing me. I just...well, I wanted to say thanks. I know this is an odd kind of job."

I laughed. "*Odd*? You think this is *odd*?"

It felt weird to stand there, practically looming over her, so I sat down, careful to keep a few inches between us.

"Okay, if you want, we can call it outright *insane*." She sniffed primly, crossing her legs, and folding her hands in her lap. She gave me a look of mock affront, but I could see the humor dancing in her eyes.

Already some of the worry and fear were melting away, and I struggled to hold onto them. I couldn't forget why I was doing this. Slowly, I sat down on the huge slab of wood that served as a coffee table in this decadent hotel room. My flat back in Sydney hadn't been this nice. Not even close.

"I should be the one thanking you, really," I said, meeting her eyes.

"Why?" She laughed. "You've always wanted to get hooked up to a crazy chick with parental issues, and then get dragged to a family reunion where you'll be the object of stares and awkward questions about a baby that doesn't exist? That's what will happen, you know. They'll assume you got me knocked up and we had to get married."

"They do realize it's not exactly 1955. That isn't how things go anymore." I meant it jokingly.

But Piety wasn't smiling when she looked back at me. "They do in my world. You'll see when you meet them. And trust me, by the time this is all over, you'll think you're getting ripped off."

"No, I won't." The sadness in her voice tugged at

me, so I did something stupid. I touched her.

She looked up at me, and I felt myself drawn even closer. Instead of moving back, I brushed her hair away from her face, then skimmed my fingers along her jawline. She had silky, soft skin. And she smelled so good – so damn good.

"It won't be all that bad. You'll be around, right?"

She laughed weakly. "That's not much of a bonus, Kaleb. I'm the one who got you into this mess to begin with."

"See, I *should* be the one thanking you."

"You're sweet." Her gaze dropped, and it hit me straight in the chest when I figured out just where she was looking.

Straight at my mouth.

I'd been careful not to spend too much time checking her out today, although I was probably wasting my time, trying to hide the fact that I found her attractive. We'd already ended up in bed – and married. But this…

The tension between us began to simmer, and when she laid her hand on my cheek, I decided that I was overthinking this. Why bother being cautious about this of all things?

I was just about to kiss her when she leaned forward and pressed her mouth to mine, taking the debate out of my hands.

Her taste…

I groaned and reached for her waist, pulling her toward me even as I went to my knees in front of the couch.

She came willingly, and I wrapped one arm around her, pushing the fingers of my other hand into her hair. Her breasts went flat against me, and in the back of my mind, an image flashed, my hands on those pretty little

49

tits, her tongue stroking out to dampen her lower lip.

Then it was gone – and so was she.

"Damn. I'm sorry," she said, breathing hard as she backed away from me.

"You're sorry?" Catching my lower lip, I sucked it into my mouth, savoring the faint taste of her as it faded. "I don't think you need to be apologizing, Piety."

"I...look." She blushed, and it was so adorable, I wanted to grab her, pull her against me, and never let go.

But then she turned away, her shoulders hunching protectively, and that was when it clicked – something wasn't right.

"Look, I'm not paying you to sleep with me," she blurted out, bolting upright just as the last word escaped her lips.

For a minute, I didn't quite get what she meant. When I did, I tried to hide my laugh by turning it into a cough. It didn't quite work.

She glared at me as I stood.

"I'm sorry," I said, shaking my head, and holding up a hand as she took a step toward me, looking like she wanted to throttle me. "I'm just...look, that never crossed my mind. When a beautiful woman kisses me, do you think I've got my mind on anything other than her mouth on mine? Or..."

I didn't intentionally drop my gaze, but...well, I had other thoughts in my head besides her kissing me, or me kissing her. And all of them involved us naked and touching each other. None of them involved money.

That was foolish, because right now, everything I did should involve thinking about money, whether I was taking a piss, eating or trying to figure out how to stretch five dollars into twenty.

But Piety shut my brain off.

And I loved it.

Her chest hitched.

If I hadn't been staring at just that portion of her anatomy, I might have missed it, but her breasts rose and fell in an erratic rhythm several times over, and I didn't let myself think about the steps I was taking to close the distance between us until I'd already done it.

And then I was only thinking about it because there was still too much space between us even though, unless I had her naked and under me, we couldn't get much closer.

Right. Clothes. I wanted those off right now.

Her hands twisted in my hair while I reached for the zipper at the back of her sundress. It was surprisingly difficult to concentrate on something so simple as a zipper when her tongue was stroking across mine. My fingertips brushed her shoulders as I pushed her dress off, and a zing of electricity went through me.

I needed to feel her skin. All of it. I needed it more than I needed anything else in my life.

Her bra went next and I couldn't stop myself from shifting enough to get my hands between us. She moaned the moment I cupped her breasts, and I made a similar sound when I felt her nipples harden against my palms. I'd never given much thought to whether I had particular type when it came to women, but I couldn't imagine a set of breasts more perfect than the ones I was touching right now.

Her hands were at my waist, tugging at my shirt, so I tore my mouth away to deal with it. I wouldn't have done anything more than that, but as I lost the heat of her body, it suddenly occurred to me that I needed to find protection before things got even more heated.

Where in the hell had I put my condoms?

I knew I had a pack. Somewhere.

"Kaleb?"

The uncertainty in her voice had me looking up, and the sight of her perfect, porcelain skin, those high, firm breasts...she took my breath away.

"Just being safe, sweetheart." I tore my eyes away from her as I dug through my pack until I found what I was looking for.

In the two minutes it took me to find them, Piety had plastered her front to my back, and I could feel the soft, silken smoothness of her curves, the hard, pebbled flesh of her nipples. I had to close my eyes. Her hands slid across my stomach, and my muscles twitched beneath her palms. Her touch was light as she toyed with the button on my jeans. In short, she was going out of her way to drive me out of my mind.

And she was damn good at it.

Turning back to face her, I caught her in my arms and guided us onto the wide couch. She laughed breathlessly, the sound fading as I put her under me. I allowed myself another moment to appreciate the sight of her body, bare except for a pair of tiny white lace panties.

If I would have known she was wearing those under that bloody dress of hers, I would've been hard pressed to resist as long as I had.

"You drive me insane, you know that?" I caught her lower lip between my teeth and tugged.

"Stop talking and kiss me." She put action to words and pulled my head closer, licking at my mouth until I kissed her.

Sliding her hands between us, she reached for the button, freed it. Then she dragged the zipper down, and I groaned the second she shoved her hand inside and wrapped her fingers around my cock. Her teeth scraped against my lip, and I tightened my hold on her hip.

Thrusting into her touch, I ground down against her hand, pleasure coursing through me at her touch.

She laughed, the sound wild and hungry. "You better not enjoy that too much. Wouldn't want you to miss out on the main event."

"We couldn't have that," I agreed.

Shoving up onto my knees, I hooked my fingers in the elastic of her panties and pulled them off, her eyes locking with mine as she raised her hips and let me pull them off. Her legs settled on either side of me, revealed dark curls and pink flesh.

Fuck.

I fumbled the condom out of my pocket and tore it open. As much as I wanted to taste her, I needed to be inside her more. Without another word, I settled in the cradle of her hips. The heat was unreal, and when I brushed against her, we both shuddered.

Hooking one of her knees up over my arm, I drove into her, listening to her cry bouncing off the walls as I slid home. My head fell forward as her wet sheath gripped me tight. She moaned, low in her throat, and I pressed my lips to the satiny skin just above her pulse.

She reached for my shoulders, sinking her nails into me. The sweet little bites of pain went tripping down my spine as I rocked back, then thrust deeper still. Her pussy contracted around me, squeezing me like a fist. She opened her eyes, and we stared at each other.

This was too good.

Too perfect.

The pleasure so acute I couldn't even process it.

I gave up trying and just let it go. Let my body sink into hers, move with hers. Each stroke sent another ripple of pleasure through me, each breath rubbing her nipples against my chest. Unlike women I'd slept with in the past, she was tall enough that I managed to bend my head down to capture one pale pink nipple between my lips without missing a single thrust.

She arched her back, nails scratching at my scalp even as she pressed my head closer to her breast. Not that I had any intention of releasing my prize. Her sounds of pleasure were almost enough to send me over the edge, and I knew I'd want to hear them again. And again. And again.

Piety was hot and sweet, her cunt rippling around me with sensations that became tighter and tighter as she moved closer to climax. She writhed and moaned and twisted under me, her nails scratching against my back and chest until my skin stung.

Neither of us spoke, and for that I was grateful. I didn't want to lie to her, to say things in the heat of the moment that I couldn't keep to later. Better to show her how attracted I was to her, how much I enjoyed being with her. I couldn't make her promises, but I could make her feel good.

I buried my hand in that thick, soft hair and used it to tilt her head back, baring her throat to me. I could feel her trembling around me, beneath me, and knew she was close. I pulled her leg up high, her ankle on my shoulder, and leaned down, opening her wider. As I pushed in deep, I bit down on her soft flesh, worrying at her skin with teeth and tongue until she exploded. The sound she made was something so primal, so real, that I came, unable to hold back any longer.

Fuck.

Dropping my head down so that my forehead rested between her breasts, I closed my eyes. Her arms and legs were still wrapped around me, holding me to her, as if she was worried I would run away.

She…this…all of it.

Dammit!

Why couldn't I have met her some other time?

Some other place?

Chapter 8

Piety

"This family reunion, is it something your family does every year?" Kaleb asked.

His fingers drew small circles on my side as we lay on the bed. We might've moved from the couch to my bedroom, but we still hadn't gotten around to ordering pizza. We would have to get something eventually, because my belly was growling, but I wasn't in any hurry. I didn't think he was either.

I was entirely too comfortable with him. I hadn't been with too many other guys, but I couldn't think of a single one who had been so easy to just *be* with.

It was nice.

"Every two years. And that's about five years too often." Grinning, I reached up to run my hand through his hair.

He caught my hand. "That math doesn't add up."

"I know. It's not that I don't love my family, but they're not the easiest people to be around en masse."

"Why not?" he asked, rubbing his thumb over my inner wrist.

I bit my lip, considering how to answer. He watched me, not pushing, not judging, and I answered as honestly as I could. "Have you ever had anybody who expected certain things of you? I mean like all the time?"

He started to shake his head, then stopped and shrugged. "In a way. I don't think it's quite the same thing you're putting up with." He kissed my hand. "But I think I get it. It can be exhausting."

"You nailed it." I curled in closer to him, enjoying his warmth. "Thank you. I know you don't want to hear it, but thanks for helping me."

"I've already told you, I should be thanking you. The money...well, I need it, so you're helping me." As he spoke, a dull flush rose to stain his cheeks, and the tips of his ears turned red. It was oddly charming.

"Family stuff?"

He gave me a lopsided grin, but offered no real answer. His eyes shifted away, distancing himself even if his body stayed close.

Understanding the need for privacy, I rested my head on his shoulder so he didn't have to feel like he was avoiding looking at me.

"You know, twenty-four hours ago, I was brooding and pissed off. I had no idea I was going to be doing this today. I had no idea I would be meeting you." I laughed a little. "All in all, I'm pretty pleased with how the day is going. Granted, last night..." I exhaled a long breath. "My mind is still kind of blown. I wish I could remember everything that happened."

"According to Astra, we got hitched." He said it in a tone dry enough to make me laugh again.

"That's not what I meant." I nudged him. "Well, not entirely. I'm talking about..." Now was my turn to blush and avoid his gaze. "I mean, last night. We slept together, but I don't remember anything. Considering how amazing what we just did was, I sort of wish I could."

He cleared his throat. "I kinda have an answer about that I think."

I pushed up and turned around, facing him. "What do you mean? You know what happened?" He wouldn't meet my eyes directly, and he didn't answer right away, so I prodded him, poking him in the side. He flinched a bit, and I tucked that into the back of my head. *Ticklish...* "Come on, tell me."

Kaleb sat up, scooting until his back was against the headboard. "I don't think anything happened."

"But this morning..." I stared at him. "There was a condom wrapper on the nightstand, and you were..." I cleared my throat. "You had a condom on."

"Yeah, about that." He flushed bright red. "It...ah...well, it wasn't used."

"But..." I couldn't think of a single response to that.

"Maybe we were just both too drunk. I don't know."

Baffled – and oddly disappointed – I stared at him for the longest time, uncertain of what I wanted to say. I couldn't think of a single thing, although there were a hundred stops and starts inside my head.

"Mystery solved, right?"

"Yeah." I managed a weak smile. "Mystery solved." I leaned against him and snuggled in closer, tucking my head into the hollow between his neck and shoulder.

His arm came around me, and it fit – *we* fit. We felt...perfect together.

Why did I feel so disappointed that we hadn't had sex last night? I didn't understand it, but there was this strange hollow feeling inside me.

"Are you okay?" Kaleb stroked his hand up and down my back.

"Oh, I'm fine. Just thinking." I was careful not to let my voice reveal anything. I'd become all too good at that. That was a skill you picked up early, being a politician's daughter. Certain things, a girl just didn't let show.

From where my head rested against his chest, I could feel the steady beat of his heart, and it was oddly soothing, comforting. My hand was on his stomach, moving up and down with each breath, and in that moment, it made a deep, gurgling noise. With a little laugh, I straightened. Before I could tease him about it, my belly rumbled in agreement. "I guess we should get around to ordering that pizza. What do you think?"

"Sounds like a plan."

I kicked my legs over the edge of the bed and grabbed the first thing that came to hand. It happened to be his t-shirt, but I pulled it on without a second thought. It came to mid-thigh, and the scent of him wrapping around my body made me shiver a little.

"Hey." His voice had a low sexy rumble to it that made my pussy throb.

I glanced back at him.

"Did I say you could borrow that?" The glint in his eye said he was teasing me.

Two could play at that came.

"Well…" I reached for the hem.

"Don't." He groaned and looked away. "Keep it on or we'll never eat, and I'm starving."

I laughed and blew him a kiss. As I moved over to the phone, though, I could feel his eyes on me, and when I glanced back at him, he was watching me with heavy-lidded eyes.

Heat swept through me, and I averted my gaze as a voice came on the line. By the time I finished ordering the food, I could hear water coming on in the bathroom, and I thought about joining him. We had half an hour.

Might as well enjoy the time…and it would conserve water too.

* * * * *

Between the two of us, we pretty much demolished an entire extra-large pie and several beers.

Now, belly full and pleasantly buzzed, I stretched back out on the bed, studying him.

"I've been thinking," I announced. He'd pulled a pair of jeans on after we'd gotten out of the shower, and while I was kind of sorry to see him wearing any kind of clothing, at the same time, it'd been a good idea. When he was all naked and beautiful in front of me, I lost track of important things…like breathing.

He glanced at me over his shoulder, a golden brow arched. "Just what have you been thinking about, Miss Piety?"

"I've been thinking…" I said slowly. I rolled to my hands and knees and crawled to the edge of the bed as I grinned at him. "That you and I need to be able to convince my parents and the rest of my family that we're comfortable together, that we fell head over heels in love…or at least in lust with each other."

"Well, that is what you're paying me for," he said, turning to face me. Eyes locked on mine, he reached out and traced a bold finger down my cheek, my collarbone, then dropped his hand down to cup my breast through his shirt. "Are you saying I haven't I done a good job of proving there's a fair amount of lust on my side?"

I was having a difficult time concentrating as his thumb moved across my nipple. "I think…it's safe to say there's a fair amount of lust on both sides."

He lightly pinched my nipple and I moaned, fighting the urge to wrap myself around him and tell him to just do me.

It took a supreme effort of will to continue.

"We have to convince them. We should…" I cleared my throat, heat rushing up to stain my cheeks red as he dipped his head and raked his teeth down my neck. He'd already left one mark, but I wanted him to leave another. But first I had to finish my thought. "We should be comfortable together."

He pushed his knee between mine as he wrapped his hand around the back of my neck. "I don't feel comfortable right now. Maybe after I've had you wrapped around my cock for a little while longer, after I've made you scream my name and I've emptied myself inside you…then I'll be comfortable."

Fuck me. Every cell in my entire body was practically vibrating.

"That's not what I…meant."

He grinned down at me, ice-blue eyes blazing hot. "What did you mean?"

"We should start sleeping together."

"Haven't we done that?" He caught the hem of my shirt – his t-shirt – and started to drag it up, letting his fingertips trail across my skin as he went. "Let me refresh your memory."

"Again, not what I meant." But I wasn't going to complain. Not when I could still feel what it was like to have him inside me

"Oh." He let the shirt go. "You meant…share your bed."

"Yes."

He looked thoughtful.

My body burned as I waited.

Then he nodded. "I'm fine with that."

He turned away from me and my stomach dropped.

"Wait! What are you...?"

He looked back at me. "We're sleeping together, right? I'm tired, so I'm going to get ready for bed."

"But..." Glaring at him, I folded my arms over my chest, knowing my nipples would be clearly visible.

He slowly shifted back around to face me, his gaze flicking down and then back up. "Is there a problem?"

"You started something. Aren't you going to finish it?"

He came toward me, a loose-limbed prowling gait that was unbearably sexy. "So...sex *and* sleeping together. This is getting complicated, Piety."

There was a teasing glint in his eye, though, one that made me want to smile, want to tease.

Smoothing my hand down the front of my borrowed shirt, I hitched up a shoulder. "Not so complicated. Don't you need to get your shirt back so you can pack it? Be ready for tomorrow."

He caught my hips, and the feel of his rough hands against my smooth skin sent a shiver through me.

"You sound like you're a big believer in being prepared."

He said the words against my lips.

Before I could respond, he was kissing me.

No...no, I really wasn't a big believer in being prepared. I just would've said anything to get him to touch me again. What did it matter anyway? No amount of preparation could have ever gotten me ready for him.

Chapter 9

Kaleb

Waking up felt strange.

For a minute, I didn't entirely understand why.

I lay there a few more minutes, trying to process. That didn't take too long, but even after I'd figured out why things felt different, I didn't move.

If I did that, it might break the spell.

It had been years since I'd woken up with a woman.

I couldn't really count yesterday. We'd been hung over and irritated, and I'd been in a stupor for several minutes even after Piety had rolled out of the bed.

This though...

This.

It had been years since I'd had this.

I hadn't realized I'd missed it. There'd been no time for a relationship, not really. Even the few I'd had when I was younger...hell. Nothing had felt as easy and right as this.

That in and of itself was just insane, because *this* wasn't real.

Piety was paying me.

Not to sleep with her, but she was paying me money to stay with her, and if it hadn't been for the money, I wouldn't have been around for any of this. And that bothered me more than I wanted to admit.

I couldn't lose sight of the reason I was doing this. I couldn't afford to. And I couldn't afford to have feelings for this woman, even though it would be damn easy *to* have feelings for her. She was…funny. Sweet, but in a subtle way. There was a sharp, sarcastic side to her that hid that softness. I liked all of it, and suspected the more I was around her, the more I'd like it. Like *her*.

Which meant if I was smart, I'd get away and stay away.

Rising from the bed, I moved over to the window and stared outside. Under my feet, the carpet was plush and thick, feeling as foreign to me as the rest of the room, as strange and different as the woman lying on the bed behind me.

I didn't fit in here.

Brooding, I looked back at Piety, but that only made me want to climb back into bed with her.

The temptation was so strong, I jerked my gaze away and headed for the small pile of clothes at the end of the bed. Grabbing my jeans, I headed for the bathroom.

I didn't bother putting them on until the door was closed behind me. Once I was lost in the relative privacy, I checked my phone to see if there had been any calls.

No.

Not that too many people *would* call.

But Camry should have.

But, of course she hadn't. I squeezed my phone around the casing, hard enough that the plastic cracked a little. Then, slowly, I lowered it and punched in her number. She didn't answer. Big surprise.

I waited till the voicemail started and once it beeped, I left a message.

"Hey, Camry. It's me. Listen…something's come up, and I've got to leave the city for a little bit. When I get back, I'll have money. I'll have everything I need to make all of this right again. It's going to be okay."

Make it right again…

I wanted to laugh at my own stupidity.

Instead, I disconnected the call and shoved my phone in the pocket of my jeans.

How could I make things *right*? How could I possibly hope to do that?

Frustrated, I wrenched the door open, half thinking I'd go for a walk or something.

And I came to a dead stop at the sight of Piety lying stretched across the bed, taking up two-thirds of it. She had the sheets wrapped and twisted around her, her face turned toward me, a faint smile on her lips.

The sight of her was like a blow straight to my chest, and without thinking – without *letting* myself think – I went to her and laid down, curling around her. I tucked my face against her hair and breathed in the scent of her.

In a few days, a few weeks, this would be over.

I'd go back to my life.

She'd go back to hers.

She'd probably forget this whole interlude. All she wanted was for her parents to get the idea that she was her own person. She was a grown woman. A fact that the body pressed to mine made abundantly clear.

Me, though…I'd go back to my life and do what? Do what I'd been doing for years?

This was my escape. *My* escape, brief as it was. I was doing what I needed to do, yeah. I couldn't deny that. But I *wanted* to do it. I hadn't wanted to walk away from

Piety yet. From the moment I'd first seen her, I'd wanted her. And then I'd wanted to know her.

When it was all over, I'd go back to a life I was just now recognizing as completely empty.

Yes, I was going to try to fix things with Camry.

How could I not?

But nothing was going to be *okay*.

Things hadn't been *okay* in a long time.

So I might as well enjoy this for as long as it lasts.

Piety made a low, humming sound and stretched.

I slid my hand down her hip, and she covered it with her own. The cool metal of the new ring she'd bought brushed against the matching ring I now wore. She'd insisted on it – her parents would never buy that she'd gotten married without an appropriate ring – for both of us.

It hadn't felt right letting a woman buy something so…personal for me.

But when she'd grinned at me so playfully, then slid it on my finger, I realized how *personal* things between us already felt. She'd told me that once this was done, I could keep the ring – sell it or do whatever.

I would keep it. I already knew that. Even after we annulled this farce of a marriage, I'd keep it. A little piece of her.

She stretched again, wiggling her ass against my cock. I closed my eyes as blood rushed south. When she did it again, I realized she was holding her breath a little. Little minx.

"Something tells me you're doing that on purpose."

She broke out in a laugh. "It took you long enough." She did it again.

I rolled onto my knees, dragging her along so that her back was flush against me. She gasped as I slid a hand around and down, pushing my fingers between her thighs. She was already wet, the slick heat making my cock even harder. She moaned as I rubbed my fingers against her clit until she swore. Her head fell back against my shoulder as she rode my hand, rocking back against my cock, until I thought I just might embarrass myself.

"Come for me, sweetheart," I spoke through gritted teeth just before I pressed against that little bundle of nerves. She cried out, her body jerking as she came.

Damn, she was beautiful like that.

I eased her down onto the bed before I eased away and tore open one of the last remaining condoms on the nightstand. We'd need more. Had to remember that. No matter how much I loved the idea of sliding into her bare. I would do at least one thing smart here.

I rolled the condom down, as I trailed my eyes up along the curve of her spine. As I watched, she lifted up on her hands and knees, threw her hair back, and turned her head to smile at me over her shoulder.

It was a sweet, wicked little grin that made my heart flip over and my stomach clench.

Groaning, I grabbed her hip with one hand and held her steady, wrapping my other hand around my cock. "I think you want to drive me mad."

"No, I just want *you*."

Such simple words, but the things they made me feel...

Swearing, I buried myself balls-deep inside her pussy with one thrust. We both cried out, our voices mixing together even as our bodies joined. I gave us both a moment to gain control before I started to draw back. She clamped down tighter around me, like she was trying to keep me trapped inside her. I wouldn't mind staying like this, wrapped inside her, where I belonged.

My balls went tight as I eased back, then slid forward. Slowly at first, then building in speed, I drove into her. Each time, she tightened around me, friction and pressure forcing me higher. I could feel my orgasm coiling in my stomach, fighting to break free. But I wasn't going to give in, not until she came first.

Bracing my hands against her hips, I bent over her, sweat blooming on my skin, need knotting in my gut. I slid one hand under her and rolled her nipple between my fingers. She moaned and arched her back.

"Touch yourself," I ordered. "Rub your clit and come for me again. Let me feel that hot little pussy of yours squeeze me."

I pinched her nipple, then tugged it as I felt her shift. She shivered as her fingers began to move over her clit. I pulled her nipple again, twisted it, and she called out my name, the sound one of pure pleasure.

Fuck. I wanted to hear that again.

"Say my name, sweetheart." I could feel her body trembling around me. "Say it and come."

I grabbed her hair and yanked her back against me. She came apart as she yelled my name and I didn't fight my release any longer.

I started to climax, curses pouring from my mouth alongside her name. But the only thing that really mattered was her name.

* * * * *

"You were cussing me out."

Her words broke the silence that had fallen as we'd

recovered, and I felt my face going red as I looked over at her.

Piety was propped on her elbow, staring down at me, a curious look on her face. "Well?"

"Well, what?" I asked.

"I'm just…well, it's not like I've slept with a lot of people or anything, but there've been a couple of guys." She flushed. "And I've never had a guy swear at me when he came before."

Shit. Throwing my forearm over my eyes, I tried to explain. "It wasn't you. It was…"

Unable to find the words, I lowered my arm and stared at her. After a moment, I caught her and rolled until I had her under me. She wasn't upset. I could see it in her eyes now. She was actually smiling. She always seemed to be smiling, even when it wasn't quite genuine.

"You know the cartoons you see in the paper? Or online where one of the characters stubs his toe or something, and all he says are exclamation marks and such? It's because cartoons don't cuss…but sometimes it's more effective, even though silence can say more than words at times. But then, there are times when swearing says more than words."

Her face softened as she reached up, cupping my cheek.

I covered her hand with mine. "I've been caught in a shit storm for a while, and now there's you. You're like an oasis." Balancing on one elbow, I slid a hand down her belly and cupped her between her thighs. "Just being with you would be sweet. But having you moan out my name, fucking you and knowing you want everything I can do to you – that you want to do the same things to me…"

"So, fucking me is like stubbing your toe. You can't express yourself in any way other than cursing?" She cocked an eyebrow even as she closed her thighs, rocking up against my hand.

"Yes." I offered her a weak grin. "It's just…well, in a good way. Almost like hitting your funny bone or…well, you get the point."

She pushed against my shoulders until I went to my back. She grabbed the last condom from the bedside table, then threw a leg over my waist.

"Let's see if we can hit that funny bone again."

Chapter 10

Piety

Walking around the airport in Las Vegas wasn't too different than walking around outside in the city itself or in one of the casinos. Okay, it was definitely cooler in the airport than in the city, but you got the same sense of excitement and desperation from many of the tourists.

There was such a wide variety of people, and I loved people watching. It always baffled my parents when we'd traveled, although I got better about getting caught watching as I'd gotten older. Mom had never approved.

Piety, sit still…stop gawking. It's so unseemly.

A stern look from Dad had been enough to communicate the same message, but it hadn't stopped my…*gawking* either. I'd just learned to be more subtle about it.

Now I didn't need to be subtle, but I'd learned it was more…well, polite not to so openly stare.

I wasn't trying to be *nosy* exactly.

People just fascinated me. All of them.

Of course, some of them pissed me off, like the mom who was yelling at a baby who couldn't be more than six months old, telling the poor thing to quit crying.

Just as the thought went through my mind, Astra noticed as well.

"Like yelling at her is really going to make the baby stop crying," Astra said, sarcasm thick in her voice – and she wasn't quiet about it either.

The slim blonde heard and whipped her head around, glaring at us.

But Astra was already talking to Kaleb. "I mean, don't *you* find it soothing when somebody yells at you? Especially when you're in a loud, noisy unfamiliar place and you're probably tired? That's exactly what makes you feel better, isn't it, Kaleb?"

The look on his face made it plain as day that he didn't know if he wanted to laugh or hide behind the menu. Taking pity on him, I laid a hand on his arm. "Half the time, being in an airport is enough to make most people want to cry – or yell."

I gave the mom a smile and hoped she'd take the out, and give her baby one too. We all got stressed after all, but the baby shouldn't suffer for it.

After a moment, her eyes fell away, and she started to bounce the little girl, patting her on the butt as she rocked her back and forth. A moment later, the pitiful wails subsided and the baby shoved her fist into her mouth.

"I'm *starving*," Astra announced, studying the menu. "Why did we get on such a late flight? I could have sworn we were flying out earlier."

"We were." I glanced at her over the top of mine. "We changed it to a later one so we could all three fly first class."

"You didn't have to…" Kaleb went quiet at my look, miming that he was sealing his lips shut and tossing away a key. He'd already lost that argument.

Laughing, I patted his arm. "Figure out what you want to eat, okay?" A small market across the way caught my eye, reminding me. "Hey, I forgot my ear plugs back at the hotel, so I'm going to go grab some."

It wasn't the only thing I needed, but I definitely needed those, and gum. Hopping off the stool, I looked at Astra. "Order me an omelet and some bacon. I want something messy and fattening before I head to the reunion. I'll be eating canapes and the rest of that crap that looks pretty and tastes like cardboard."

"You got it. Don't worry, PS. I'll stay here and keep Kaleb company." She gave me a serene smile.

Inside the small shop, I found a box of condoms and the ear plugs I needed for the trip. My ears always killed me when I flew. I also saw a book from one of my favorite authors and grabbed it. On impulse, I picked up an action thriller for Kaleb. I had no idea if he liked to read. If he didn't…well, I wouldn't hold it against him *too* much. After all, Astra and I were best friends, and I only nagged her about her lack of love for reading every now and then. Like once or twice a week.

As I made my way to the cashier, a voice caught my attention. Plaintive, young…almost desperate. "Please, can you try again? It's the last credit card I have, and I'm out of diapers."

"Ma'am, I've already tried twice, and I've got other customers."

The young mom.

My gaze locked on her as she stood there, rocking her baby, and holding her credit card out to the cashier while a couple of other customers shifted restlessly behind her.

One of them, an older businessman behind her, said,

"Can you move? I have a plane to catch."

My temper snapped. Striding forward, I pulled out my wallet. "Here you go, sis."

Heads whipped my way as I nudged the businessman aside, just as he had been trying to do to the young mom. I swiped my card, smiling serenely at the cashier and ignoring the surprise on the girl's face. She really was just a girl. Nineteen, maybe twenty. "I need cash too. What's the max?"

"Excuse me," the dude in the suit snapped. "You weren't next."

I glanced at him. "Oh, I know. My *sister* was. The girl you were being so rude to? We'll be done in a second."

I withdrew the maximum amount I could, then stepped out of line, holding out the diapers to the girl who was standing there, staring at me, still rocking the baby.

She didn't take them. "What's this?"

"Diapers, sweetie." Nudging her out of the line, I continued to hold the package out to her.

"I…" She firmed her jaw. "I don't need charity from some rich bitch."

"It's not charity." I didn't let the barb get to me. I was rich. I could be a bitch. And so could pride. I understood pride really well. "It's called kindness…and help. Sometimes everybody needs a little."

Her cheeks flushed hot and red. "I don't–"

"Doesn't your baby?" I kept my voice soft.

She deflated and reached out, slowly taking the diapers. "We're going to meet her dad. He's in the army, stationed out in Virginia, and I…" Her eyes filled with tears. "We're getting married. I'm moving out there. All my stuff is already on the way, but it took all my money, and I'm about broke. My parents won't help me."

She looked like she wanted to just break down and cry.

"Then your parents kind of suck," I said with a sympathetic smile. Gently, I turned her around and pushed the diapers into the bag hanging from one narrow shoulder.

Then I turned her back around to face me. "Here." I started to give her the money I'd withdrawn, but then I stopped and pulled out my wallet, taking the rest of my cash. It added up to nearly three hundred dollars. Nothing I'd miss, and it'd make a difference to her. "Make sure you both have food and formula before you get on the plane. And put the rest of the money somewhere safe. The diaper bag is too easy for people to steal from."

She gaped at me, dark eyes wide. "Why…why are you doing this?"

"Because I can. Because you need it." I brushed a wispy lock of hair back from the baby's forehead and then smiled at her. "Go on…I think she needs her diaper changed."

I headed back into the store and almost walked into the businessman as he headed out. He glared from the girl to me. "Square things up with your sister?"

"Yep." Breezily, I edged around him and took my place in line.

"That was nice of you."

I jolted at the sound of Kaleb's voice coming from just over my shoulder.

Whipping around, I met his eyes. "What…where did you come from?"

"Same place you did. I put my order in then came over here. I needed…something." His gaze slid down and lingered on the box in my hands, his lips twitching in amusement. "Looks like great minds think alike."

I flushed. "Well, I'm taking care of it. You can go back to the restaurant."

"I don't think one box will be enough," he said easily, gaze heated. "Again, that was nice of you."

We shuffled forward as the customers in front of us each paid and went on their way. It was down to the last one before he spoke again.

"Nothing to say?"

Huffing out a sigh, I said, "What's to say? She needed a break. I gave her one."

"Just like I needed one." He didn't sound angry, but he wasn't happy either.

"No, you're doing *me* a favor," I said quickly, shaking my head.

"I'm the one getting paid to–"

Spinning around, I clapped my hand over his mouth. "Shh…" I didn't give a quick look around, although I was tempted. "Be quiet, you…" Huffing, I dropped my hand and turned back to the counter just as the last person in front of me moved off. "Just hush," I said grouchily.

I dumped my stuff down in front of the cashier, hoping she hadn't noticed the interaction between Kaleb and me.

I suspected she had though.

If for no other reason than the fact that she was gaping at him.

He seemed to inspire that reaction quite a bit, not that I blamed any of them. He was *gorgeous*.

And for a while, he was mine.

Instead of making me smile, though, the thought made me a little sad.

He was mine…but only for a while.

* * * * *

"You can't do that," I said, focusing on my irritation instead of the thought that had been circling through my head since we'd left the store.

Astra had wandered off to check out some purses in the store we'd just passed, giving me the chance to finally talk to Kaleb about what'd happened.

We still had an hour to wait until boarding, and Astra couldn't sit still for that long, especially not with a plane ride ahead of us. I didn't want to talk to him in front of her, not when I knew she'd see more than I wanted her to.

"I can't do what?"

Kaleb was wearing a pair of sunglasses now, and I wanted to tug them off, look into his eyes.

"Say things about me paying you." Self-consciously, I glanced around and then met his eyes. At least I assumed I was meeting his eyes. The lenses of his glasses were opaque. "I get recognized sometimes. Not as often out here, but if a person is a journalist, especially on the political beat, it's not a stretch. I can't have anybody hearing that I'm *paying* you. It will get back to my dad, and this is all for nothing."

"And they might assume you're paying me for something else." He wagged his eyebrows.

I laughed even as blood rushed up to heat my cheeks. "My father would have a heart attack." I was only half-joking about that. Offering him a smile, I said, "Just...don't do it, okay?"

"No problem." He slung his arm around my neck. "Shall we find our gate, my darling wife?"

"We shall." I pasted a smile on my face, hoping it would hide the hollow ache settling inside.

77

* * * * *

It was the shortest flight ever.

Or it felt that way.

As we collected our luggage, Astra watched me with gleaming eyes, and I had to poke her in the side and give her a death glare to keep her from saying something.

I didn't know what she wanted to say, but I had no doubt it would be something embarrassing. When Kaleb made a quick stop by the restroom, I found out.

"You two almost look like this is...*real*," she said, her voice low.

"That's the idea." I managed a non-committal shrug.

"Except there's no reason to play it so well right now. And I don't think you're *playing*." She tapped a bright pink fingertip against equally pink lips. "You like him. I mean, *really* like him."

"Well, yeah." I kept my eyes on the restroom. "What's not to like? We get along. He's funny and sweet. He's *not* into me because of my parents or my money."

"All good things," she agreed. "But this is just a temporary thing, remember? You don't really know him. So why does it seem so *not* temporary?"

"You're imagining things." I waved it off and started to add something, but a tall, blond figure caught my eyes, and I gave her a quelling look to keep her from pursuing it.

She arched an eyebrow, but lapsed into silence.

A moment later, Kaleb joined us and took his luggage, a single duffel bag which he hefted over his shoulder with ease. He also took my suitcase and Astra's, leaving us with our carry-ons and purses.

"It's so nice having a big, strong man around the house," Astra said, sighing lavishly.

"Stop it." I smacked her on the arm and moved to his side, gesturing toward the exit. "Our car is on the way. Won't take long."

"Your car?" he asked.

"We always have a town car pick us up," Astra said, checking her phone. "It's so much easier than trying to deal with parking and lugging our own luggage around. Of course, if you asked Piety's daddy, he'd insist that we take a limo."

I rolled my eyes. "Astra, stop. Your dad isn't much better."

"Oh, I know. Sometimes, he's worse." She flashed a sunny grin our way. "That's why we never tell anybody when we're going out of town. Then we don't have to worry about unexpected chauffeurs showing up at our loft."

We moved past the crush at luggage pick up and got outside just as the driver texted that he was there. "Perfect timing," I said, gesturing to the car. "It's Roy."

We had a favorite, a guy we usually requested and most of the time, we got him. His worn, friendly face creased in a smile as we waved him down, and he studied Kaleb with curiosity as he held the door for us. Kaleb hesitated, eying the bags.

"I'll get them, sir," Roy assured him.

"Come on," I said, tugging on Kaleb's hand.

After another moment, Kaleb climbed in after me, sinking back onto soft leather, but looking uncomfortable. "He's..."

"If you let Roy hear you calling him old, he'll have

your heart on a platter," I said, keeping my voice low. "He thinks he's still thirty-two. Besides, he likes his job. He does this so he can help with his granddaughter's college. Doesn't have to. He retired from the military, but he wants to help."

"Sounds like you know him."

I nodded, but I didn't go into any detail as Roy slammed the trunk shut and came around to the driver's seat.

Kaleb still looked like he wanted to say something, but when I took his hand, he twined our fingers and slowly relaxed.

"So…are you ready for this?"

He stared out of the window as we pulled away from the airport, the Philadelphia city skyline slowly revealing itself. "Ready as I'll ever be, I guess."

* * * * *

"Welcome home!" Astra threw back the door and stepped into the loft we shared.

I still stood next to Kaleb, holding his hand.

The doorman was taking care of the luggage, yet another thing Kaleb was clearly not used to.

My life must seem so strange to him.

I didn't mind carrying my own luggage. I was usually the one carrying it down when I left – Astra too. But when we got back, the staff in our building, like Roy, made us feel like we were doing them injury if we didn't let them handle it. Granted, I think they appreciated the tips, and I had a feeling we tipped better than most of the people here, so maybe that was part of it.

But Kaleb was clearly not used to having his luggage handled for him or doors opened, and the expression on his face made me re-evaluate every little thing, even though I always told myself not to take anything I had for granted.

I didn't think I did. Many of the people Astra and I knew growing up didn't know what to make of us. While they'd been partying and shopping and heading off to Cancun for vacations in high school and college, we'd wanted to get involved with Habitat for Humanity. We hadn't been able to in high school, no matter how much we begged, so we'd done it in college, never even telling our parents.

Over the summers, we backpacked through Europe, staying at hostels instead of the lavish hotels our parents had pushed on us.

I knew I was a little spoiled, but I didn't want to live my entire life never seeing beyond the silver spoon.

Astra and I got along so well because we both felt the same way.

Now, though, I felt like I was seeing my life through somebody else's eyes and it was…weird.

I wasn't sure I liked it.

Shaking off the feeling, I pulled at Kaleb's hand. "Come on. Astra can wait for the luggage. I want to show you around."

"Ah…yeah. Yeah, sure." He looked a little dazed, eyes lingering on the huge windows that dominated one wall, facing out over the city, the river sparkling off to the east.

"We moved in the year before we graduated from college, handled all the designing, picking out the furniture." We walked into the large, wide-open living room space. "Our mothers kept insisting we let somebody from their circle recommend a decorator. But we didn't want a designer space. We wanted something comfortable."

"It's gorgeous," he said. Then he smiled a little. "And comfortable. I could sleep on that couch for a month, I bet."

"I've tried." Then I laughed.

I took him through the entire place, room by room, although I only gestured toward Astra's rooms. "She's a bit of a messy roommate, and the lady who cleans for us has been on vacation in Puerta Vallarta this week. You don't want to look in there."

"It can't be any worse than…" He stopped, trailing off and shaking his head. "Never mind. I'll take your word for it."

I paused by another door and opened it. "One of the guest rooms. We have three. Sometimes we have a party here, and we'll let a guest stay over in case…" I rolled my eyes and mimed drinking from a bottle.

"You're a good mate."

"And this is my room." I bit my lip as I led him inside, still holding onto his hand.

It wasn't as large as my childhood room, but it was *mine* – decorated by me and only me. A rainbow of colors that shouldn't have worked erupted around us, cheerful and chaotic and wonderful. Orange and red and pink, blended with the colorful carpet I'd bought from a street vendor on one of my trips out of the country with my parents. It had appalled my mother, which made me love it even more.

The silk comforter on my bed was pink and orange, and it might have been too much for some, but I loved it. The walls were the only thing lacking in color. They were a pure, soft white, but there were bits and pieces of art, pictures, silk wall hangings that echoed the color design.

"I feel like I've fallen into a flower," he said, smiling as he turned to look at me.

"Is that a bad thing?"

"No." He smiled. "I like it. It's kind of like…you. Crazy and wild and…soft."

"Oh." Something I didn't want to think about made my throat close up. "Well, I think I like that."

"Good." He cleared his throat and ran a hand through his hair. "Well, should I…um. Any particular guest room I should take or can I just pick?"

I moved closer.

His pupils spiked, getting a little larger as I reached past him and nudged the door closed.

"I was kind of thinking that you could just stay with me."

Chapter 11

Kaleb

Stay with me.

Her words lingered with me all through that night, clear into the next morning.

Standing under the hot, pulsating spray of the shower, I braced my hands against the wall and told myself to quit thinking about it – about *her*.

I needed to be thinking about my problems, of which there were many.

I still hadn't heard back from Camry.

I'd left more than a couple of messages. She should have called by now. I didn't know if I wanted to be pissed or scared. I was a little of both, but I couldn't do anything about it here. And I couldn't leave until the bloody money was in my hand.

It was quiet, not even a whisper, but the brush of chilled air against my skin let me know that the shower door had been opened. I turned just as Piety pressed flat against me, her breasts warm and soft – *everything* about her was warm…and soft enough. She definitely had an athletic build. She had the look that made me think she could take a run down the beach and maybe even join me when I went out surfing.

It made me wonder if she'd ever gone surfing herself.

If not, I could teach her.

She pressed her mouth to my neck, and I reached out, gripping her hips. "If you need the shower, I can let you have it in a few minutes," I said, head falling to the side as she bit down.

Fuck.

"Hmmm. But I climbed in here because you're here." She eased back, blinking the water out of her eyes. She pressed her hands against my chest and let them slide down, the path made slicker by water. "I was thinking we could engage in some…water conservation."

She slid her hand down to my cock.

"That's…an important issue," I said, the words rough.

She tightened her grip as she neared the tip, rotated her wrist as she moved closer to the base. It was enough to drive me to madness.

"Isn't it?" She licked water from where it ran down the midline of my chest, then she sank lower, giving me a view that I knew men would kill for.

Then she closed her mouth around my cock.

"Oh, shit."

She chuckled, and the reverberation had me slamming a hand against the wall. When she leaned forward, I eased my weight completely against the tile and threaded my fingers through her hair, shaking the water out of my eyes as I watched her swallowing my cock. I'd had her more than once since we'd met, but we'd both been too eager to take the time for this.

When the water clouded my vision again, I fumbled for the faucet and turned the spray off, shuddering out a groan as she paused a moment to lick the water away from my belly and left thigh.

"Didn't want to waste that water, since we're trying to conserve and all?" she asked, giving me a sly smile.

"Can't have that."

I grabbed her hair and tugged her mouth back. I clenched my teeth as she took me back inside, the wet heat almost enough to undo me. This time, she sucked on me with a fervor, not letting go until I was panting and half-mad. When she finally did, my cock slid from between her lips with a little *pop* before she stood up in front of me, raising onto her toes until our lips were pressed together.

The brush of her belly was damp against my cock, and I swore. I needed her again.

Spinning her around, I bent her over the built-in bench seat and drove inside.

She was even more wet and soft than usual, slick like satin.

And *naked…*

No.

"Shit. Condom," I said, groaning.

I started to pull away.

"Don't stop." It was a weak whisper, and I told myself to ignore it. To do the smart thing.

Then she reached down and closed her fingers around my balls. My eyes crossed and hot licks of pleasure-pain went shooting straight up my spine. Talk about having someone by the balls.

"Shit, Piety, I…fuck, we need a rubber."

"I brought one. But…" She wiggled her ass back against me. "Do we really need it? You feel so good. I'm…safe. Protected."

I rolled my hips against her, told myself again to pull

out.

"Please, Kaleb. You feel so good like this."

She looked over her shoulder, her eyes deepened to indigo.

How the hell was I supposed to say no to her?

"Yes," I muttered, knowing I was doing something incredibly stupid. But if I was going to be stupid about something, I might as well be stupid for her.

And maybe for myself…a little. This once.

She squeezed my sack again, and I thrust against her again. I could only withdraw so far with her holding onto me, but the friction was perfect, sweet and tight. And then I heard her cry out and knew that I'd found her sweet spot.

"Fuck me, Kaleb." She released me, using both hands to balance herself.

She didn't have to tell me twice, not when I finally knew what it felt like to be skin to skin with her. I doubted I could ever have it another way after this. I reached underneath us and found her clit, stroking it as I thrust into her, long, deep strokes that would get us to our climax quickly.

I planned on having her again in her bed, and then I'd take my time.

As I felt her clench around me, heard her gasp out my name, I wondered if I'd be able to let her go when the time came. I pushed the thought from my mind as I let my own orgasm roll over me. I pressed my mouth against her shoulder, murmuring her name as I emptied myself inside her.

I wouldn't think about the future. Not now. I'd enjoy what time I had with her. All of it.

* * * * *

"Think of a happy place."

Glancing at Piety, I asked, "Are you telling me or yourself?"

"Myself." She sighed glumly as she parked her car, a sexy little McLaren that had almost given me a hard-on just climbing inside. Riding next to her had done the rest.

I'd almost asked if I could drive, but I thought that might be pushing it.

"I think this car is a damn happy place." I thought a moment, then smiled. "And the shower. That's a very happy place. Between your legs, that's a favorite. Should I continue?"

"Thinking about me crawling between my own legs isn't exactly making me nice and calm." But she smiled over at me.

"Oh, it's not making me *calm*." I took her hand, threading our fingers together. "It's giving me nice thoughts. Or dirty thoughts. Some might not consider those so nice, but whatever. Why do you look so nervous? This was your idea."

"Actually, it was Astra's." She rested her head on the padded headrest.

I did the same, enjoying the luxurious leather. These were moments I'd remember the rest of my life, and not just because I was sitting in a supercar that would make most men weep from the sheer beauty of it. It was the beauty *in* it. Piety was turning me inside out and we barely knew each other.

"She manages to talk me into the craziest shit. Always has. This wasn't any different. Hell, I think this was the easiest of all." She rolled her head on the seat and looked at me. "Because of you. You're incredibly easy to say yes to, you know that, Kaleb?"

"Am I?" I lifted her hand to my lips and kissed it. "I'd say the same of you. I'd say yes to just about anything you asked at this moment."

"Hold on to that thought," she muttered. She turned her gaze back toward the house. "You might not think so in a bit."

"Come on. They can't be that bad, can they?" I'd said something along those lines before. They'd raised Piety, after all.

But she gave me that grimace again. "Just remember…go to your happy place."

* * * * *

"I can't *believe* you did this."

I stood off to the side, remaining silent for the most part while Piety stood in front of her parents, looking like a queen. Her parents viewed themselves as royalty at least, no denying that.

Her father, one Senator Silas Van Allen had taken one look at me and dismissed me with barely a flicker of his lashes, right up until Piety had pressed a kiss to my cheek, and said, "Daddy, meet Kaleb Hastings. My husband."

Her mother had gasped in outrage, and looking from me to Piety and back like she expected us to tell her it was all some big prank.

"What are you going to tell Windsor?" her mother asked, her voice low, as if I wouldn't hear them.

Of course, I was standing right there, and she damn well knew it.

"What do you mean, what am I going to tell Windsor?" Piety asked calmly. "I'm not going to tell him anything. Well, unless I run into him at a fundraiser or something. We hardly know each other."

"You've been dating," Silas said, his voice just as neutral as his daughter's. But his eyes were…cold.

How could these two have created somebody like Piety?

She was so warm. So alive.

And they were like a couple of wooden dolls, complete with sticks up their respective arses.

"No, Daddy. You *wanted* us to date. I went out with him once or twice to get you off my back." She lifted a shoulder and turned away, moving over to a long table stretched against the wall.

"Is that what this…this farce is about?" Silas demanded.

I tensed. I really didn't like the way they were talking to their daughter.

His eyes came to mine. "Is that it…what did you say your name was?"

I didn't respond. If he was smart enough to handle the political claptrap, he was smart enough to remember my name. He just wanted me to feel like I wasn't important enough.

Fuck that.

"Kaleb," he said slowly. "It *is* Kaleb, correct?"

"Yep, sure is, mate." I exaggerated my accent and gave him a glib smile. If Piety wanted to piss him off, I might as well give her – and him – her money's worth. "I'm a bit of a bastard, really, going and stealing Piety away like I did, marrying her without so much as inviting

90

you. But we just couldn't wait, could we, sweetheart?"

Piety was back at my side now, and some of the stress had melted from her eyes as she leaned against me. "No. We couldn't." Head resting against my arm, she gave her mom a dazzling smile. "Maybe we can plan a real ceremony here in a few months…something we can invite *everybody* to. The drive-in Vegas chapel thing was so…lame."

"You got married…" her mother paused, a hand pressed to her chest, "you went through one of those *drive*-through chapels?"

Piety waved a hand, forgoing the answer, which was probably a good idea since neither of us actually had any idea how the ceremony had gone. "It was just making things official. Kaleb and I knew what we wanted."

Damn, she was good at this.

Sliding a hand down her back, I glanced at her father. He was still skewering me with his eyes.

"Just what do you do, Kaleb?"

"Right now? Not much of anything." I shrugged and turned my head into Piety's hair, nuzzling her neck. "I had to quit my job so I could be with Piety."

She gave me a smile so warm and sweet that my heart ached a little. Then it ached more as I reminded myself that this wasn't real. None of it was. We enjoyed being with each other, but that was as far as it went.

"How…thoughtful of you," Silas said. I could hear the fury pulsing in his voice. "And what was it you did before you quit?"

"Well, I didn't hold the job long. I'd only taken it mainly to get some money and get over here to the States." I had a feeling that would piss him off – and it did. His mouth tightened, and I could see the redness slowly creeping up his neck. He looked like he wanted to punch me already. And I hadn't even gotten to the good part. "Back in Australia, I did a bit of this, bit of that. Planned on opening up my own surf shop, but that didn't pan out. Anyway, I came over here after Flames Down Under took me on."

"Flames…" It was her mother who said it. Amara's face went white, and she looked from me to Piety before covering her mouth with her hand.

I bit back a smile. Her mother knew what Flames Down Under was. I'd have to point that out to Piety later if she hadn't caught it already.

"You'll have to help me out there, Kaleb." His jaw was tight, yet he managed to sound calm, casual even as he continued. "I'm not familiar with Flames Down Under. Is it a restaurant?"

"No. It's a dance troupe…of sorts." I paused and then added, "We're – well, it's not *we* anymore since I quit – but Flames are kind of like the Aussie version of the Chippendales. Strippers."

I added the last part in even though it wasn't necessary. He'd figured it out.

"You married a *stripper*," he said, finally giving up the pretense and whirling on Piety with rage stamped all over his features.

"I married *Kaleb*." She lifted her chin and stared him down. "I'm hardly a child, Dad."

"That's hardly evident!" He flung a hand in my direction. "He just outright admitted that he came over here for money, shakes his ass…*for money,* and you went and married him. You don't even know him!"

"I know what I need to know." Piety looked over at me and the smile on her face did little to calm the anger that had started to burn in me.

The anger had nothing to do with what her father was

saying about me – I didn't give a damn about that – but he had no right to talk to her like that.

Bastard.

"And just what is that?" Silas held up a hand. "Never mind. I don't want that answer. This is insane, Piety. I won't stand for it."

After a moment, he turned on his heel and moved to pick up a phone. He spoke quietly into it and then replaced it before looking at me, eyes hard and cold as steel. "I'm having a car brought around. The driver can take you...wherever. But I need to speak with my–"

"I'm not going anywhere without my wife." I took Piety's hand. "Not unless she wants me to."

"This is my house, you son of a bitch," Silas said, voice choked.

"And he's my husband." Piety tightened her hand around mine. "If he's not welcome...well." She glanced up at me. "Come on, Kaleb. Let's go."

"Piety, wait." Amara rose as she spoke for the first time in several minutes.

"I won't stand here and have Dad talk to me like I'm an infant." Piety lifted her chin.

"Then stop acting like a child!"

I turned on the senator then. "Exactly what is your problem?"

He blinked, clearly caught off-guard by the *stripper* daring to talk to him.

Next to me, Piety tensed.

I continued, "I couldn't understand it, the whole way here. Piety has been so...well, she's amazing. I've seen her give her heart to people. She laughs, and she makes me laugh. She's kind and sweet and funny and confident. And then on the way here, all that changes. Now I get it – she was worried about dealing with *you*."

93

He opened his mouth, but at that moment, a towering man appeared in the doorway, his bald head gleaming as if it had been polished with wax. The thought made me chuckle, and I shook my head, amused at the absurdity of it all.

"You think this is *funny*?" Silas asked, the words grinding between his clenched teeth.

"Sir, how may I be of assistance?" The giant eyed me narrowly.

"You aren't needed, Timothy," Piety said. "Dad was trying to make my husband leave, but if he can't stay, neither can I. We're both going."

"Your husband..." Timothy – the giant – studied us for a moment, then nodded at Piety. "Congratulations." Then he nodded at the elder Van Allen's and left.

"She makes me happy," I said without thinking. For a minute, this wasn't a scam, wasn't anything I was doing for money. I was just seeing the rage, the disappointment, all the negative emotions in the older man's eyes – emotions directed at Piety – and it pissed me off. "And I think I make her happy. If you love her, I don't understand what your problem is. Unless, of course, you're more worried about your life than hers, and that makes you the son of a bitch here."

A soft gasp escaped Piety at my words, and I decided I needed to stop before I said something stupid – or more stupid. Taking her hand, I lifted it to my lips. "Come on, love. Let's go."

* * * * *

94

"Thank you."

We'd been driving in relative silence for the past ten minutes, and the soft words were loud.

I looked over at Piety. "You're not mad?"

She laughed. "No. I…hell, Kaleb. There have been so many times I've almost said those exact same words to him."

"Not being related to the uptight bastard makes it easier." Grimacing, I added, "Sorry. He just…I don't like how he talked to you."

"It's okay." She smiled, her gaze locked on the road. "My parents love me, Kaleb. I know that. They just don't understand me. Anyway…it went about as well as we could hope. Now we just…well, we've got the family reunion. Then you and I will have some massive blow-up, and we'll call this quits so you can go on your way. I've got the money I promised you – half of it now, the rest after the family reunion. Okay?"

I swallowed hard. "Sounds good."

"Oh, by the way…" She glanced at me. "Astra's cousin is a lawyer. I don't know if you're wanting to stay over here or go back to Oz, but we can talk to him. He can help you figure things out."

"Brilliant."

But I wasn't paying that much attention.

In a few more days, this would all be over.

I should have been relieved. I could focus on what really mattered. I could deal with Camry. Do what I'd come here to do.

Yet I wasn't relieved.

And even though she was sitting right there next to me, I was already missing my wife.

Chapter 12

Piety

I checked the time.

Again.

It was only ten minutes later than when I'd checked the last time.

Sighing, I dropped down onto the couch, determined to find some way to fill my mind.

Something underneath my butt managed to preoccupy my thoughts...for maybe two seconds.

I frowned as I pulled out a cell phone. Not mine.

"Kaleb's."

Had to be.

I rubbed my finger along the surface of it for a moment, nibbling my lower lip. Then I put the phone down and dropped my head back to the couch. He wasn't here, and I was slowly going out of my mind.

Astra had indeed worked her magic and gotten him a meeting with her cousin Samuel. Whether or not anything solid would happen today, I wasn't betting on it, but at least they could start the ball rolling.

I'd feel better if I was with him, but Kaleb had told

me there was no need for me to go. Something told me that he wanted to go alone.

So I stayed home.

I wasn't *hurt* or anything. It wasn't like he needed me to hold his hand, and our marriage wasn't about a green card for him. Besides, I could use a little more downtime and relaxation before heading back to work next week. I certainly wasn't going to be getting any over the weekend.

I snorted at the thought and tried to picture how things would go when my dad already looked like he wanted to explode just thinking about Kaleb.

Dad had tried calling, but I'd ignored him.

He'd even broken down and texted even though he'd always insisted that texts were so impersonal. He didn't like emails, either, but understood they were how people communicated these days.

But texts?

Senator Silas Van Allen didn't *text*.

But he had sent me one earlier.

You need to stop acting like a child and talk to me. Please join your mother and I for dinner.

I'd responded with a simple question. *And Kaleb?*

We haven't been able to spend time with you in several weeks. We need time to catch up. He can join us some other time.

I'd given him a simple answer.

No thank you.

That had set him off, and Mom had taken over from there, but I was ignoring her too.

It was weird how freeing this was. Granted, it was all a farce, and I needed to think through how things would be after this, but for the first time, both my mother *and* my father had stopped trying to talk *through* me, stopped

97

looking through me.

Yes, they were angry, but I could handle that.

I couldn't keep handling how they spent more time worrying about how *my* life was going to affect *theirs*.

If they were that hung up on it, they should have had a poodle instead of a daughter.

I checked the time again without any conscious thought, then groaned. It was going to be another hour, maybe two, before he was done with Samuel.

I was about to go out of my mind...

The phone next to me buzzed again and I looked down at it automatically.

A pretty girl's picture flashed up across the screen, along with the notification that he'd gotten a message.

"Don't do it, Piety," I muttered to myself.

He was a good-looking guy. He probably got messages from a *lot* of girls. Of course, he hadn't told me that he was involved. I hadn't asked.

But...

I'd married him, and we were having sex. It wasn't just about me, since I knew where we stood with each other. I didn't want to be the other woman. At least that was the excuse I gave myself as I swiped my thumb across the phone to unlock it.

Her name was Camry.

That was the first thing I noticed.

She was also flashing a wide, open grin into the camera.

She looked...happy. Sweet and young and happy.

Who was she?

The phone jolted in my hand as another message came through.

Are you there, K? Come on...I need to know. Things are getting desperate here. You got the money or not?

A strange, heavy sensation settled in my gut, and I closed the messages, putting the phone down.

I knew Kaleb needed money. He'd been honest about that from the beginning. Or had he?

Had he known who I was from moment one? Astra said she remembered how things had gone the night Kaleb and I had gotten married, but how reliable was her memory.

Had Kaleb been playing me this whole time?

And just who the hell was Camry?

Part Two

Chapter 1

Piety

While I waited for my husband for hire to return from his meeting with Astra's cousin, the lawyer, I was dealing with the uneasiness I'd felt ever since I read the message on his phone from Camry.

Camry.

Who was she?

How did he know her?

Did she mean anything to him?

Of course she did. Her picture was in his phone. She called him K.

But did any of that matter?

And why was she asking him for money?

But even as that thought occurred to me, I brushed it aside. I'd had people I barely knew hit *me* up for money, guys I'd dated just a couple of times would ask me to hook them up, telling me about this *fascinating* idea they had and just how much they could change the world if they only had a *little* bit of financial help.

Money didn't mean somebody mattered – it meant the *money* mattered.

But the rest?

I pushed the question aside as I heard the familiar

sound of a key in the lock, and I slid off the couch just as the door opened. He caught sight of me coming toward him and paused, as if I'd surprised him.

I wrapped my arms around his neck and kissed him. For that brief moment, as my lips touched his, the chaos in my head faded away to nothing, and it was just the two of us. It seemed that some tension drained out of him as well, and I wanted to curl myself tighter around him, pretend the world was gone.

But the world would just come back and find us. It always did.

So I took a step back, rubbing my lips together to hold on to his taste a moment longer.

"How did it go?"

He shrugged, his voice flat as he answered, "It went."

He kissed my forehead before he stepped around me, and the feel of his lips lingered in the sweetest way. I turned, watching him as he moved deeper into the loft.

"You left your phone," I said. There. Nice and easy. I didn't have to mention I'd gone snooping and seen his message, right?

"I noticed," he said nonchalantly as he pulled out a bottle of water from the refrigerator. He grinned at me. "I discovered that...oh, two minutes before I was supposed to meet the lawyer."

"Could have been worse. You could have left it back in Vegas."

"True."

Looking down, I fought the ugly monster brewing in my belly. I didn't have all the facts, and even if I did, we hadn't made any real promises to each other. This was a business transaction.

With sex.

"Who's Camry?"

The words popped out without any conscious thought from me, and I would have sucked them back in if there'd been any possible way of doing it. But there'd wasn't, and I stood there, feeling blood rush to my face as he slowly lifted his head and met my eyes.

"What?"

"Ah…" Face flaming, I shifted from one foot to the other, feeling awkward and out of place. It wasn't a feeling I was used to, and I didn't like it – at *all*. "She…um…well, she texted you. I'm sorry. I didn't think. I just picked up the phone and saw the message. She wanted to know about money."

I half-expected him to just brush it off. *Oh…it's a woman I met on the tour…she's always bumming money for a smoke.* Or *It's a lady from home, sometimes she runs short right before payday.*

It would be something small and easy.

But a muscle jumped in his cheek as he stared at me.

"She's…" He turned away, the muscles in his spine going tight. He stood so rigid, I thought he'd break. I wished I hadn't said anything. He clearly didn't want to talk to me about her.

"Camry's my sister."

Oh. A harsh breath escaped me, the nervousness draining away to be replaced by giddiness.

But all of that evaporated in an instant when Kaleb looked back at me.

"She needs money to pay off her dealer. That's why I came to the States, the reason why I joined the Flames. She's in trouble." He shook his head and barked a bitter laugh. "She's been in and out of trouble since our parents died, and I can't do shit to help her. But I can't just ignore her, either. She's my baby sister. I have to at least try."

Chapter 2

Kaleb

I expected any number of possible reactions from Piety, everything from apathy to outrage. After all, it was one thing to have told her I needed money. Telling her it was to pay off a drug dealer was something else.

What I didn't expect was for Piety to come over and take my hand, then lead me to the couch and tell me to sit. She sat down next to me and curled up against me, her presence soothing me more than I deserved. "I think it's time you tell me what's going on."

"I just did."

"No. You told me you had a sister who owes money to a dealer...that's like saying Captain America is a movie about a soldier."

Her comparison tugged a smile out of me. "You mean there's more?" I tilted my head and smiled at her, suddenly exhausted.

"Kaleb."

Sighing, I dropped my head forward. I owed her that much at least. "Okay."

Closing my eyes, I tried to figure out where to start.

How did I wrap up the last decade of my life in a way that wouldn't take hours or months to explain? She deserved to know, but I hated the thought of having to relive all of it.

"Our parents died ten years ago. It was rough." Shaking my head, I stared off into nothing. Rough didn't even describe it. "Before that, we were normal. So fucking normal, you'd almost get sick. Dad and Mom would dance around the house at night, and they'd laugh and tease each other. I used to act like I hated it but..." I shrugged, smiling a little. I didn't let myself remember the good times enough. "It was good. They were good. *We* were good. Then they were killed in a car crash, and nothing's been good since."

"I'm so sorry," she said, her quiet words full of emotion.

I looked over at her. "We were sent to live with my dad's uncle – he's the only family we had left. He tried, but he never had kids, hadn't wanted any, and he didn't know what to do with us. Especially Camry. She was only eleven at the time. She cried a lot. Caused trouble. Started skipping school and by high school, she got into drugs and was already drinking...fuck."

This was why I didn't like to think about it. I felt like a failure. I hadn't been able to help her. At all.

"Sometimes she hated even being around me, hated *me*, I think."

"No." Piety touched my cheek. "Why would she hate you?"

"Because I had them longer. I know it doesn't make sense, but she was so young when they died. Nothing makes sense when you're a kid who's lost her parents."

"But you're her brother."

"Fat lot of good I've done her." My heart twisted at

her words, and I wished it could be that simple. "Camry…well, hell. If Mom and Dad had still been alive, there's no telling what she might have gone on to do. She was always smart. Even as much trouble as she got into, school was still easy for her. She even managed to get an international scholarship to go to college over here. The University of Nevada, in Las Vegas."

Piety brushed at my hair. "You must have been proud of her."

"I was." I only wished it could've lasted. "But I got worried fast. She had trouble after the first few months. She ended up losing her scholarship and left school. But she didn't come home. She stayed in Las Vegas. Now…hell. I don't know all the details, but I know she owes a shitload of money to a piece of shit drug dealer, and when I try to call, I can hardly ever get hold of her. The one time she does call…" I laughed, bitterness leaving a foul taste in my mouth.

Getting up, I paced over to the wide window that faced out over the panorama and stared outside.

"I talked to Samuel about helping us getting new visas to stay in the States," I said quietly. "When I signed with Flames Down Under, I got a work visa, but since I'm not in the show anymore, I need to find another way to stay. I have to…for Camry's sake. She's an addict. She needs help, more help than I can give her. I want to get her into some sort of program. I'll find a job."

She opened her mouth to ask a question, but I held up a hand.

"Not stripping either," I assured her. "I was…*am* a good surfer. I worked at a surf shop in Sydney. I wanted to run my own surf camp eventually. Teach people how to surf. When I first got here, I had this crazy idea I could get her debts settled, then we could find some place. In

California, maybe. I could work at a surf store, maybe give lessons." He shot me a quick smile. "Nobody surfs like an Aussie. Except maybe down in Hawaii. But it was an idea. I don't know though. Nothing is going the way I planned."

Hearing her get up, I started to turn, catching her arms just as she would have slid them around me.

"What are you doing?" I asked softly.

"Hugging you." She gave me an easy smile. "You look like you need it."

"I…" The words died in my throat as she slid her arms around me and tucked her head against my chest, snuggling in close. Damn. What had I done to deserve her?

"It'll work out, Kaleb. You'll see."

I cupped the back of her head in my hand and breathed in the scent of her. I really, really wanted to believe that.

She smoothed her hands up and down my spine, but the worries continued to eat inside me. When she took my face in her hands and kissed me, offering the sweetest of distractions, I didn't have the strength to refuse. She tasted so good, felt so soft. The heat of her mouth on mine, her hands in my hair, it was too much and not enough.

She leaned into me, deepening the kiss as she slid her tongue into my mouth. I gripped her waist, swallowing her moan as I pulled her against me. It wasn't close enough. We had too many clothes between us, and that was a problem that needed rectified immediately.

I pulled back, looking into her eyes as I caught the hem of her skirt, slid it up her toned thighs. She didn't look away from my gaze, not even when I ran my finger along the crotch of her panties and found it damp.

"I want you," I said, the need slamming into me like it had been lying in wait all day.

"Then have me," she said as she leaned in and bit my lower lip.

I groaned as it sent waves of heat blasting through every neuron in my body.

"Right now? Right here?" I asked, staring into her eyes.

"Right now. Right here. No roommate to bother us." Her tongue flicked out to wet her lips. "Astra's gone for the day...out doing things. Going to be gone...all day...oh..."

She clamped around the fingers I'd just slid through her damp folds, then up into her wet channel. Fuck. She was so tight and hot. My cock throbbed just thinking about being inside her again.

"That's...convenient." I twisted my wrist, using my knuckles to rub against her g-spot.

She rocked against me, her lashes fluttering. She slid a hand down and gripped my wrist, her mouth parting on the sexiest groan I'd ever heard. She started to ride my hand, and I almost laughed, even as my dick began to pulse. *Fuck*. I wanted to have her riding *me* like that.

But there was time for that.

Later.

Right now, I wanted to watch her come on my hand.

She moved against me, demanding and hungry. I braced my free hand on the wall over her head and looked down, watching my hand move under her skirt. When I circled my thumb around her clitoris, she shivered, a delicate reaction that started at her shoulders and went all the way down.

Damn.

Her nipples went tight and I swore. I wanted them in

my mouth. Wanted to use my teeth on them until she'd feel it for days.

But that would require moving, and I didn't want to do that until–

"Kaleb!" She clenched around me and climaxed, hard and quick, her hips bucking against my hand even as she cried out my name.

I waited until she was done before I moved, and it was the most pleasurably excruciating moments of my life.

Then, as she sagged against the wall, looking insanely pleased with herself, I yanked my pants open, pushed them down far enough to free my aching cock, and grabbed her hips. She laughed when I picked her up, then swore as I thrust inside her. I moaned as I felt the mini tremors still going through, and I had to grit my teeth against the sensation because it just felt too damn good.

"You're...fuck me, Piety. You're going to kill me."

She chuckled and clung to my shoulders, grinding down on me. "But what a way to go."

"Yeah." Lashing everything down until I almost had myself under control, I eased away enough to look into her eyes as I withdrew. After a moment, I eased back inside. "I love watching you. Love touching you."

"I love having you touch me..." The words broke on a sigh, and she arched, clamping tight around me with a moan.

Orgasm number two.

If I hadn't been so close to coming myself, I would've been smug.

"Don't..." I hissed out. "Don't do that, sweetheart."

"I can't help it." She shoved away from the wall, closing the small distance I'd put between us, and wrapped her arms around my neck. Then she started to move again, riding my cock this time. All sleek muscle and gorgeous female, she used her thighs and hips to move herself against me.

"*Fuck.*" I grabbed her ass, dragged her up and then let her sink back down, driven by her weight. Then I did it again, grinding her against me. The angle would be putting friction and pressure on her clit, and when she whimpered, I knew I had to do it again.

And again.

Again.

I would do this all day if it meant she'd keep making those mewling sounds.

"Please!" The word was weak, but I knew it would've been a scream if she'd had air.

Lurching forward a half step, I put her back against the wall and drove into her. Deep, hard, over and over, until we came together and it was violent, almost painful.

And absolutely fucking perfect.

Chapter 3

Piety

"Are you nervous?"

Sliding on my earrings, I glanced into the mirror and met Astra's gaze. I shrugged and answered honestly, "Some, I guess. I mean, this whole thing rides on him not..."

I trailed off, because I couldn't understand why he *wouldn't* say anything. My parents had been awful to him. The people around us later today would be just as bad, although they might not say anything outright. Still, it wasn't going to be fun, and I knew if I had people digging at me like that, I'd want to strike back.

"He won't say anything," Astra said, reading my mind in that annoying way of hers.

I stuck my tongue out.

"You're so mature." She clucked her tongue, then flopped back down on my bed to stare up at the ceiling. "He's not going to. He's just got that kind of...oomph to him. You can trust him. He's the guy you call at two in the morning when you've got a flat. Even if you're an hour away, he'd come help you out, and wouldn't ask for anything in return."

"Yeah." I had that kind of feeling from him too. Maybe that was part of why I was so nervous. Granted, this had been my idea – okay, mine and Astra's – but he'd be the one to deal with some of the harsher things said by people. Sure, they might say things about me and my *judgment*, but I'd dealt with that plenty already in my life.

They wouldn't be insulting his *judgment*.

They'd be insulting him, and what was worse. Now that I knew why he'd made the decisions he'd made, it made him a better man than I'd thought possible.

Groaning, I rubbed my forehead.

"Next time I offer somebody a ludicrous amount of money to do something for me, tell me to ask them why they need it so badly first," I told Astra, moving to sit next to her. After a moment's debate, I flopped down flat right alongside her, and we lay there, studying the ceiling.

"You like him, don't you?"

"Yeah." Closing my eyes, I blew out a breath. And told her the whole truth. "I really, *really* like him."

"Tell him."

A knot settled in my throat, but I forced myself to ignore it. "No point. He has things to do back in Las Vegas, a life to get back to."

"And you know this because…?"

Sitting up, I looked over at Astra and shrugged. "We've talked. Some. I…I think he kind of likes me too. But the things he's got going on comes first. I don't blame him. But it's too complicated for a relationship."

"If it's the *right* relationship, nothing is too complicated." She sat up and hooked an arm around my shoulders, hugging me. "You seem happy with him, PS. Do you really wanna give that up?"

Putting my hand on her arm, I leaned into her. "I'm

not even ready to think about that yet. Besides, I can't control the things in his life."

Even though they weighed on me.

Even though Astra wasn't entirely wrong.

There was a knock on the door, and I squeezed Astra's arm. "Gotta go. That's him."

"Say hi to Mummy and Daddy for me." She blew me a kiss and wagged her eyebrows,

"You sure you don't want to come?" I picked up my purse from the foot of the bed and went to open the door.

She followed me out into the living room to answer. "You'd have to get me even drunker than you were in Vegas before I'd consider going through one of your family reunions again. And I'd have to *stay* that drunk. All day. I'm pretty sure that's not good for the liver."

I laughed as I opened the door. "Probably not."

She winked at me. "Toodles!"

"Toodles." I made a face at her as I stepped into the hall and reached for Kaleb's hand. Turning my attention to him, I asked, "Are you ready for this?"

"Are you?" He threaded his fingers between mine.

"Why wouldn't I be?" I gave him a brilliant smile and squeezed his hand. "Let's do it."

* * * * *

The madder my dad got, and the more my mother clutched her pearls – she *literally* clutched her pearls – the easier it got.

Sinking down on a padded chaise lounge next to my great aunt Agatha, I gestured to Kaleb. "Aunt Agatha, have you met my husband?"

She gave him a narrow look and a short nod. It was one of the politer receptions he'd gotten, but her attention on him didn't last long. She was too interested in me.

Holding a cocktail in one hand and a book in the other, she studied me.

"Just what are you up to, Piety?" she asked, dark eyes far too shrewd for my liking.

"I'm introducing you to my husband," I said innocently.

"Humph."

She took a lusty sip of the cocktail and put her book down. It was a romance, one of those kind featuring a bare-chested man with a woman bent over his arm, her boobs all but falling out of the dress. The sight of it made me grin, but her next words wiped it all away.

"Your husband. What's his middle name?"

It caught me off-guard, and I felt like an idiot – I didn't *know*.

"What's yours?" Kaleb asked, interrupting smoothly. He sat down on the chaise next to me and gave Agatha a mega-watt smile. "If I'd known Piety was holding out on me, I might have told her no."

To my surprise, a laugh boomed out of Agatha. "*She* proposed to *you*?"

Some of the suspicion leaked from her eyes, and she sighed, reaching out to pat my knee. "Keep your secrets, Piety. I won't blab. But it's going to take more than this for them to leave you be." She leaned back and settled more comfortably against the chaise. "It's going to take *you*."

I wasn't even going to try to follow that line of thought, and she didn't give me the chance. "Here," she said, pushing her nearly empty cocktail glass into my hand. "Go refill me. I'm thirsty, and I want to admire the arm candy you brought."

Wariness flooded me. "Aunt Agatha…"

"Oh, relax. None of them will bother him if he's with me." Aunt Agatha gave me a serene smile, then one final pat on my knee. "Go on now."

Sighing, I did as she said, knowing I'd never get a moment's piece from her until I did.

As I made my way through the crowd of aunts, uncles, cousins, and various other relations, I told myself I didn't need to hurry, that Aunt Agatha wouldn't expose our secrets.

Then, I wished I would've hurried, because I came face to face with one of the few cousins I would have done *anything* to avoid.

"Well, well, well." Tabitha smiled at me. She was my father's niece, and she looked far too like me, save for the hair. Hers was a bronzed sort of blonde, and the stylist she used teased out shades of gold and caramel. She was shorter and softer, a gentler reflection.

At least physically.

Inside, Tabitha was a piranha.

"How's life for the newlyweds?" She gave me a look of innocent curiosity. "I hear you married an exotic dancer. Does he still…perform?"

"Hi, Tabitha." I chose to ignore everything else.

"You see, a friend of mine is getting married, and I'm in charge of the entertainment for the bachelorette party." She took a step closer and gave me a devious smile before glancing toward where I'd left Kaleb with Aunt Agatha. "And he is *certainly* entertaining. Easy on the eyes."

"Nice try," I said. With a casual smile, I smoothed out a non-existent wrinkle in my dress. "But you and I know none of your friends are warm-blooded enough to enjoy a man like Kaleb."

"Oh, I don't know." She smiled, though her idea of a smile was just the slightest curl of her lips. Heaven forbid she do something that might lead to wrinkles. "A girl has to...experiment every now and then. You clearly have...and look at you. So, what do you say? Does he...hire out his services?"

I didn't need to be a mind reader to know she wasn't talking about stripping.

But instead of sinking to her level, I stepped aside and gestured. "I'll tell you what. Why don't you go ask him? He's right over there...talking to Aunt Agatha."

The first few words were all she processed for a moment, and the cat's smile came, brightening her eyes.

Then she heard the rest. *Aunt Agatha.*

She sucked in a breath. "You left him with *that* old hag? Talk about a man-eater."

"What's the matter, honey? Jealous?" I asked. "Go on then. Go talk to him."

She turned on a toothpick heel and stalked off. We both knew she'd never do anything that might even resemble confronting somebody near Aunt Agatha. The woman was a lioness, and you had to have a spine to deal with her.

Tabitha was vindictive, petty, and cruel. Brave? That wasn't her.

I managed to get Aunt Agatha's drink – and one for me – without too much additional drama, and I got back to find my aunt and my husband laughing as if they'd known each other for ages. It was enough to make me smile, and I turned Aunt Agatha's drink over to her as I sat down next to Kaleb, leaning against him without thinking about it.

115

"Hmmm…" Aunt Agatha made a low noise as she sipped from her drink, the sound making me slide her a narrow look.

"What's that for?"

"Oh, nothing. Nothing." She waved a hand at me and took another sip, looking rather pleased with herself. "I just thought I had this whole mess figured out, and you just went and dashed it all to bits, that's all."

"What mess?" I took Kaleb's hand, hoping she wasn't going to say what I thought she was going to say. "We're not a couple of specimens sitting on a slide in your lab, Aunt Agatha."

She'd worked for a biological research facility for years after her husband passed away, choosing science over pursuing a family. A rather strange idea for a woman of her time, she'd once told me.

"Everything and everyone is a specimen, in a way." She reached out, one hand extended.

I took hers, and she squeezed my fingers.

"Go on, now, Piety." She smiled at me and let go. "Mingle and make sure you kiss that sexy Aussie of yours a time or two. Shock the hell out of that stodgy old nephew of mine."

I blushed at the thought of kissing Kaleb – or anybody else – in front of my father.

"Enjoy the rest of your day, Aunt Agatha," I said.

"You too, darling."

As we lost ourselves in the crowd, I hooked my arm through his. "What did you think of her?"

"She doesn't seem to fit." He glanced down at me. "A lot like you."

I laughed, delighted. "That's the best compliment I've ever received. Thank you."

"That's the best compliment you've *ever* received?"

116

We'd reached the stone balustrade that separated the wide terrace from the landscape. There, we stopped, leaned against it, and looked back over the crowd. Some of them weren't paying us any attention. Others were good at pretending not to. But some didn't even try pretending. I ran out of fingers counting the ones who weren't even being subtle about their interest in us.

"Look at everybody here. I didn't have too many role models growing up." I shrugged, swirling my straw through my drink. "It's not that any of them are...well, *bad* people. But they have a certain view of the world that doesn't fit with mine. Is it any wonder that I clicked with Aunt Agatha?"

"No." He dipped his head.

He was going to kiss my cheek.

Whether it was because so many were still making such little effort to hide their interest, or their disdain, I didn't know, but I turned my head just slightly so that his lips brushed my mouth instead of my cheek.

He paused, hesitated.

Against his lips, I whispered, "Kiss me."

And he did.

It wasn't a deep, *I'm gonna get you naked,* kiss. But it was far from chaste.

And when he looked back at me, my heart was pounding, my throat was dry...and I wanted to get *him* naked.

* * * * *

Night wrapped around us in a cool, dark embrace by

117

the time we finally reached my room. It wasn't that it had taken forever to get home. It had just taken forever to get from the elevator to the door, then across the living room and finally to here.

There was a breadcrumb trail of clothing marking our progress and later, much later, I'd be a little embarrassed, because no doubt Astra would see it and tease me.

But for now, all I could think was that he wasn't completely naked and he wasn't inside me. And I needed both things immediately.

Fumbling with his belt, I leaned against the wall as he reached under my skirt and yanked at my panties. A tearing sound accompanied the burn of fabric being pulled tight against my skin, and then a faint touch of cooler air moved against my already wet flesh.

"Open your mouth, Piety," he said against my lips. "Open…damn it, can't get enough."

I laughed shakily, thinking the same thing.

He caught my lower lip and bit down. At the same time, he caught my hips and lifted up. I wrapped my legs around him and arched, pulling him against me.

I was already slick and ready for him, and I didn't want to wait anymore. We could go slow later. Right now, I needed him. He was hard, and the head of his cock passed over me, once, twice…

I gasped, shivering as he teased me. "Stop it," I demanded. This time, I was the one doing the biting, pulling at his bottom lip.

"What…stop this?" His dick slipped against me again.

"Kaleb," I whimpered.

"Do you want this?" He teased the head over my clit, and it wasn't nearly enough friction or pressure to ease

118

the ache inside me.

"I want you in me. I want...*you*."

His eyes met mine, and there was something utterly raw about the emotion there as he sank into me. Something too intimate, something more than sex. Part of me wanted to look away, but another part...couldn't.

"Have me then," he breathed the words against lips. "And I'll have you."

His mouth covered mine as he began to rock against me, slow, subtle moves that barely counted as thrusts, but I felt every nuance of him, every stroke.

Felt it in a way that was more than physical. Straight to my soul.

And when I came, it was so, so sweet...

Chapter 4

Kaleb

The world looked terribly small from thousands of feet up in the air.

I guess it only made sense.

The weird thing was how small I felt, how isolated.

For the first time in a week, I was alone with nothing more than my own thoughts in my head, and I didn't like it.

I'd spent most of my life alone, so this shouldn't have been anything new. And yet...

And *yet*...

The checks Piety had given me burned a hole in my pocket. There was no way this plane could land soon enough. I'd done what I had to help Camry, but part of me wished Camry had never been in the picture – and I hated that part of myself.

Hated it, and hated that it was growing bigger and bigger.

For a few days, I hadn't had to worry about taking care of my sister or anybody else.

Oh, the worry had been inside me, rubbing around

like an annoying bug, but I hadn't felt the need to constantly watch my back, or wonder when she'd show up, or if I'd hear from her – or the cops.

Now it was all rushing back, and what I really wanted to do was board the first flight back to Philadelphia so I could see Piety again.

But I had responsibilities – a sister to take care of.

I didn't have time to dream about something that never would have worked out anyway.

But I couldn't stop thinking about what it would be like when she came back to annul the marriage. We'd agreed I had to handle Camry first, but then I'd see Piety again. See her and…

Let her go.

The words made something ugly and hot fester inside me, and I admitted to myself that at some time during the past week, a part of me had begun to wish this whole thing was real. And at least a part of me wanted the chance to make it real.

So, yeah, we didn't know each other all that well – we hadn't had that chance – but everything I knew about her, I liked. I wanted the chance to know more, and I wanted…everything. A little more of everything when it came to Piety.

And that wasn't going to happen.

Closing my eyes, I dropped my head back onto the padded headrest just as one of the airline attendants came by and offered a cocktail. Even though I hadn't asked for it, Piety had done everything first class, including booking my trip back to Las Vegas. I had a wide, comfortable seat, and I'd already been given a snack and offered wine or a premium beverage. I'd declined both.

When the attendant asked again, I requested scotch, and when she started to name the offerings, I just shook

121

my head and asked for the best.

A few minutes later, something smooth and powerful was gliding down my throat, and I silently toasted the woman who was my wife for a few more days.

Once the scotch was gone, I closed my eyes and put her out of my mind.

I had to move on.

All that mattered now was Camry.

* * * * *

"Have you got the money?"

The man on the other end of the line made me want to do something brutal, ugly, and violent.

I managed to keep that desire out of my voice as I responded. "That's why I'm calling. When can we meet?"

"Well..." Stefano drew the word out.

I already knew he would try to make it seem like he was doing me a favor. Bastard. If I could put my fist all the way through his face when I saw him, I would.

But I already knew that would just cause more problems for Camry.

When she'd gotten herself hooked up with a crook like Stefano, she'd outdone herself. He wasn't the first asshole she'd been with, but he was, by far, the worst. He sold drugs and flesh, and while he might not be the one who got his hands dirty, he didn't like being double-crossed either. I'd been doing my research on him, the best I could. Law enforcement had tried to arrest him more than once, but the piece of shit kept slipping free.

No, the best chance was to just get Camry away.

"I think we can make something happen tonight. You bring that money, pretty boy, and no cops. You hear me?" Stefano said.

"I hear you."

He named a place and hung up. I shoved my phone into my pocket and stood there, staring at nothing. The hair on the back of my neck stood on end, and my gut was raw. I didn't like this, didn't like any of it.

But what the hell else could I do?

* * * * *

There was an air of desperation to this hellhole of a strip joint. Even the dancers strutting up and down the stage looked just this side of panicked, like a mouse caught in a trap or cornered by a cat. A particularly cruel one that wanted nothing more than to play with its food.

When Stefano glanced at one of the girls on the stage, she put a little more heart into her act. I could've sworn I saw her hands start to shake as she ripped off the tiny top that had barely covered her nipples.

I wanted to grab her off the stage and give her my shirt – and a damn sandwich. She was so skinny, her ribs showed, and her hipbones jutted out against her skin. She looked like she hadn't had a good meal in weeks, or longer. What sort of man was attracted to that?

"Like that one, do you?" Stefano gave me a leering smile.

The asshole was almost as tall as me, and bulky. The kind of guy who liked to stare at his muscles as he worked out and flexed, if I had to make a guess.

123

He looked about the way I'd thought he would, dark eyes, dark hair, and a sleazy smile that made me think he'd been born straight out of a grease trap.

Everything about him was slimy.

"Tell you what," he continued. "You can have her for the night. A freebie. Once we wrap up business."

Just the suggestion made me feel dirty.

"I don't think so." I met his dark brown eyes. "I don't need to pay a woman to have sex with me."

A muscle pulsed in his cheek.

Should have kept my mouth shut.

But he just smiled. "Sometimes we all like it a little wild, you know. A bit *rough.* Just thought I'd do you a favor. My girls will do *anything.*"

I looked past his shoulder, staring at the woman on the stage. "Yeah. I see that." Then I met his gaze and put the envelope down on the table. "Here. The money you say Camry owes. Now, take me to her so I can get her out of here."

He laughed as he took the envelope and started to count its contents. "So you want to save your sister. What makes you so sure she wants to be saved?"

I shifted restlessly in the chair, thinking about the two grand I hadn't put in the envelope. It would be enough, I hoped, to put the two of us up in a hotel for a little while so I could find a decent job, see about getting her help–

"You're short."

I shot him a narrow look. "No. I'm not. I counted it twice. You said she owed you ten grand. That's ten grand."

"Ten grand just covers her drug debt." Stefano lifted a shoulder. "But if she goes with you, I'll lose another ten-grand easy – just within the first few weeks. She's a favorite. Won't be easy to replace her."

"You arrogant–" Coming out of the chair, I slammed my hands down on the table, glaring down at him.

He smirked, his eyes flicking left then right.

I knew without looking that some of his goons had come up and surrounded us. Son of a bitch! Mother. Fucking. Asshole. I was tempted to beat him shitless just for existing.

But Camry needed me.

"You got this easy enough," Stefano said, smacking the envelope against his hand.

"I don't have another ten grand." I started to understand the desperation some of these women must feel. Or at least a shade of it. I needed to get Camry away from this scum.

"Then you better get it." Stefano leaned in, still smirking at me. "Until you do...she's mine. But I'll be reasonable. I'll give you some time. A few weeks...interest-free. Hurry it up though. You wanted to do business with me, now we're doing business."

Chapter 5

Piety

I'd put entirely too much time into my appearance, and I knew it.

I'd even gone shopping.

Not that I minded shopping, but how many women went shopping to buy an *annulment* dress?

A wedding dress, sure.

A dress for a date? Or even when you knew you'd see your ex and you wanted to knock him dead, just so he'd know what he was missing out on. Hell, even a dress to celebrate a divorce from an asshole.

But this wasn't any of those.

I was going to see my yet-to-be-ex and sign annulment papers, and I wanted to look good. Not because I wanted him to know what he was missing out on – but because I wanted to look my best.

I'd chosen a sheath that was almost the same color as my eyes and paired it with shoes the same shade. Keeping the makeup light, I'd done my best to look *good* without making it obvious I'd spent nearly an hour getting ready.

I hardly slept the night before. I was too anxious about seeing Kaleb again, and I didn't want the effects of a sleepless night showing on my face.

"Is this the place, Ms. Van Allan?"

The driver of the car I'd hired met my gaze in the rearview mirror, and I looked out the window, already reaching for my phone to double-check. But I didn't have to.

I saw Kaleb.

He was sitting on a bench outside the towering spiral of glass, and just the sight of him made my heart race.

"Yes. This is the place."

The driver parked, and before I climbed out, he passed me a business card.

"I won't be any more than ten minutes away, so call me when you're done," he said, smiling.

"Of course." I slid out of the car and started toward Kaleb, hoping none of my nervousness showed on my face.

My heart thudded against my ribs. Just seeing him again had my belly twisting inside. It hadn't been long – just a couple of days – but it felt like forever. I wanted to go to him and kiss him and run my hands over him…

He looked up, and my pounding heart tripped a beat or ten.

Forgetting my mental decision not to let him see my emotions, I rushed closer and caught his hand just as he stood up. I placed my other one on his cheek, frowning at the shadow across his eyes.

"What is it?" I asked.

"Nothing." He gave me a tired smile and nodded toward the skyscraper at his back. "You ready to get inside and get this done? Get you out of the heat. You aren't used to it."

I wasn't enjoying the Vegas heat, but instead of saying *yes*, I cupped his face and asked my question more firmly. "What's wrong?"

"I…" He sighed, and it was like the energy drained out of him with that expulsion of air.

Sweat beaded on my neck and began to trickle down my spine. "Come on. There's a coffee shop over there." I nodded toward it and took his hand. "Let's get something to drink. The meeting isn't for another half hour."

"I thought you said…" Kaleb frowned, checking his watch.

"I asked you to meet me here at two. I didn't tell you when the meeting was." I flashed him a smile. "I wanted to see you."

A ghost of his old grin came and went. "Come on."

Inside the coffee shop, I got both of us iced tea.

Sitting at a booth in the back gave us some semblance of privacy. I took his hand again, not wanting to waste a single moment that I could be touching him.

"Talk to me," I said. "Please."

"I met with Camry's dealer." He looked away, jaw clenched tight. *Everything* about him seemed tight, like he might shatter. Or explode.

I wanted to go around the table and sit next to him, but this wasn't about what I wanted, so I stayed where I was.

"I guess things didn't go as planned."

"No." He laughed, and it was a terrible, broken noise. The sort of sound that tore at my heart. "Son of a bitch. Scum-sucking, bottom-feeding son of a bitch."

"Tell me how you really feel."

He stared at me, then a faint smile curled his lips. "I'm being polite, actually. Piety, this man…shit, I'm not even sure if he qualifies for the title. I'm not even sure he qualifies as human. He's cold-blooded…a snake."

It wasn't that much of a leap to figure out what'd happened. "He's stringing you along, isn't he?"

Kaleb closed his eyes, his entire body sagging. I squeezed his hand and he turned his over, threading his fingers between mine. The connection hit me hard, straight down to my soul, and I tightened my grip.

"How did you know?"

Lifting a shoulder, I said, "As angry as you are, as frustrated as you sound. Wasn't hard to guess. I...ah..." I licked my lips, debating on how to answer. "I know girls who've gotten caught up with men like him – or at least men who seem to have things in common with him. He sounds like a predator."

"He is." Kaleb clenched his jaw. "We met at a strip joint he owns. There was this girl." He shook his head, his voice tight and sour. "Piety, I swear, she didn't look like she'd had a decent meal in weeks. I wanted to put some clothes on her and feed her." He dragged a hand down his face. "That sounds awful, I guess. I was taking my clothes off for a living just a week ago, and here I am, wanting to help some girl who's doing the exact same thing."

"You and I both know that's not the same thing." Rubbing my thumb across the back of his hand, I willed him to look at me. "There's a difference between somebody who wants to strip for a living, and someone who is either coerced or forced into it. And it sure sounds like that's what's happening here"

"He offered her to me."

My jaw dropped.

Now he did look at me. "She looked so sad and scared standing up there. There was nothing sexy about it at all, but there were men cat-calling at her, and I was thinking about how pathetic the whole thing was. He saw me looking at her and said I could have her for the night. Free. That she would do *anything* I wanted."

129

Somehow I managed to close my mouth.

"I wanted to beat the shit out of him."

"Now I do too," I said. I wasn't...*surprised*. Not exactly. The shelter I volunteered at took in a lot of girls who were trying to get out of prostitution, and we had to deal with pissed-off pimps quite a bit. Men who treated women like they were nothing more than just commodities, a product to be sold or traded.

But *knowing* it and having it happen to the relative of someone I cared about...It made me sick just to think about it.

"You look like you want to make him eat his own face," Kaleb said.

"Ew." I blinked at the disgusting mental image, then laughed. "Then again, it would be a nice punishment. Have any suggestions on how to make it happen?"

"No. But I'll think about it." He leaned back, his eyes staring off at nothing. "He wants another ten grand. Says the money I paid him only covered Camry's drug debt, but that he's entitled to get the money he'll lose when she leaves him. She's one of the *favorites* – like she's some kind of piece of meat."

"Kaleb..."

"Look, I'm sorry." He started to slide out of the booth. "We should head on up to the lawyer's office, see if they're ready for us. If not...I don't need to dump this on you. You've already helped me enough."

I tightened my grip on his hand. "What are you going to do?"

He stared down at me. "I'll figure it out."

"You've been trying to do that ever since he dumped this on you, haven't you?"

He didn't answer, but the dull red flush creeping up his cheeks told me all I needed to know.

"Come on." As I led Kaleb out of the coffee shop, I used my free hand to send a text to the driver, then turned to meet Kaleb's eyes. "My driver's on his way back. We'll get this figured out."

He frowned, and I could see the wheels turning as he tried to figure out what I was doing. Without giving him an explanation, I called the lawyer's office next. His gaze grew more intense as I canceled the appointment, explaining that something urgent had come up and I'd get back with them when I needed them – so terribly sorry.

"What are you doing?" he demanded as I ended the call. He gestured toward the entrance doors for the office building, just a few hundred feet away. "It's right there."

"You've got bigger problems, Kaleb, and I'm going to help."

"It's not *your* problem, Piety," he argued, pale eyes flashing. "I've got to fix this on my own."

"I'm your friend." The word felt…funny. We were friends, I thought. But that was such a mild term for what we had. "Friends help each other, right?"

"And what do you propose we do?" He crossed his arms over his chest, staring me down. "Are you going to pay me to stay married to you for another week or two? Give me more money so he can jerk me around again? Is that the solution you have in mind?"

"No." Then I shrugged. "Actually, I don't have a solution. But this guy is a user. You'll never be free of him as long as you play his game, so I don't think paying him is the answer. But I'm not walking away and leaving you – or your sister – alone to deal with him."

"My sister isn't your concern," he said gently, reaching up to cup my chin.

As he angled my head back, forcing me to meet his gaze, I tried not to let him see how much I loved having

131

him touch me again.

I'd missed it – missed him – every second.

I'd felt the loss of him every second.

It had been hard enough to convince myself that I needed to come out here and handle the annulment. The only thing that made it even semi-tolerable was knowing I'd see him again. But the thought of walking away now when he was dealing with this was just intolerable.

"She is." I leaned in and brushed my lips across his. "Because she's yours, and I'm concerned about *you*."

Chapter 6

Piety

I'd booked a room at the Bellagio before I'd left Philadelphia.

Now, as my driver came to a stop at the elegant, grand entrance, I tightened my hand around Kaleb's. He was staring at nothing, and I knew part of him wasn't here.

He was thinking about his sister.

I wished I could take the worry away, but I was too acutely aware of the sort of trouble she might be in. The first month I'd been at the shelter, I'd worked with a girl who'd tried to get away from her pimp. She'd tried so hard. One day, she left the part-time job at a coffee shop, and he caught up with her, saying that she still owed him.

When she'd stood up to him, he'd beaten her senseless. She had permanent vision damage, and we still had to convince her that it wasn't her fault.

People like this Stefano were bottom-feeders. We

had to find out how to help Camry.

"Thanks, Delano," I said as he helped me out of the back of the car. I passed him a twenty. "Would you be available tomorrow if I need you?"

"You just give me a call, Ms. Van Allan." He tipped his hat to me and nodded at Kaleb as he climbed out.

Offering my hand to Kaleb, I waited for him to take it before we started inside.

The concierge had seen me coming, and he already had my room key ready and a bellboy was on hand to take the luggage Delano had unpacked from the trunk.

"I still can't get over that," Kaleb said abruptly.

I glanced at him, puzzled.

He gestured to the bellhop walking in front of us as we started down the hall. "You didn't even have to check in. They were just…waiting for you."

"Ah…" Blood rushed to stain my cheeks red. "Well. Yeah."

He laughed, and while there was still an edge to it, it was better than what I'd heard earlier. "You're embarrassed by it. I imagine your dad would be furious if a place like this wasn't ready to get down on bended knee the moment he walked through the doors."

"Probably." I nodded at the bellboy as he held the elevator doors for us, nudging Kaleb in the ribs so he'd stop with his observations.

But he either didn't get the hint or refused to take it. He met the bellboy's eyes. "What's it like? Working at a place like this?"

"It's a good job, Sir." He smiled politely.

"I'm not a sir." Kaleb snorted. "I'm only here because I'm lucky enough to be hooked up with her. Otherwise I'd be…hell, a week ago, I was taking my clothes off for a living."

"What was that like?" The bellboy smiled again, still polite, but I saw a hint of amusement in his eyes. "Working at a job like that?"

"Good one," I murmured. Then I winked at the bellboy. "Ignore him. He's had a rough few days."

"Of course, Miss."

Once he had my suitcase in the room, he nodded at us and accepted the bill I extended, then left, closing the door softly behind him. Meeting Kaleb's eyes, I said, "When I've had a bad day, I get a little bratty, just to make myself feel better. It looks like we share that in common."

"Sorry if I embarrassed you."

"Oh, it takes more than that to embarrass me." I sat down and reached for the ankle strap of my shoe. "But questions like that to an employee, in a place like this? The wrong kind of answer, overheard by an asshole sort of manager could get somebody fired. I think that would make you feel like shit if that happened."

Kaleb hissed out a breath and turned away, shoving both hands through his hair. "That doesn't make sense. I was the one being an ass."

"But this hotel is meant to cater to the guests. If a manager thought that the kid had somehow insulted you..." I shrugged. "Things are different here when it comes to that sort of thing. People are more uptight a lot of the time."

"You're not." He looked back at me, eyes darkening with a familiar desire. He came toward me, going to his knees as he reached me.

I'd been in the process of reaching for my other shoe, but at the look on his face, my body started to feel curiously lax and limp, overheated too, like a puddle of hot wax. He leaned down, pressing his lips to one knee, then the other, sending a new ripple of warmth across my skin.

"I missed you," he murmured. "I didn't expect that to happen, but it did. It's like you're my own addiction, Piety, and I'm not certain I like it."

He reached for my remaining shoe and sat back on his heels, staring into my eyes as he freed the strap and slowly slid the shoe off, his fingers lighting caressing my skin.

"I wasn't expecting any of this to happen either," I said truthfully. "But I'm not exactly unhappy with it."

It stung that he might be, but I didn't say that.

"I didn't say I was *unhappy* with it." He ran his thumb along my instep.

It sent a shiver through me, and I had to swallow a sigh when he began to dig his fingers into the tight muscles of my left calf. I hadn't truly realized how much I craved his touch until now. His word choice, *addiction*, was an appropriate one.

"You're the best damn thing to happen for me in ages, sweetheart. But I don't have time for this...for you...for all the things I feel for you." His fingers moved higher. "And damn me if I give a flying fuck."

My breath caught in my lungs, stuttered, and hitched there.

Then he straightened, coming up in front of me, his hands sliding up over my hips to my waist. He tugged me to the edge of the bed until we were eye to eye, chest to chest, belly to belly, my body burning with the need to feel his skin against mine.

"I get around you, and it's like nothing else matters. I don't like that, Piety. I have to think about my sister and you make me not want to care about anything."

I could see the struggle on his face, and I wanted to

tell him that I understood, that I'd be the responsible one and walk away.

Except I couldn't. And not just for me, but for him too.

"You've spent most of your life taking care of her." I traced my finger across his upper lip. "It's okay to want something for yourself every now and then."

"She needs me." His gaze fell away, his hands resting on my hips.

For a moment, I thought he'd walk away, but then he looked back at me.

"But, dammit, Piety, *I* need *you*." He leaned in and kissed me, his mouth hot and demanding.

I didn't even have time to brace myself, but that was okay because he had me. His fingers dug into my hips until I knew I'd have bruises, but it still wasn't enough. His tongue plundered my mouth, and I could feel the hard length of him pushing against me.

"Tell me you want me," he said against my lips.

"More than I've ever wanted anything." And it was nothing but the truth. I'd never felt this way about anything or anyone before. It should have scared me, but at the moment, it just felt right.

He tugged me closer, and I thought he just might pull me down onto his lap and take me right there, but he went for the hem of my dress instead, peeling it up and off until I stood naked in front of him. The surplus cut front had let me go without a bra, and I shivered a little, the cool air drawing my nipples into tight, hard buds.

He made a greedy, desperate sound in the back of his throat, and it made things low inside me tighten. Then his mouth closed over my breast, and it was heat and wet that made me shiver, made me cry out.

I shoved my hands into his hair, and he scraped his

teeth over my nipple. I swore, my head falling back. I clung to him, not trusting my legs to hold me as he moved to my other breast. With each pull of his mouth, my pussy throbbed.

When he slid one hand between my thighs, I whimpered and spread them wide, eager for more.

But he didn't touch me.

Instead, he lifted his head and stared down at me.

Panting, I waited, watching him. If he stopped now, I was going to kill him. "What are you doing?"

He shook his head and caught my shoulders, easing me down to the bed.

When I lay flat, he kissed the underside of my left breast, rubbing his chin back and forth across my flesh so that the faint stubble growing on his chin rasped over my skin. He kissed my belly. My hip. The inside of my thigh

I arched up, whimpering, needing, pleading.

When his breath kissed my damp skin, I whimpered and curled one leg around his upper torso.

Then he licked me, opening me with one long stroke of his tongue and I arched up, screaming, but the sound was breathless and broken.

He did it again, then circled my clit with his tongue.

"Piety…"

Even the touch of air on my skin felt like too much, and I fisted my hands in his hair, trying to draw him closer. "Please," I moaned.

"Tell me."

I couldn't, another moan choking out the words.

He caught my wrists and dragged them from his hair, holding them easily in one hand. "Tell me what you want, baby. Do you want my mouth on you?"

"Yes…please…fuck…yes. Your mouth, your tongue…*you*."

He flicked his tongue over me again, raked my clitoris with his teeth.

Then he pushed two fingers inside me and pressed up.

I came in a rush, startled by the suddenness of it, my body shaking. Before it was over, he was inside me, the thickness of his cock stretching me as he filled me in one smooth stroke. I cried out, the sensation pushing my climax even higher. I closed my eyes, spots dancing behind my eyelids as pleasure overwhelmed me.

"Look at me," he said, tangling his hands in my hair and arching my head back.

Forcing my eyes open, I stared at him, whimpering as he twisted his hips and sent the head of his cock sliding and rubbing over my already sensitive G-spot. Grabbing for him, I clutched at his sides, my nails sinking in deep.

"I don't want to think about being without you," he said against my lips, only a second before he kissed me.

I caught the words, clung to them. I wanted to ask him what they meant – did they mean *anything at all*?

But he was stealing the breath and soul from me, riding me fast, and I couldn't think, couldn't breathe.

"Come again for me, Piety…come."

Like I had any other choice.

* * * * *

We lay curled against each other, the room dim and quiet, sweat drying on our bodies as we stared at each other in silence.

It should have been awkward.

There were no words spoken, nothing that I could think needed to be said in that very moment.

I'd come to need him, and it could either be the best

thing that had ever happened…or the very stupidest thing I'd ever done.

I didn't yet know which.

But right then, I didn't care.

Snuggling in closer, I rested my head on his shoulder and sighed in satisfaction as he curled his arm around my shoulders.

The silence, warm and comfortable as it was, stretched out, but it couldn't last forever.

Finally, he said the words. "We need to talk."

"I know." Rubbing my cheek against his chest, I slid my hand up, then down his abdomen. Muscles jumped and clenched under my touch. Lifting up on my elbow, I stared down in his eyes. "But do we have to do it now?"

"No." He cupped my cheek and kissed my forehead. "We don't have to do it now."

"Good. Because I'm not ready to."

"Me neither."

Chapter 7

Kaleb

The earth had moved.

Okay, maybe not literally.

It wasn't like there was an earthquake shaking Las Vegas.

But as I laid there with Piety wrapped around me, I understood why some people talked about how being with a certain person made the world shake under their feet.

She'd changed something in me.

She'd changed *me*.

I didn't know if this was what it was like to fall in love – maybe it was the start of it. Maybe it was something else entirely.

I don't know, but things felt…different.

And I couldn't tell her any of it.

Whatever it was between us, it was only temporary, and I would be an idiot to think otherwise.

Maybe I was an idiot anyway because, instead of keeping whatever distance between us I could, all I wanted to do was grab up every second possible.

My hand was in her hair, and I could feel her breasts

moving against me with every breath. She fit perfectly against my side, as if she had been made specifically for me. Nothing had ever felt so good in my life. Her hair was silky smooth, her body soft and warm.

"What are you thinking about?" she asked, her voice drowsy and soft.

"The same thing I think about a lot these days," I replied honestly.

"Your sister." There was a world of understanding in her voice.

I should have felt more than a little guilty.

Camry should have been on my mind.

She hadn't been though. Not when I was with Piety.

Turning toward her, I met Piety's eyes. "I'm thinking about you."

She pushed up onto her elbow and looked at me. "Really?" Her eyes glowed as she smiled, and it sent a jolt of heat right through me.

"Yeah. I like thinking about you."

She laughed, and the sound was bubbly and soft. "I like thinking about you too."

There were a hundred other things I wanted to say, but before I had the chance to put even the first one into words, my cell buzzed, letting me know I had a call.

Sighing, I reached for it.

It showed only a number, but I recognized it. Setting my jaw, I answered, careful to keep my voice neutral.

Stefano's voice came through as lazy and arrogant as always. "Kaleb, you don't sound too happy to hear from me. Why is that?"

Because now I'm thinking about you instead of the woman in bed with me, I thought. I didn't say it though. "Don't know what you mean, Stefano. It's a delight to hear your voice."

"Yeah, I can tell." He laughed, amused. "Look, I was just...you know, checking in. Wanted to make sure you hadn't thought about taking off and leaving your sister to hold the bag. You wouldn't want to do that, would you? Leave your sister to fend for herself in this big, bad world?"

Fury flooded me. I fought the need to hit something. "I don't plan on leaving her, Stefano. I'm working on the problem."

"So you've found a way to come up with the rest of the money you owe me?"

The money I owed him? He was fucking unbelievable.

Slowly, I sat up, easing away from Piety and staring at the wall as I willed myself to stay calm.

Completely unaware of the anger simmering inside me – or simply not caring – Stefano continued, "See, you better work fast. Otherwise, the price will just keep going up and up."

"I want to see my sister." My eyes burned, and the fury bubbled in me like acid. "I want to see my sister and make sure she's okay before this goes any further."

"Nah, that ain't going to happen," Stefano said confidently.

"Then..." I sucked in a breath, blew it out through my teeth. "You know what? Fuck you. You've got my sister dancing like a puppet on your strings, but I'm not your puppet, Stefano. I'll help her, but I want to make sure she's okay first. If you can't make that happen, then shove that money I gave you up your ass and don't expect to see a penny more."

I disconnected the call, feeling sick as I rubbed my shaking hands over my face, wondering how bad I'd just fucked things up.

"What did I do?" I whispered. The bed shifted behind me and I turned toward Piety. "What the fuck did I just do?" The words came out in a shout this time.

She didn't even blink as she rose from the bed and came to me, reaching down to cup my face in her hands.

"I think…" she said slowly. "You did exactly what you had to."

"No, I…I…" A torrent of disjointed words came bubbling out, and she leaned in, kissing me softly.

"You did what you had to," she repeated more firmly. "You want to make sure he's not screwing you over, and you want her safe. If that's her pimp, then that's what they do. He'll push you as far as he can. You just made it damn clear you're nothing like your sister."

She sounded calm, strangely grounded, and I felt like I'd explode into a thousand sharp, jagged bits.

I started to say…something, but the words died as the phone rang. I went to grab it, but my fumbling fingers knocked it to the floor. I didn't answer until the third ring. "Yes."

Stefano was laughing. "Well, I'll say this, *mate*…you've got balls. Tell you what. I'll let you see your sister. Then you pay me my money."

"I've still got to collect it," I said, my mouth going dry. I'd see Camry, know she was okay.

"That's fine, that's fine. But you keep this shit up, boy, and the price will continue to rise. You got me?"

"I got it." Swiping the back of my hand over my forehead, I looked at Piety.

She met my eyes, her strength holding me steady.

"Where do you want to meet?" I asked. "Somewhere public. No offense, but I'd rather swim bloody and mangled with a great white than be someplace private with you."

"Aw, I'm hurt, Kaleb. And here I thought we could be friends. But that's fine. I'll text you the place. But Kaleb...?"

I started to lower the phone, but now I pressed it hard against my ear. "Yeah?"

"You bring a cop, and you'll be sorry. But Camry will be even *more* sorry."

* * * * *

"What if he freaks about you being here?"

The cooler night air whipped my hair back from my face while blowing Piety's long locks into hers. She spoke in a calm, sure voice. "He told you not to bring a cop. I'm not. You brought your wife. And trust me, he won't mistake me for a cop."

Taking my hand, we started walking in a circle around the top of the hotel. We were back at the ride where we'd come the day after our crazy wedding. Our impromptu, insane honeymoon.

Abruptly, somebody stepped in front of us, half crashing into Piety.

"Hey, watch..."

The words died in my throat as I realized who it was.

"Camry," I whispered.

My sister gave me a sharp smile and then looked over at Piety, contempt written across her face. "Ditch the rich bitch, and we can go talk, Kaleb."

"Hi." Piety ignored the insult and held out a hand. "I'm Piety. Your sister-in-law."

Camry looked at her for a long moment, then at me.

145

Finally, she shook her head and muttered, "Whatever. Come on. I don't have much time."

We ended up in the nearest restaurant, sitting in a booth with Piety next to me, Camry across from us.

"What do you want, Kaleb?" she asked, her voice cool.

"What do I...?" I cleared my throat and tamped down the flash of temper her words had triggered. "What the hell does that mean, what do I want? I'm here to help you."

She lifted a shoulder and started to pick at the metallic blue polish on her nails. It was a shade or two lighter than the skinny-strapped top she wore. It kept falling over one bony shoulder. She looked like she hadn't seen a decent meal since she'd left home.

"Are – *have* you been sick?" I asked carefully.

"What?" She lowered her hands and stared at me, her crystal blue eyes clouded.

"You just...you look like you haven't been eating."

She tossed her hair over her shoulder, the light brown waves looking dull and brittle. "Oh, puh-leeze. I eat when I'm hungry, not because the clock says I should. I refuse to be one of those cows who can't fit into a pair of skinny jeans."

"You're right," I said, keeping my voice neutral. "You're not a cow. A skeleton might work, but a cow? Not in a hundred years. I've seen refugees in better shape than you."

She flinched but covered it quickly with another of those harsh smiles. "Fuck off, Kaleb." She directed her next comment toward Piety. "So, just how did *you* come to be?"

Piety narrowed her eyes and took a deep breath, then seemed to relax as she exhaled. "Well, once upon a time, my mommy and daddy decided they wanted a little girl…" Piety stared at her with big, wide eyes.

The sharp retort caught Camry off guard, and I caught a flicker of my old sister in the admiration crossing her face.

"Wow. Aren't you a bitch?" Camry said.

"Takes one to know one. Or so they say." Piety thanked the server who appeared just then with our drinks. Beers for both of us, but a double bourbon, no ice, for Camry. "I mean, maybe I'm off base here, but I thought you'd have some appreciation for the brother who came here to help you out, but all you're doing is being a bitch yourself. I guess they show love differently in Australia."

For a moment, just a brief one, Camry looked shame-faced. Then she tossed her drink back. "You know, I'm pretty sure I don't *need* his help."

"So, you weren't ten thousand dollars in debt to a drug dealer?" I snapped.

She opened her mouth, then shut it, her teeth clicking together with the gesture. She crossed her bony arms over her chest, giving me a good look at the track marks she wasn't even trying to hide. Her jaw jutted out as she glared at me.

"I gave up my job, Camry. My life. I was *this* close to talking Mac into letting me buy him out. It was all I'd *ever* wanted, and now I've lost my chance." I smashed my fist into the table, the fury I'd been suppressing all this time rising and grabbing me by the throat. "*This* close. And now it's gone."

"So go back!" she shouted. "Tell him to give you your job back. I didn't ask for your help."

"The hell you didn't!" I shouted back, feeling sick. "A dozen times at least. Remember all those nights when you called, half out of your mind, crying about how much trouble you were in?"

"I was high," she said with a dismissive wave. "Just…just go."

"I can't." I felt like I'd been punched in the chest. She was all the family I had, and she didn't care about how much she'd hurt me. "Hell, maybe I could, but the job's gone. He's already sold the store. I gave it up for *you*."

She stared at me.

I waited for a sign. For something.

"Yeah, well." She shrugged. "You didn't have to. I'm *fine*."

Piety covered my hand, squeezed. "Then I guess he doesn't need to pay the other ten grand." From the corner of my eye, I saw her staring at my sister. But there wasn't disgust on her face. It was…pity. "I mean, I guess you heard that your pimp wants more than what you shot up your arm. But if you're *fine*, then I guess you don't need anything else, right?"

Camry opened her mouth, then closed it, looking at me, then at her. "Bitch, why don't you mind your own fucking business?"

"I am." Piety's voice was still even, controlled. "He's my husband, and you're jerking him around."

I opened my mouth, but before I could say a word, Stefano arrived and sat next to my sister. He nodded at me, then eyed Piety, muddy brown eyes gleaming.

"Who's the broad, Kaleb? Are you bringing her as a trade for your sister? I might just consider that."

I tensed, ready to break the bastard's nose. Only Piety's fingers tightening around mine kept me in my seat.

He laughed as he slung his arm around Camry's shoulders. Pulling her close, he pressed his mouth against hers. She didn't so much as blink, and my stomach churned.

"Having a good dinner, baby?" he asked.

"Fine, thank you," she said woodenly.

"Satisfied now?" He looked at me. "She's good."

I just stared at him and he kept his eyes on me as he nuzzled her cheek, let his hand slide down until it covered one of her breasts. His other hand was under the table, but I didn't have to see it to know it was under my sister's skirt. I reminded myself that beating this shit out of this bastard would only land me in jail, and then probably on a plane back to Australia. I had to be smart about this.

He stood. "Now it's time for you to quit jerking me around, or the price will just keep going up…and up…up. Fuck me over and see what happens."

He snapped his fingers at Camry and she got up, tugging her tiny skirt back down over her ass. She took his hand when he held it out, a flush creeping over her pale skin.

"Where the hell are you going?" I said as they started to walk away.

She looked back at me.

He didn't.

"It was good seeing you too, Camry. Always great to catch up," I said, not raising my voice an iota.

She flinched, but still followed the asshole out the door.

Chapter 8

Piety

"It's not personal," I said softly, covering his hand with mine.

He stared out the small rectangle at the world below us, although I knew he wasn't seeing it. He'd barely acknowledged anything since we'd left the restaurant. The only time he'd even talked had been when I'd booked our flight back to Philadelphia.

I'd managed to convince him there wasn't much he could do here that he couldn't do back east. In fact, he might be able to do more for her if Stefano didn't know what he was up to. Which meant that coming back to Philadelphia with me could help the situation rather than hurt it. I couldn't even imagine what he was going through right now, but I wanted to make it better, do something to comfort him. I'd been reaching, I knew, but it had gotten him away from the people who were manipulating him so badly.

Finally, he looked over at me, anguish etched on his face.

"How can it not be personal?" he asked. "That

150

asshole talks about her like she's nothing more than a slab of meat, right in front of her, and she just takes it. Then she talks to me like I'm nothing to her, and I'm the one who's supposed to get her out of the mess she's in?"

"No." I brushed his hair back, leaning as close to him as the seats allowed. "Maybe you're not supposed to dig her out of this mess. It's not easy to save someone, who doesn't want to be saved."

"So I *shouldn't* pay Stefano off?" His jaw went tight.

I didn't think he should, but I wasn't going to tell him that. It wasn't my place. "That's got to be your decision, but I can tell you that he's jerking you around. As long as he thinks he has you on a leash, he's going to use it. And Camry is...well, she's your leash."

He stared at me hard and tension pulsed, beating in cadence with my heart. Had I gone too far? I knew I was basing this on experiences I'd had at the shelter, but he didn't know that.

Finally, he looked away and swore. "Fuck. You're right. What else am I going to do though? Leave her to deal with that prick on her own? She hasn't been able to do it so far."

"Maybe she hasn't been trying."

Icy eyes cut to me. His voice was sharp. "What's that supposed to mean?"

"It's just..." I sighed and looked away. I hated this. All of it. Hated that he was hurting. That his sister was caught up in drugs and whatever else Stefano had her doing. "Kaleb, did she seem like she was scared of him? Frightened? Desperate to get away?"

"She...that's bullshit, Piety." His voice started to rise. "She's the one who called me."

"I know." The airline attendant approached, and I lapsed into silence until she'd gone by. Biting my lower

151

lip, I struggled for the right way to explain this and hated that I felt so uncertain. "He's got her so suckered in right now, if he asked her to dance the hula naked on the front lawn of the White House, she'd get herself shot trying. That's how this works. She'll do anything to keep him happy, because by keeping *him* happy, he keeps *her* happy."

"So..." He blew out a harsh breath and tugged his hands free. Reaching up to scrub his hands up and down his face, he let out a stream of low profanity. "Are you telling me you don't think he's been threatening her at all?"

"Hard to say. But..." I lifted a shoulder. "She looked like she was maintaining pretty well. She could carry on a conversation. Wasn't jittery. If she was in such bad shape that she ended up in debt to the tune of ten grand, I think she would have been looking worse than she was. Which would leave her in not so great shape for his...um...other business. That makes her valuable to him. Men like him...they'll use someone who's that bad off, but someone like her, who can still function, that's who they prefer. Hooked enough that they don't want to get away, but not so much that johns don't want them."

His eyes flew to mine and blood stained my cheeks.

"How do you know all of this stuff?" he asked, voice rough.

"I do some, ah, counseling of sorts."

"Of sorts how?"

"I've been working with a shelter off and on for a few years. I was finally taken on full time last year. Most of my work is with women in...similar situations." Nervous for reasons I couldn't explain, I rubbed my hands together and resisted the urge to bite my nails. I'd quit that habit years ago, but now found myself practically smacking my hands to keep from nibbling.

"What sort of counseling?" Kaleb's suspicion had only grown.

Huffing out a breath, I crossed my arms over my chest and glared at him. I didn't want to have to say it, but I didn't think he'd listen any other way. "The kind of counseling you give girls who are trying to get away from negative influences in their life. For some reason, I seem to have a knack for it. And I can tell you this – your sister is playing you."

Something hot and furious lit his eyes, and I watched as his chin went up, and he prepared to argue. Then, slowly, he lowered it, and the tension drained out of his body.

"Shit," he muttered.

"Tell me about it."

* * * * *

"So what do we do now?"

The rest of the flight passed in silence, and I ended up drifting off. Now that the plane had landed and taxied in, I was brooding over what lay ahead.

As we moved through the Philadelphia airport, I glanced over at him, debating on what to tell him. I didn't like it, but I think I was going to have to...hedge.

If I was upfront, he'd want to come with me, and some of these things would just be easier to investigate if he wasn't there.

I wasn't trying to hide anything, but I could move quicker if I wasn't answering questions, and I already

153

knew he'd have a hundred. Or more. I didn't blame him. I would too. But I also knew we didn't have time for a hundred questions, or even one. I could answer questions after I told him what I'd accomplished. And if I failed...?

Shit.

Then I'd give him the money, and we'd go back out there, and I'd offer Stefano *more* money if he'd just kick Camry to the curb right then and there. I could offer him enough that he'd do it too. Camry would be pissed, but he was her anchor and maybe if she was cut off from him, she'd realize how much trouble she was in.

But that was my *last* option, not my first.

That was the logical reason. The emotional one was that this was hard enough on Kaleb as it was, and I didn't want to make things worse if things didn't go as planned.

"I've got some stuff I need to do for work," I said finally, looking over at him.

His mouth compressed into a tight frown.

"We'll take care of her. I'll make sure you get the money, and we'll work on it tonight and tomorrow." I didn't like lying. In a way, I *was* telling him the truth, or a shade of it. I'd given my heart and soul to helping girls like Camry out. It didn't matter to me that she hadn't come into the shelter asking for it. She'd come across my path, and she needed it, so that was good enough for me. I'd probably be doing the exact same thing if she hadn't been Kaleb's sister.

But as I watched him nod, resignation settling on his face, I knew I'd go above and beyond for Camry because of who she was.

Chapter 9

Kaleb

"Wow. Something smells *amazing*," a voice announced behind me.

I glanced back at Astra, then immediately whipped my head back around to focus on the omelet sizzling in the skillet.

She wore a whole lot of nothing. Okay, not *nothing* – there was a tank top that didn't quite reach her panties and those panties covered very little, so she might as well be wearing nothing. It was true some could argue that I wasn't really all that married, and yes, I was neither blind nor dead, but still…she was Piety's best friend, and I was more than a little crazy about Piety. Seemed wrong to notice that her best friend had curves like that.

She chuckled behind me.

"I'll go put on a robe, Kaleb. Sorry, not used to having people in here other than me or PS. It's cute, though, seeing a guy blush."

"You're a pain in the arse, Astra, you know that?"

This time, it wasn't a chuckle, but an all-out laugh. "Don't suppose there's enough to share, is there?"

I stiffened and she laughed again.

"The food, Kaleb. I'm talking about the food."

Heat suffused my face and I scowled down at the pan. "There is." I figured she'd wake up once she smelled breakfast. One thing about Piety and Astra, they both enjoyed eating and made no bones about it. I checked the bacon in the skillet on the back and turned the burner off before reaching for my coffee.

I'd started breakfast more to have something to do than anything else. Piety had left early that morning, telling me that she had to work. She'd smiled when she said it, kissed me, then just...left.

I couldn't quite put my finger on what it was, but there was something she wasn't telling me. She'd been gone most of the day yesterday too. Once we'd gotten in from the airport, she'd had the driver bring me to the loft, and she'd left, not coming home until late. She hadn't offered an explanation, and I hadn't asked, but my gut said something was going on.

Since I knew I'd go crazy if I did nothing but sit and think about how crazy my life had become, I'd decided to make breakfast. After that, I was going to clean the place. Not that it needed much, but I wasn't used to sitting around and doing nothing.

I'd been working my ass off since my parents died. Not having something to do went against everything I knew, and it was driving me crazy.

"Okay, Crocodile Dundee. I'm decent."

I smirked. "That's a bit of a dated reference, Astra."

"Hey, I'll have you know I enjoyed the very best education. I immersed myself in the eighties culture and know all the best movies."

I grinned as she came to join me at the counter, taking a cup and pouring herself some coffee, staring down into the dark brew.

She looked at me sideways. "I'm a little nervous here. I'm picky about my coffee."

"So am I."

"Let's see if you make the cut. Otherwise, I'll have to boot you out, just to save Piety the heartache." She winked at me, then took a sip. A moment later, she sighed and leaned against the counter. "Okay. I give you my stamp of approval."

"So glad to know." Nodding at the plates in front of her, I said, "Hand me one and I'll dish you up."

A few minutes later, we were sitting down to eat.

It wasn't until Astra had cleared half her plate that she asked where Piety was.

"She said she had to work." I kept my attention focused on the plate in front of me, eating with mechanical focus and not really tasting any of the food. I didn't want to look at Astra, because I had a feeling she'd read more in my eyes than I wanted her to.

"Huh."

Slanting a look at her, I echoed her response. "Huh." I popped a bite of omelet into my mouth, chewed, swallowed, then asked, "What does that mean?"

"It's just a noise. Do you plan on doing anything to amuse yourself?"

"Not really." I wasn't about to tell her I'd located some cleaning supplies and was already making a game plan on what I'd do once I cleaned up the dishes. I had a feeling she'd tell me it wasn't necessary. Better to already be doing it before she realized what I was up to.

"Well, I'm not due back at work until Monday, so I'm going to enjoy being *lazy*." She made a show of an exaggerated stretch before picking up her coffee cup.

Grateful for something inane to talk about, I asked, "Where do you work?"

157

"Get ready to be surprised." Over the rim, she gave me a rueful smile. "I work at a homeless shelter. It's a sister shelter to the one where Piety works. I love it, but sometimes I need a break. I dragged Piety off to Las Vegas after I finished handling a rough case. She needed to get away from her folks, but she needed a vacation too, even if she won't admit it. Her job is rougher than mine. At risk youth...I couldn't do what she does."

She'd told me about the work she did, but I couldn't deny that I was a bit surprised that Astra was involved too. Those two were so much more than they appeared at first glance.

"Piety's parents definitely play up the photo ops when they get a chance, but it's never been about that for her." Astra smiled. "She has a social science degree, did you know that? Graduated from Columbia at the top of her class. All she's ever wanted to do is help people."

Not for the first time, I found myself wondering what I'd done to deserve someone like Piety in my life. "That's amazing you two do that."

Astra's voice trailed off, and she shrugged. "I'll admit, it's hard. The place I'm at works with at-risk youth and runaways. We try to get them placed with...well, affluent families who are good at reaching troubled kids. The sort of people who want to make an impact on a kid's life. It makes a difference. Not all the time, but most of it anyway."

She looked away, but I stayed quiet, wondering where she was going with this. She seemed like there was more she wanted to say.

"Piety, though...she's at a shelter that specializes in helping abuse victims. Women whose husbands or boyfriends or whoever beat on them. Her job is to not only get them away physically, but to work on the mental, and sometimes physical dependency they have."

Her description sounded like one Piety had probably given.

"Sounds like hard work," I said softly, staring into my coffee.

"It is. She's good at it. Sometimes, though, it...hurts."

Tightening my hands on the cup, I thought of how Piety was helping me with Camry, and wondered what it was doing to her, wondered how much Astra knew.

Across from me, she sighed. "She should take more time off. But sometimes I think she doesn't feel like she has the right."

"What's that mean?"

Astra caught sight of my scowl, and she shrugged. "It's not logical. We were both born lucky, we've got so much, and others don't have hardly anything. I don't know if she feels like she has to balance the scales or what, but she pushes herself like she has something to prove...or something to repay."

Was that why she was doing this? Trying to balance some sort of unseen scale?

I didn't know, and that bothered me more than I liked.

*****

"What are you doing?"

The confusion in Astra's voice told me I'd been right on base when I'd elected not to tell her about my exciting cleaning plans for the day.

Looking up from the table I was dusting, I cocked

159

my head and then looked at the rag before examining the can in my hand.

"It would appear that I'm cleaning." I gave the table a final swipe and then moved to the bookshelves.

"You don't need to do that." She sounded mystified. "We have somebody who comes in twice a month. She'll be here next week, and we pick up our own clothes. We even launder them ourselves. We're not totally helpless."

"I never thought you were," I said, laughing under my breath.

"Then why are you doing this?"

She came around to stand in front of me, and I looked from the bookshelf to her. With a sigh, I met her gaze. "Because I've got nothing else to do. Piety isn't here. I don't know this city, and I really don't feel like playing tourist. I've got a shitload on my mind, and if I just sit around and watch the fucking television, I'll go flat out crazy."

Her eyes widened a little.

"Sorry," I said shortly, going back to the task at hand.

"Hey, I've said bad words before. A lot."

Looking back, I saw understanding mixing with the humor in her eyes. She smiled at me. "It's cool," she said softly. "I get it."

"Thanks."

I went back to work on the bookcase, acutely aware that she was still watching me.

After another moment, she turned away. "I'm going to take care of some stuff and then order in something for lunch. How do you feel about Chinese?"

"I feel just fine about it." I wouldn't have minded cooking lunch, but that would require a trip to the store, and I had no idea where one was, and Philadelphia was nothing like Vegas, or back home.

I half-expected her to disappear back into her room, but Astra set herself up on the couch, laptop perched across her thighs, a pair of glasses on the tip of her nose. She focused on the screen with single-minded determination, and after a while, I forgot she was there.

Nearly two hours passed before she interrupted me.

"Chicken or pork? Sweet and sour? Kung pao? What's your poison, Kaleb?"

"Huh?" I threw the rag into the bathroom and swiped my arm across my forehead. I'd thrown myself into the cleaning with more intensity than it really needed, thanks to a text from Camry a half an hour ago.

What's going on, Kaleb? Where are you? Are you going to help me? I'm sorry I behaved that way. I do want to leave Stefano and come home with you.

I hadn't replied.

I didn't know what to believe anymore.

I was…tired.

I'd come here to help my baby sister, and then when I'd finally talked to her, she'd acted like I was just there to be a pain in her skinny, underfed backside.

"Kaleb?" Astra's voice was soft.

"Sweet and sour chicken," I said, bending back over the bathtub. "That will do."

"Are you okay?"

"No worries, Astra." No fucking worries at all.

She left me alone, and I scrubbed at the already gleaming bathtub as if I could scrub all the misery out of me.

*****

161

It was nearly ten when the door opened.

Astra flashed me a bright smile and bounded up from her chair.

The remnants of pizza still sat on the coffee table, and I stared at the box for a long moment before standing and cleaning it all up.

Piety's soft voice behind me didn't even have me turning around. "I'm sorry I left you alone so long."

"No worries. It's not like I need a babysitter." I glanced at her as I carried the box into the kitchen. "There are two slices left if you're hungry."

"No. I…ah…grabbed something while I was out." She slid her hands into her back pockets and looked around. "What did you do all day? Astra show you the city?"

"No. I'm afraid I'm not much up for playing tourist with everything going on." I placed the two remaining slices on a plate, wrapped it up, then put it in the fridge next to the leftover Chinese from lunch. Once that was done, I tore the box down and placed it near the trash to dispose of in the morning. While she watched, I cleaned up from the rest of the mess from Astra and I's late dinner.

"Seems like you figured out where everything is," she said, giving me a smile. I think she tried to keep it light, but it just looked strained.

"Yeah."

I waited, wondering if she'd say anything else, offer me anything. She'd said I should come back here while we figured out what to do, but so far, she'd spent the past two days out of the loft, hardly talking to me. I was running out of ways to tell myself that I'd figure something out on my own.

162

Piety toyed with the braided belt on her dress, but instead of waiting any longer for her to speak, I said, "I'm tired."

Heading past her, I paused just long enough to kiss her cheek, then went straight into the guest bedroom where I'd put my stuff yesterday, closing the door behind me.

I heard voices just a few minutes later, low and soft, but I didn't try to listen to what Astra and Piety might be discussing.

I was too tired to deal with this.

Tired and feeling empty and just about out of hope.

*****

A second restless night led to me sleeping past ten, and when I woke up, the loft was empty.

A note was under a cup next to the coffee pot.

Kaleb,

Astra and I need to see to some business details. We'll be gone for a while. I plan to be back in time for dinner, though. Don't make plans.

She signed it with a *P* inside a heart.

I reached for the piece of paper and crumpled it in my fist.

"What kind of fucking plans does she think I'll make?"

Unless there was somebody on Craigslist looking for a kidney or something, I was shit out of options, and I needed to figure something out fast because, clearly, Piety had forgotten all about my sister. Good for her. I couldn't do that.

Head pounding, I started the coffee pot.

It hadn't even managed to get me my first miserable cup when somebody knocked on the door.

Frowning, I walked over and looked through the security hole. Nobody had called up, and security here was tight – I'd already seen that. So whoever it was must be somebody the building security knew. Unless that somebody knew how to get in undetected.

I didn't know the guy in the hall, but what did that mean? I could count how many people I really *knew* in this city on one hand and have fingers left over.

Eying the distinguished-looking man, I felt an immediate rush of dread and distaste fill me.

"Can I help you?" I asked through the door.

"Mr. Hastings? Hello, my name is Stuart Rushmore. I'm a friend of Piety's. I was wondering if you had a few moments."

As I watched, he smoothed his tie down and beamed a brilliant smile directly at me, clearly aware I was watching him – or maybe he just liked to smile.

"A few moments for what?" I asked.

"Well, to be blunt, Mr. Hastings, I'm here to help you. If you could allow me in…?"

"How about you tell me who you are first?" For all I knew he could be working for Stefano. Not likely, but still…

"As I said, I'm a friend of Piety's. To be more direct, I'm a friend of your in-laws."

Oh, shit. Dread dropped down on me like a leaden weight, and I wanted to tell him to get the fuck out. But instead, I unlocked the door and studied the man in front of me for a long moment.

He did the same.

He probably found me wanting. He looked expensive, in a lightweight summer suit and a tie the same shade of green as his eyes.

"It's a pleasure to meet you," he said after a few moments.

Before he could hold out his hand, I turned away. "Something tells me I'll need coffee for this. Bourbon, too, but it's kind of early for that."

He followed me inside. "I wouldn't mind a cup of coffee myself. But you can relax. I don't have anything hard to tell you. It will make your life so much easier, in fact."

* * * * *

I stared at the check.

"What's the catch?" I asked flatly.

"Not much of a catch, really."

The moment I'd seen Stuart Rushmore standing at the door, I'd decided he was probably an arrogant piece of work. I was right.

He was also a prick.

He smiled at me like we were friends, leaned forward, and gave me that *we're cool* look as we talked and did all sorts of things that would have irritated me even if I'd liked him. But I'd disliked him from the get-go, so it made it even worse.

"You just need to end this farce of a marriage. My clients know it's not real. You know it's not real. Why keep it up?" Elbows resting on his knees, he gestured with one hand and shook his head. "This was just some

165

stunt Piety pulled to upset her parents. She got her way. She wanted attention, and she got it. They'll talk. You'll get the money you clearly need–"

"*Clearly?*" I asked, keeping my voice calm through a sheer act of will.

"Both Mr. Van Allan and I know what a desperate man looks like," he said, his voice almost kind. "Perhaps if you hadn't involved his daughter, he would have been more open to helping without getting me involved. As it is, you're lucky he's willing to make this offer."

He put the check down, then a folder.

"Take the check. Sign the annulment agreement. Leave the city. Everybody gets what they want."

The numbers on the check staggered me.

It would take care of what Stefano wanted. Get him to let Camry go.

It would be more than enough, even some to start a new life back home. Open the surf shop I've always dreamed about.

All I had to do was leave.

Leave Piety.

"How do I know he won't cancel the check the moment I leave?"

"I'm going to the bank with you." He smiled benignly. "Then to the airport. I've already secured you a first-class seat back to Las Vegas. But this is a very limited time offer."

Chapter 10

Piety

"Kaleb!"

I felt awful about how I'd left him alone in a strange city for the past two days, but I had news that was well...promising. Not one-hundred percent *good*, but definitely heading in that direction.

And I could *tell* him now. I hadn't wanted to get his hopes up, and I hadn't wanted him coming along until I knew more about what I needed to do.

Thanks to Samuel, Astra's uncle, and his contacts, I was able to get the DA in Las Vegas interested enough in the case to open an inquiry into Stefano. Maybe even get him off the streets, away from Kaleb's sister. Granted, it would need the corroboration of Camry, but it could work. It was a shot. A good one.

Now that I had answers, I could finally tell him.
Everything.

The dinner I'd planned to be a distraction could now be almost a celebration.

Things were going to work out.

I knew it.

"Kaleb!"

There was no answer, though, and my voice almost seemed to echo back in that odd way a place had when it was empty.

Not just because somebody wasn't there, but when they were...*gone*.

"Hey, PS." Astra came rushing in after me, all smiles. She wagged her eyebrows. "Are you two heading out?"

Turning back to the empty apartment, I lifted a hand. "It looks like he's already gone."

Astra looked at me, confused. "What? I thought you told him you wanted to go out to dinner?"

"I did. I wrote it in the note I left him." Then I frowned. Maybe he hadn't seen it.

But when I checked, the note was gone.

I turned around and saw Astra dumping her purse in the chair. "Maybe he just got hungry and went to the store. It's not like we keep a bunch of stuff on hand." She kicked her shoes off and groaned. "Those shoes are adorable but murderous."

"Maybe. But wouldn't he have left a note?"

Turning back to the empty loft, I looked around, searching for some clue as to where he might have gone, but I didn't see anything.

"He probably wasn't planning on being gone long. You've been out late the past two nights, so he probably figures he has time." She shrugged and leaned back, rotating her feet at the ankle and glaring at the discarded shoes. "You know, you did a good thing, helping him. Maybe he can stop being so serious all the time. He doesn't seem to enjoy life much."

I'd filled Astra in on some of the details – some, not all – earlier because I needed her help.

"Yeah, I hope so," I said absently as I wandered around the main room of the loft. Something was missing. I couldn't figure out what it was.

I walked into the room he used last night and looked around. I hadn't minded him sleeping elsewhere, not in a logical way, since I knew I'd be up early and home late. Now, I was looking forward to him being back in my bed again. The bed was made, but I'd already figured out he was a neat freak. Astra told me how he'd spent half the day yesterday cleaning. It wasn't that either of us were particularly messy. Both of us wanted a clean space, so we'd learned how to pick up after ourselves between professional visits.

I walked back out, frowning without really knowing why. The place was now spotless. There wasn't even a speck of dust to indicate people even lived here. I went into my room and looked around, lingering in the door, searching for whatever it was that was tugging at the back of my mind.

Something's missing…something's missing…

Not even a speck of dust, I thought.

Nothing to indicate anybody even lived here…

"Shit," I whispered. Spinning on my heel, I rushed back into the guest bedroom, coming to a stop in the doorway as I looked around.

For some reason, it felt like somebody had punched a hole in my chest and ripped out my heart. "It's not here," I said. I could hear the panic in my voice, and it didn't make sense.

Astra stared at me, confused. "What's not here?"

"His suitcase," I said. "His suitcase isn't here. Neither is his jacket. He left in hanging on the hook by the door. It's not here."

"Why would he need a jacket?" she asked. "It's the

middle of summer."

"He brought it with him from Australia."

I rushed back into the bedroom and flung open the door, hoping I would see the jacket or his suitcase hiding in a corner, but it wasn't there. "He's gone, Astra."

"That doesn't make sense." She offered me a smile, but it was hesitant and uncertain. She came to stand in the doorway where I had been just a few moments ago, watching as I went through the bedroom searching for some sign of him. It wasn't like I'd find his suitcase, or him, hiding in one of the drawers. But I was desperate and not feeling particularly logical.

As I came striding toward the doorway, she stepped out of the way and trailed after me as I continued my mad search of the loft.

It didn't take long. There was no sign of him, and worse, not even a note. "Why did he leave?" I asked. I wasn't asking her, I was asking myself, trying to figure out some sort of answer. Did he think I wasn't going to help him?

And *how* could he leave? He had to do something for Camry, and he was nearly out of options. But…hell. I didn't know what to think. Covering my face with my hands, I emptied my mind and tried to calm my thoughts, desperate to think everything through.

"Maybe he thought it was something he should handle on his own," she said gently. "It sounds like he's been doing everything on his own for a long time."

"But where will he come up with that kind of money on his own?" I demanded. That piece of shit Stefano wasn't exactly giving him a lot of time. I shoved my hands through my hair and tugged, feeling more and more helpless, more and more frustrated.

"How about instead of driving yourself crazy," she

suggested, "you call him." She pushed my cell phone into my hands and guided me over to the couch. "Call him and get an answer. That's all there is to it."

Touching my phone, I looked up and gave her a wan smile. "You know, every now and then, you really make sense."

She gave me a wounded look. "Only every now and then? I thought I made sense all the time. You're just not superior enough to understand my unique way of thinking."

"Yeah. You've got a unique way of thinking, alright." Sighing, I pulled up Kaleb's number and hit the call button.

One ring.

Another.

Then a third.

And fourth.

As it rolled to voicemail, I closed my eyes, unable to stop the sinking sensation of dread inside me. I left a message, hoping I didn't sound as desperate as I felt. When I disconnected, I shot Astra a look. The look on her face had me wincing.

"That sounded pretty pathetic, didn't it?"

She held up a hand and wiggled it. "You could have sounded a *little* more needy, but that's okay. You like the guy. Right?"

She sat down next to me and hooked an arm around my neck, hugging me closer.

"Don't worry. He'll call back soon, and you'll figure out what's going on, and we'll all feel better."

* * * * *

171

But Kaleb didn't call. Not that hour.

Not the next.

It was almost eight when somebody knocked on the door, and I lunged for it, ready to yell at him and hug him and kiss him and throttle him.

But it wasn't Kaleb. Feeling deflated, I stood there, staring at my parents' lawyer, unable to say anything.

"Aren't you going to invite me in?" he asked, offering me a smile.

"Um, yeah." I looked around the loft, feeling like I'd never seen it before. It already felt empty without Kaleb there. How insane was that? "Come on in."

I stepped aside and waited for Stuart to come in, although I had no idea why one of my parents' personal legal lapdogs might be here to see me.

He moved deeper into the main area of the loft before he turned and met me. Astra had retreated into her room earlier, and it was just the two of us. Probably a good thing. She didn't like Stuart any more than I did, and she didn't bother to hide it.

"Why are you here?" I asked, feeling too drained to bother with courtesies.

He sighed, smoothing his tie down. "We need to talk, Piety. I…look, I don't want to be rude, but can I have a drink? It's been a rough day and I could use it."

The grave expression in his eyes hit me a moment later, and my heart seized inside my chest.

"Are my parents okay?" I asked, forcing the words out through an already tight throat.

"Yes, yes…" His eyes softened. "Of course. They're fine. They…well, I told them you might take it better coming from me."

"Take what?"

"That's what I'm here to discuss." He put his briefcase down and came toward me. Within moments, he had me sitting on the edge of the couch, holding my hands in his.

I don't know how he managed it. It was one of the reasons he was so good at what he did – managing people. He hadn't stayed with my parents for so long by *not* being good at it, that was for certain.

"Piety, you look so tired."

"I've had a crazy couple of days," I said shortly, tugging my hands free.

He nodded his understanding, as if he knew exactly what I'd been dealing with the past forty-eight hours. "That's part of what I'm here to talk to you about." He patted my knee, then got up and went into the kitchen.

Make yourself at home, I thought sourly. But I remained quiet as he cracked open a bottle of scotch – my brand *new* bottle – and poured both of us a drink. He came back to me, concern stamped across his features as he gave me the glass.

"You'll probably need it in a moment, sweetheart."

I took it but didn't lift it to my lips. I just held the glass in my lap as he sat back down.

"How about you cut the bullshit and just tell me what's going on?" I said.

"You are so much like your father." He shook his head and took a sip of the scotch.

"Insulting me won't help me feel any better," I fired at him.

Shock danced across his features. "That wasn't an insult."

"Maybe not to you." I took a sip too, then put it down. It hit my raw belly too hard and too strong. "But I'm not feeling too friendly toward the man right now.

173

Sue me. He wants to control my life, dictate who I'll marry, and when I *do* marry, he insults the man, ignores me–"

Stuart interrupted me, his voice calm and placid. "And he protected you today."

"What?"

He didn't repeat himself, just reached inside his briefcase and withdrew a manila folder. "Kaleb went to see your parents today. Did you know that?"

"He...no. What?" Confused, I shook my head, eying the folder like it might bite me.

"Piety..." He sighed. "Look, I know you have your differences with your parents, but surely you know they love you."

"Yeah." I jerked a shoulder in a shrug, still eying that folder. What was in it? And why was he here? "Why are you here? I've already asked once."

"Kaleb attempted to blackmail your parents."

"I...he what?" Shaking my head, I shoved upright and paced a few feet away. Once I had some room, I took a deep breath. This was bullshit. It had to be. Something Stuart and my dad had cooked up.

But where's Kaleb?

"He paid them a visit and told them things weren't going quite the way you two had planned. You're not happy – he's not. Anybody can see that. But he didn't want to give up on a good thing so easily – or that was the implication. But if they wanted to make it easy...well, he said he'd agree to an annulment if they agreed to help him out financially." Stuart's eyes fell away at the end, like he couldn't stand to look at me as he said it.

"No." Denial swelled inside me at the very first word. Shaking my head, I repeated, "No. That's bullshit."

It had to be. It wasn't like we had planned on anything between us being real to begin with. This had to be a joke. He was getting money from me to help his sister, and I was getting…

What was I getting? I *thought* I was getting back at my parents.

But that seemed an empty reason now, especially considering what Kaleb was dealing with. But what Stuart was saying was just bullshit because we *knew* the marriage was a farce.

Nobody else did.

"No," I said again, louder, with more force in my voice. I practically shouted it.

It was loud enough that Astra appeared in the doorway, looking from me to Stuart then back.

Distaste flashed in her eyes for a moment when she saw him, but it was quickly hidden when she met my gaze. "What's going on?"

"Nothing," I said, my voice shaking. "Stuart here is just feeding me a load of crap that he and my parents cooked up."

But I didn't sound entirely convinced.

I didn't *feel* entirely convinced.

Why hadn't he called me back?

Why hadn't he texted?

"Have you talked to him?" Stuart asked softly. "Maybe there was a…misunderstanding on your father's part."

"I bet," I muttered, shaking my head. But I pulled my phone from my pocket, checked the messages, and tried to call *again*.

Nothing.

"When did he…?" But I couldn't bring myself to finish the question. Shaking my head, I turned away.

"Piety, I spoke with him myself at the reunion. Kaleb seemed – in my opinion, at least – to have a great deal on his mind. If he was desperate, perhaps…"

"Desperate." I jerked my head up, staring at him. "Why do you say that?"

"I know desperate men, sweetheart." He held my eyes levelly. "The man who went to the bank with me was a desperate man."

"You went to the…" I stopped and sucked in a breath. "You went to the bank with him?"

"Your parents agreed to pay, as long as he sign the papers as promised." Stuart stared at me with a solemn, sad expression. "Then I accompanied him to the airport. They wanted to make sure he'd actually leave as promised."

Leave.

Agreed to pay.

"Is this really happening?" I whispered.

"Piety…"

"Stuart," Astra said softly. "Shut up."

She came to me and rested a hand on my arm. "Are you okay?"

I looked at her, unable to answer.

Maybe he'd just been desperate, I thought. No, there was no question of that. He *had* been desperate. Whatever he'd done, it wasn't done out of malice.

"Why didn't he wait?" I whispered. "I was trying to help."

"Help with what?" Stuart asked. "Never mind. It doesn't matter. Look, this boy has led you around by the nose–"

"Shut up!" I shouted. Spinning away from him, I shoved my hair back and tried to think. Why hadn't I told him? I mean, I knew *why*. I'd been trying to make sure I

176

had everything in place. I hadn't wanted to get his hopes up and then have things fall apart.

But if I'd been upfront with him about everything I'd been trying to accomplish over the past couple of days, he would have known I hadn't just *forgotten*.

He wouldn't have been so desperate.

"It's my fault," I whispered, tears trying to burn their way up through my throat.

Stuart misunderstood. "Honey, you made a bad choice."

"Oh, shut *up!*"

Both Astra and I shouted it at the same time. He looked caught off guard and backed up a step before realizing what he'd done. Mouth flattening out, he lifted a hand. "I think you need to take a deep breath and calm down."

Shaking my head, I looked over at the folder Stuart had brought with him. The annulment papers. I didn't *want* to calm down.

"You can go now, Stuart."

"Piety…"

"I said you can go!" I turned away, and when I didn't hear movement behind me, I shouted. "*Go!*"

Chapter 11

Piety

I hadn't touched the scotch from earlier. Now, I wished I'd poured it out. The smell of it made me sick.

Astra sat across from me on the opposite couch, watching me with worried eyes as I stared at the annulment papers as if they were a snake ready to bite me.

I almost wish that was the case. A snake bite would be less painful than this.

It didn't make sense. It wasn't like we had anything real, right? So why did it hurt so much to hear that he'd walked away?

"Just because it wasn't real doesn't mean it won't hurt that he just up and left," Astra said.

Dazed, I looked up at her. "What?" Then I realized I must have spoken out loud. Shaking my head, I said, "It just doesn't make sense. I know he didn't plan to stay, but–"

"That doesn't mean you expected him to use the marriage to blackmail your parents into a payoff." She offered a weak smile and shrugged. "But it sucks. Not that your parents aren't jerks, but you still don't want to see them being used."

I snorted. "Hell, my parents excel at using people. Maybe I should celebrate that they got used for once."

I rubbed my burning eyes and swallowed around the knot in my throat. I would feel better if I could just cry, but the tears refused to come. I was pissed. Pissed-off and hurt. I wanted to cry, *and* I wanted to scream, *and* I wanted to throw things. But none of those would solve anything.

"Why couldn't he have just waited?" I asked, my voice cracking. "I was trying to help."

"Oh, honey…" Astra got up and came around the table, wrapping her arms around me.

A tear finally managed to break free, and it rolled down my cheek, followed by another, then another. As the dam started to break, I wrapped my arms around Astra and rested my head on her shoulder.

"Why couldn't he just wait?" The question came out as a sob this time.

"Maybe it's better that he didn't," she said gently. "If you're hurting this bad already, think about how much worse it would have been the longer you two were together. This was never meant to last anyway."

"But I think I wanted it to." I finally admitted out loud what I'd been feeling almost from the moment Kaleb and I had begun this charade. Astra wrapped her arms around me and did the only thing she could do. She held me while I cried.

It wasn't supposed to be real. But it hurt like it was.

Part Three

Chapter 1

Kaleb

"Piece of shit bastard," I muttered, fuming. I disconnected the call and slammed the phone down although it didn't do anything to cool the temper burning inside me.

I'd called Stefano so many times, I'd already lost track.

The same could be said for Camry.

Neither of them bothered to call back or even send a text. That was only one of the things that had me in a foul mood.

Piety had called numerous times that first night and left several messages. But since then, she'd only called twice, and each call had been late. At least late for the eastern part of the United States. She hadn't left a message, and she hadn't texted anything either. I almost answered each call. I almost called her back more than once.

But what the hell would I tell her? That I'd accepted the money from her parents so I could help my sister? That it had been driving me crazy sitting in Philly, doing nothing while she worked on anything?

Would I tell her that the prick lawyer had been right

about there being nothing else I could have done? He was right, even though he was a prick. Maybe he hadn't known why I needed the money, but I had needed it. And I'd needed it bad enough to do something desperate, something that would hurt her. That had mattered more than anything.

I knew it wasn't fair to compare my sister's life to the feelings of a woman I barely knew – even a woman I wanted more than I'd ever wanted anybody. My baby sister needed me and I'd already failed her too many times.

That thought had me reaching for the phone again, but when I went to check my messages, Piety's name filled my vision. I read one of the messages again even though I'd already committed all of them to memory.

Where are you? Is everything okay? I've got some news. Call me back, please?

News. I had no idea what she planned to tell me, but that message had come through while I'd been speeding across the country on a first-class ticket paid for by her parents.

Even now the thought turned my stomach.

I went to delete the message, just as I had told myself to do a thousand times over the past couple of days. But before I could, the phone rang.

"Finally," I muttered under my breath. There was no name attached to the phone number, but I knew who it was nonetheless. "About time you called."

"Easy, easy," Stefano said. "Why are you so hot under the collar? I would have thought you'd be happy that I was giving you time to get all that cash together."

"I want to talk to my sister."

"She's sleeping. Doesn't exactly keep banker's hours." He sounded amused with himself.

181

I wanted to punch my fist through the phone, grab him by his thick neck, and strangle him.

Twice.

"When can we meet? I just want it to get it over with." I sounded calm. Maybe I should have considered an acting career.

"Yeah, well, me too. But I've been busy. I'm a businessman, you know. Your sister isn't the only fish in the sea, and I've got other fish to take care of. Although she is my favorite. I'm going to miss her when she's gone." Then his voice went sly. "Assuming she doesn't come crawling back for more. I can be hard to resist."

"Fuck you," I snapped. "Look, can we just set up a time to meet or what?"

"You're in such a hurry. But fine, no small talk." Stefano laughed and named a place.

I had no doubt it would be just as sleazy as the first place, but it didn't matter. Camry was all that mattered now. "What time?"

"Three."

He hung up, and I stood there staring at the phone. I had a bad feeling about this entire thing. But what else was I supposed to do?

* * * * *

Three o'clock came and went. It was coming up on four-thirty when he finally came in…alone.

Camry wasn't with him.

What the *hell*?

I came out of my seat, hands closing into fists.

182

He had an easy smile on his face when he saw me. I wanted to knock that smile off his face, and his teeth down his throat.

"Hey there, Kaleb. How's it going? You got my money?"

He looked so damn pleased with himself. The arrogant bastard always looked so fucking happy.

"Where's my sister?" Anger was a huge ugly knot in my gut, but I managed to keep my voice level.

"That ain't how this works." He clicked his tongue and shook his head, looking almost pained as he said it. "See, you gotta pay me what you owe me, and *then* she's free to do what she wants. But until you pay me…"

"I want to see my sister." I spoke slowly, as if that would make a difference.

Stefano's eyes went cold and hard. With a shake of his head, he shouldered past me. "You don't get to make demands here. I own her."

"Did they forget to tell you that slavery ended a long time ago?"

"So naïve," he sneered. "Where. Is. My. Money?" He enunciated each word, the cold, ugly threat coming through with every syllable.

I knew I couldn't ignore him, this time. I wasn't worried about me, but my sister? Yes.

I turned on my heel and went back to the table where I'd been waiting. I sat down and reached for the envelope I'd left on the seat. As he sat down across from me, I slammed it on the table. "There. Now, where is she?"

"See, that wasn't so hard." Stefano shoved the envelope into his coat pocket and leaned back in the seat. He dropped his fingers on the top of the table and looked around, appearing pleased with himself. "So…here's what happens now. I'll let her know that her debt is paid in full. She's free to do whatever she wants. Just like she's always been, since, you know, slavery's illegal and all that."

"If she was free to do what she wants," I said, struggling to keep my temper under control, "then she could have left whenever she wanted."

"Hey, man..." He held up his hands, looking wounded. "She owed me money. What was I supposed to do? Just let her walk out and leave me hanging?"

"Yeah. You're the injured party here." I curled my lip at him, so disgusted I could barely stand to be in the same room.

"Hey, she came to me. Remember that. I didn't snatch her or something like that. I'm legit." He hitched up a shoulder and tipped an imaginary hat in a salute before sliding out of the booth. "Nice doing business with you, Kaleb."

I almost told him to shove his *business* up his ass.

Instead, I shrugged easily. "Tell Camry I'll be waiting for her call. I want to know where to pick her up."

"Hey, I'm sure she'll be in touch...soon."

As he turned and slouched out of the club, I fought the uneasy feeling settling over me. More than anything else, that last comment set me off.

I'd been leery of this whole mess from the get go, but now I was left wondering if I hadn't just been played. By both of them.

Chapter 2

Piety

"So you see, this client last week…"

Across from me, one Windsor Kiperman droned on and on. He was a good-looking enough guy, dark brown hair, and *amazing* hazel eyes streaked with gold. But he was so hung up on work, it was amazing he hadn't choked on it.

I nodded politely, trying my best to look like I was interested.

Really, I *should* be.

He was good looking, and well off. Came from the 'right' kind family, and his father was also one of my dad's biggest campaign contributors. Had an MBA from Columbia.

In the eyes of my family, it was probably a match made in heaven.

In *my* eyes, it was a match made in the doldrums. I'd never been so bored in my entire life. It wasn't that Windsor was a bad guy or anything. He wasn't. He opened doors. He'd called up and asked if I had an opinion on where we should go to eat. He was polite, attentive during the drive over.

185

And he was so perfectly…*boring*.

Finally – *finally* – he wrapped up his conversation about the client, and I leaned forward, smiling. "What was the last movie you saw?"

If he kept talking about work, I just might cry.

He stared at me with a blank expression.

"I absolutely loved the Avengers movie that came out last spring. Did you see it?" I continued to smile as I reached for my wine, wondering if my face would hurt from that fake, plastic smile.

"Hmmm. No. Those movies don't appeal to me." His comment wasn't rude. It was just a statement. A polite, boring statement. "I seldom have time for movies. I'm rather surprised you do. I heard you do…charity work?"

He left the statement hanging, as though it was a question.

"My charity work?"

"Yes, I understand you're involved in some philanthropic sort of work." He sliced a precise cut off his steak and popped it in his mouth.

I hadn't been able to stop noticing that he cut his food in an obsessively neat way. It was like he practically measured how wide of a bite to cut, how long.

You're obsessing, Piety!

"Ah, yes. I suppose you could call it a philanthropy sort of thing." I shrugged. "I'm a social worker. I work at a homeless shelter."

"You *work* there?" Windsor arched his brows. Now, instead of slicing off another perfect bite of steak, he laid his fork down and leaned forward. Puzzlement stamped all over his features, he studied me.

"Yes. I work with abuse victims, domestic mostly, but some that are drug or prostitution related." I expected his eyes to glaze over, but he nodded, looking almost interested.

"I didn't realize you actually worked there. I assume you get a paycheck?"

I rolled my eyes. "Barely. Their budget isn't much, but I love my job, and it's an important one."

Windsor nodded slowly. "I imagine it is. I've been attempting to convince my father into getting the company more involved in philanthropy, and perhaps getting the employees to jump on board, but he's...slow to see the benefits."

"The benefits are helping people out."

"Yes, of course. That's always a positive thing, but that's not an argument that would work with him." He shrugged, his eyes sliding away. "I didn't know you actually worked at this facility. Fascinating."

I'd heard too many similar comments, most of them with more than a tinge of superiority, to be insulted. At least Windsor seemed to mean it when he said it sounded *fascinating*.

"Yes, well, my parents would much rather it be true philanthropy." I played with the napkin in my lap. "Dad loves how it looks in front of the camera, but that's the only way it appeals to him."

It sounded terrible, and it made me feel even worse than before. I felt awful about how Kaleb had taken my parents for all that money, and here I was complaining about them. The last thing I needed was more guilt. That was how I'd ended up here.

I still didn't want to believe he'd done it. But he hadn't called, hadn't texted. Without any sort of explanation, what was I supposed to think?

You're not supposed to be thinking about him at all, especially on a date.

Desperate to change the subject, I asked, "So if

you're not into movies, what do you do for fun?"

No more thinking about Kaleb.

"Well…" He shrugged sheepishly. "To be honest, I really don't do much for fun. I just don't have time."

"Oh, come on, everyone has time for a little bit of fun." I pushed my hair back from my ear and stopped myself from playing with a strand. I didn't want to look as bored and I felt. "I try to read for about fifteen minutes a day no matter how busy I am. I go crazy if I don't get in something to entertain me. Do you work out, go to the gym?"

"I work…pretty much all the time." He held up a hand. "Sometimes I play golf with a client."

"But that's work too."

He laughed. "True. I'll be able to slow down later in life. Right now, I'm still trying to get established and show my dad I can take care of the business. I'll be the one taking over when he retires, you know." He cocked his head, a thoughtful look on his face. "What about you? Have you ever thought about going into politics? Following in your father's footsteps?"

I shuddered at the thought. "Hell no."

He laughed. "You look like you just ate something that tasted really, really bad."

"I *feel* like I tasted something really, really bad. There's no way I would go into politics." I gave an emphatic shake of my head.

"So what do you plan on doing?" The genuine interest in his voice was…sweet.

But he didn't get it.

"I'm already doing it." I shrugged. "I love what I do. Sometimes it breaks my heart. Some of it drains me and leaves me exhausted. But at the end of the day, I'm making a difference. That…matters. It's enough for me."

At least it always had been.

I hadn't felt quite so ready to dive into work recently, although it wasn't *work* that was getting to me. I was just finding life in general lacking.

And I knew why.

Kaleb.

And there it was again. I was thinking about him.

Dammit!

"What about your father? Don't you think he's making a difference?"

"I think he's too busy to worry about getting re-elected to think about making a difference." I laughed a little. "Yeah, I don't really put much stock into politics when it comes to...well, much of anything positive."

Windsor seemed to realize he'd said something wrong. "I'm sorry. I didn't mean..."

I waved him off. "It's okay. Not everybody gets it, but they don't need to. I'm happy with what I do. I'm more than happy. I feel…complete. At the end of the day, I'm satisfied. I make time for myself, and I do things for fun – *now* – and I don't feel the need to do anything to prove myself to anybody. I'm good."

"I think I envy you," Windsor said softly.

Okay, that surprised me.

"Nothing is stopping you from finding what would make *you* happy – except you." I held his eyes for a moment.

"True. But my priorities are more important than just being happy."

Chapter 3

Piety

The better part of a bottle of wine sat open in front of me. I had just about emptied my glass, and I was ready to top it off. Again.

Drinking in the dark wasn't exactly the best way to end the night, but I wasn't ready to go to bed, and I had no interest in reading or watching TV.

The one thing I *did* want to do wouldn't happen.

I wanted to talk to Kaleb.

But I sure as hell wasn't going to call him. Or text him.

Again.

I put my phone away just to make sure I didn't give into the urge or get too drunk and forget the promise I made to myself.

Then Astra called to check on me, asking if I was okay.

I lied and ended the call before she could press the matter.

Part of me wished I hadn't, that I'd confessed to how miserable I truly was. If I had, she would have come back home, and we could have eaten ice cream and watched cheesy movies, and maybe I wouldn't feel so pathetic.

Maybe I should just give in to the inevitable.

My parents were just going to keep pushing men like Windsor at me. At least Windsor wasn't a total ass. I could be Piety Kiperman within a year if I played things right.

Piety Kiperman.

"Fuck my life," I whispered, the very idea making my head hurt.

Life with him would be awful.

I'd be bored within three days, if not less.

But my parents loved him, and if it wasn't him, it would be somebody else. Somebody obnoxious and truly repugnant. Mom had already sent me a text, asking how the date had gone and when we were going out again. Maybe I could grow to like hearing about work. And more work. And golf with people from work.

Tears burned my eyes, and I groaned, putting the glass down so I could cover my face.

"Crying alone in the dark plus drinking alone in the dark equals beyond pathetic."

I couldn't help it though. Everything seemed to be imploding around me and all I wanted was to go back to my nice, normal existence when I'd been content.

Except content wasn't enough now.

I'd felt what it was like to be truly happy. I'd only had a taste of it, but it had been enough. I wanted that back. I wanted something my parents had never had – passion. A partner who *loved* me, not just somebody who shared common interests.

I wanted things my parents wouldn't even understand, which was why they thought Windsor was perfect for me. Because they didn't get it.

I wanted a man who loved me so much he was stupid with it. My dad was never stupid about anything. The thought of him doing something stupid and crazy for my mother was just insane. The thought of my mother doing something stupid and crazy for my father was equally insane.

The sound of my own laughter caught me off-guard, but I'd started to think of that strange, free-fall sort of feeling I'd had when I'd climbed on the skyscraper roller coaster with Kaleb. I'd done it because of the way he'd smiled at me. I hadn't been able to stop myself despite how terrified I'd been. It wasn't even all that crazy, but my mother wouldn't have done it.

My father…on a roller coaster?

Never.

Doing something that scared them just to be close to each other.

Nope.

"Stop it!" I grabbed the bottle of wine, and without even bothering to pour it into the glass, I took a drink. Rising, I wandered into my bedroom and over to the window. I'd never felt so lonely and empty before in my life.

If I could just convince myself that I was worried about Camry, I'd feel better.

If I could just convince myself that it had little to do with him as a person and more to do with the situation itself, maybe I'd be alright.

But I couldn't do it.

Yes, I had concerns about Camry, but she wasn't what had me lying awake at night.

I'd thought there was something between us. I really had. But I must have been wrong. Maybe it had only been on my side. If we'd had anything there, wouldn't he have talked to me before he left? Wouldn't he have at least called or sent me a note? Something to let me know that he was okay?

I took another drink of wine, then put the bottle on the nightstand. Falling back onto the bed, I stared up at the ceiling.

I wanted to tell myself that things would get better, that things would turn around.

But I'd been doing that ever since he left, and so far, nothing had changed.

* * * * *

"You see...I told you a change would do you good..."

Astra's wild, bawdy laugh had me giggling. "Look at that one...the blond." My heart skipped a beat when he flicked ice-blue eyes my way.

He was so...so pretty. And biteable. And pretty. I wanted to just...bite him. Yeah. Bite him. Yum.

Astra giggled. "You're licking your lips, PS. Don't blame you though. Have you ever seen such a pretty man in all of your life?"

"Nope. Not ever." Chin resting on my fist, I stared at him and sighed. I was entirely too drunk to be sitting here, gaping at some stripper – or maybe I was just drunk enough to be gaping at a stripper. I didn't know.

I just knew I was drunk and I loved it. Maybe I was going to be drunk all the time now. That would be nice.

The beautiful blond edged closer, and the woman a seat down from us reached out and stroked her hand down the back of his calf. I wanted to smack her. She shouldn't be touching him. He ignored her, catching the chair that had been placed in the middle of the walkway and swinging a leg over it.

"I bet you anything he's just pretty though. No brain inside that head." I gestured to him, convinced that somehow made sense. "If you're that pretty, you've got to have something wrong. Right?"

"Hey, you're pretty and smart. I'm fucking beautiful and pretty damn sharp." Astra laughed until she snorted and waved at the blond. He continued to twist his spine, a movement that made it clear that at least there was one thing he was definitely not *lacking.*

My mouth went dry.

"Besides, with that face, what does it matter if he has a brain? As long as he's not a dick – I mean, I want him to have one..." She shot me a grin. "And he definitely does."

We were both so drunk, that was why it was so funny. It had to be.

He slid off the chair and went to his knees, crawling along the stage. I had a bill already clutched in my hand, and my fingers were shaking as he moved closer.

His skin was hot against my fingers, almost shockingly so. Our eyes caught, then held. I wished there was something I could say or do. Something like... Hey, you want to get a drink?

I bet that *would make me stand out. Biggest loser he'd probably had to deal with in a long time, and I was fawning over him. My fingers lingered on his skin for so long that he caught my wrist and tugged my hand away.*

But he didn't let go.

At least not right away.

We stared at each other, and I bit my lip, tugging a little harder as a bunch of women around us started to whoop. He let go, loosening his grip slowly until I felt each slow brush of his fingers as they left my skin.

His eyes, so bright, surrounded by spiky lashes, held mine for another moment. I didn't want him looking away, but in the next moment he did.

And I slumped in my seat.

That had been the most intense minute of my life – at least that I could recall, considering how freaking drunk I was. And I probably wouldn't remember it tomorrow.

"Wow...look at his ass." Astra smacked her lips. "I just want to...bite him. Like all over. Don't you?"

"Yes."

I caught the server's eye and waved my hand. I needed another drink. Desperately. Maybe if I got just a little more sloppy drunk, I could get him out of my head.

* * * * *

"It's him!"

Astra grabbed my arm and squealed. "See! It's him."

I was already staring at the guy at the bar, face shielded by shaggy blond hair, so I didn't need Astra shaking me. It wasn't helping my spinning head, either.

"Stop," I said, tugging my arm away. My heart raced harder at the sight of him, but when Astra tried to tug me closer to the bar, I dug in my heels and resisted. "No. You're supposed to be distracting me and helping me have fun. I'm drunk enough."

"I'm not taking you over there to get drunk. He's the distraction." She was nowhere near as quiet as she tried to be. Several people swung their heads to look at us as

she continued to pull me along. "Come on, PS."

He flicked a glance our way, and the sight of those eyes had my heart hitching a beat or two. He immediately returned his interest to his glass though.

He had a booted foot hooked on the rung of the bar stool, broad shoulders slumped.

There was something...lonely about him.

Maybe it was because I was lonely too, but when Astra urged me along, I stopped resisting. He continued to stare into his drink, swirling the whiskey around and around, and I continued to stare at him.

What are you looking for? *I found myself wondering.* You won't find the answers there.

Astra nudged to me. "Talk to him. I dare you."

"I stopped responding to dares a long time ago." But I found myself taking one wobbly step and then another, and before I knew what I was doing, I had settled down next to him.

He didn't even look up.

"Hi."

Nothing.

I tried again. "I saw you dancing."

He shrugged and lifted his glass. "So did a lot of other women. I don't do private performances. Sorry."

"Oh, I don't want..."

He looked up at me.

Our eyes met.

Oh...wow...

Oh...wow...

He kissed me, and he tasted like heaven.

I giggled a little bit, because the bourbon he'd been drinking had been called something...heaven something. And I knew it was closer to hell, especially on the stomach.

But it tasted pretty damn good on him, and now he was with me, his skin hot and naked on mine.

"Stop," he muttered when I slid my hand down his chest. "You've got to stop."

"Why?" I giggled again as I slid my hands farther down, his skin hot against my palms. Hot and amazing. Everything about him was amazing.

"Stop, because...fuck. I need..."

"Yes, you need to fuck." I laughed, delighted with everything. Curling my arms around his neck, I tugged him back to me. "You need to fuck me. Right?"

"Right..." He laughed this time, and then he kissed me again.

And again.

And again...

* * * * *

I jerked upright in the bed, staring at the wall.

That dream…

"Wow."

The echo of something from the dream came back to haunt me.

Oh…wow.

Had I *said* that?

Or just dreamed it?

I couldn't remember, couldn't think.

Shaking, I rubbed my hands up and down my face.

I had a headache, and the outline of the bottle of wine mocked me. I'd drank almost half of it. Not that much in the scheme of things, and not enough to give me a hangover, but maybe enough to fuel a wild dream.

Yet…it didn't *feel* like a dream.

Not really.

It had felt like…well, a memory.

"Wow."

Chapter 4

Kaleb

The pathetic little hotel where I was staying might not have been exactly a fleabag, but it wasn't much better.

The watery light made it impossible to read, but I didn't have anything else to do so I stayed bent over the book Piety had given me, ignoring the slowly building headache and focusing on the words on the page.

I had nothing else *to* focus on, unless I wanted to think about the phone that hadn't rang or the sister that was still strangely absent.

But it was getting harder and harder to keep my thoughts on anything that didn't either piss me off or make me wish I'd done everything – and I mean *everything* – differently.

I hadn't seen or heard from Stefano since I'd given him the money yesterday. Camry hadn't so much as called. I lost track of how many times I sent her a text or tried to call. I left the address of where I was staying.

She knew where I was. She knew how to get in touch with me. She could, assuming Stefano had actually let her go. I didn't see why he wouldn't. If he was trying to string me along for more money, he would have made that clear already. Right?

Shit, I hope that wasn't what he was up to.

Still, if he planned to jerk me around more, I would have expected to hear from him, and I hadn't heard from anybody. My phone had been wonderfully, miserably silent. Camry hadn't called, begging for money.

Piety hadn't called. Not even once.

Unable to tolerate the stingy light any longer, I closed the book and placed it face down on my chest. Throwing my arm over my eyes, I tried to forget about where I was and pretend I was back in Philadelphia. With her. Of course, it didn't help me feel any less miserable. Maybe I should imagine I was back in Sydney, surfing.

At least that was a little more likely to happen in the near future.

One thing I did know – I wanted to get the hell out of Las Vegas.

I hated it here.

The wind, the dirt, the sun…and there was never any darkness, never any silence.

I must have half-drifted off to sleep because the knock on the door was so unexpected, it jerked me into awareness – and confusion. I sat up, not entirely sure where I was. I was hungry, sore, and irritated, and when the knock came again, louder, I shouted, "What is it?"

"Open up, grouchy pants!" a thin, familiar voice said through the door.

Camry.

I almost fell on my face rushing to get there.

Something light, almost happy settled inside my chest, ready to explode. Finally!

And then it died, all in the span of a second.

Camry stood staring up at me, a wobbly smile on her mouth, and her pupils so huge I could barely see her eyes.

She threw herself at me and practically missed. If I hadn't caught her, she would've toppled to the floor. "Oops!" she said cheerfully. "Hi, big brother!"

"Camry."

She gave me a smacking kiss on the cheek, and then brushed me off, moving deeper into the room, bouncing with every step. Shit.

"You took *forever* to answer the door, Kaleb." She giggled and said my name again. "Kaleb. *Ka*-leb. That's a cool sound...*Kaleb*."

"You're high."

"Maybe." She held up her index finger and thumb about an inch apart. "Just a little."

More than a little. I wanted to hit something. As I fought with that urge, Camry turned in a circle, looking around the room. "Wow. This place is a *dump*. Why are you staying here?"

"I've been too busy saving every penny to pay off your drug debt, Camry," I snapped. "I'm afraid I don't have money for a room at the Bellagio."

"Ooohhh..." She smiled and spun around in a circle. "That's a nice place. Stefano's taken me there."

I clenched my jaw. "I bet he has. Did he give you the drugs?"

"Not like I'd take them from anybody else." She sniffed. "I'm *careful*."

"And that's how you ended up owing him ten grand."

"Shit, Kaleb. You're *grouchy*. You're so grouchy. You want to know why I get high? It's because I don't want to be grouchy and boring like you. Lighten up, brother. Life's too short. You're supposed to have fun."

The bed springs squeaked under her, and she laughed again at the sound, bouncing up and down. Turning away from her, I moved to the window and threw open the curtains. Immediately, the heat made me wish I hadn't. The air conditioner had a hard time keeping up already, and I could feel the scalding temperature outside beating against the glass.

I hated it here.

I wanted to go back home.

Back to Philadelphia.

Somewhere…anywhere but here.

"Maybe I should get high," I said absently. "Rack up a debt of ten thousand dollars, whore myself out too. But who will bail me out when I get in trouble, Camry?"

"Don't be mean." Camry sniffed. "You know, I could have taken care of it myself."

"Then why in the blue fuck did you call me?" Spinning around, I glared at her. "I gave up *everything* for you – my job, my apartment, my chance to buy the shop. *Everything!*"

Piety.

Everything.

"I did it because I *thought* you needed me."

She flinched, tears filling her blue eyes.

I felt terrible, but steeled myself against it. I knew better than to do this, to let her get to me. I should have known better than to even *come* here. Piety had been right about my sister. Camry sure as hell hadn't acted afraid of Stefano, and I was starting to get a bad feeling about this whole miserable mess.

Looking away from her, I focused on the wall. "Don't try and use tears on me, Camry. Not now. Not after all the shit you've pulled."

"I'm not trying to *use* anything!" She stood up, wobbling on a pair of heels that had to be five inches. She gave me a defiant glare and still managed to look pathetic and woebegone.

"Why are you doing this?" I asked. "Where did you get the money for the drugs this time?"

"It was *free*!" She flung it at me like a weapon. "He *likes* me, so he does that sometimes."

"Bastards like him likes nobody but themselves." I wanted to shake her. "Dammit, you can't fall down that hole again. I can't get that kind of money again."

"Why not?" She shrugged, not looking worried. "You did it easy enough this time."

"Easy?" I started to see red.

I'd given up Piety for her. Easy?! It had ripped my fucking heart in half.

The first time I finally found anybody who meant something to me, and I gave her up...and for *what*?

"Easy?" I shook my head and turned away. Gathering up some clothes, I started for the bathroom. I needed to cool down before I lost it. "I don't think you have any idea what it cost me, Camry. What *you* cost me. You probably never will. And I'm about ready to stop trying to make you understand."

"What does that mean?"

I paused to look at her. "Just that. You can get help. You don't need Stefano. You can get help, get off the drugs, stop sleeping with men for money or for a quick fix...whatever. But if you're going to keep this up, I won't be the one to help you back up the next time you're in trouble. You'll have to figure it out on your own."

"I've always had to do that." She poked her lip out. "You had Mom and Dad. But I only had...me."

"You had *me*." I wasn't going to do this. "And you know it. But if you want to tell yourself otherwise, then do it. Maybe it makes it easier for you."

* * * * *

I stayed in the bathroom more than long enough for her to give up waiting and leave, but when I came out, she was still there, standing in front of the window with her hands in her pockets.

"You never needed me," she said, her voice soft.

Was that what all of this was about? I didn't let myself ask her the question though. I wasn't sure I wanted to know the answer. And to be honest, I wasn't sure it mattered. Camry didn't want to get clean. I could see that clearly now. Until she was ready, there was nothing I could do to help her.

"You know, if I'm such a pain in the ass, you could just…" She laughed, the sound shrill and harsh. Turning to face me, she jutted her chin up, an indignant look on her face. "I've *tried*, Kaleb. Things aren't as easy for me, okay? I wanted my mom and my dad to be there. I wanted…things. You did too, I get that, but you coped better than I did."

"No. I just coped. You had it rough. I get that." Shaking my head, I looked away. "But instead of trying to cope, you partied, you did drugs and acted out. I'm done feeling sorry for you."

"I'm not asking you to feel sorry for me!" she shouted. "Fine! Just go! Go do whatever it is you do."

"Your entire life is a plea for attention, Camry." Already tired, I sat on the edge of the bed, staring at her. "I came here to help you. Again. Apparently, *that* is what I do – look out for you. I don't know how else to define myself. And every time, it gets thrown back at me. I'm…tired of it. I'm just tired."

"Then stop." She crossed her arms over her chest. "I

don't need you to take care of me, Kaleb. I don't need it, and I don't want it."

There was something final in her voice, and I looked up to find her staring at me.

She gave me a tight smile and then turned. I didn't even have time to process what was happening until she was already out the door. I lurched up, going after her, but she just kept walking.

There was a car waiting for her in the parking lot.

"What are you going to do?" I asked.

"Whatever I want." She glanced at me as she neared the car. "You don't want to talk to me; you want to bitch at me. So fine. I'll leave."

"You didn't come here to *talk*. You came here strung out and feeling sorry for yourself. Sorry if I'm not really in the mood for a pity party when I'm dealing with my own shit, Camry."

"Well, now you can do whatever you want. And so can I. You made that clear." She lifted her chin. For a moment, just a brief one, I thought I saw something in her eyes.

Sorrow.

Guilt.

Hurt.

I couldn't tell.

It was gone so fast, then she was too. She climbed into the car, and the driver pulled off with a spray of dust and gravel.

I stared after the car until it was lost from sight, and then, feeling oddly numb, I went inside.

I was done with this.

Everyone had told me I couldn't help her if she wasn't ready, and maybe I was a slow learner, but I finally got it. I wasn't going to sit around wasting my time trying. I wasn't going to hang around for her to jerk me around again.

I grabbed my wallet and started to shove it into my pocket, only to pause.

Dread filled me when I squeezed it.

Earlier, it'd been fat with the cash I'd put in there, half the cash I'd left over. Now, it was almost pathetically thin.

"Camry…" I closed my eyes, hoping against hope.

I had to make myself look inside, even though I already knew what I'd find. Or what I wouldn't find.

I'd stashed half the money in my wallet, and every last dollar was gone.

Flinging the wallet across the room, I swore. It hit the wall and bounced before falling to the floor. Without waiting a moment, I went to the mattress and hauled it up, searching for the small slit I'd made, and the rest of the money.

It was there.

Thank God.

I wasn't completely broke.

But what was I going to do…?

It hit me then.

There was only one thing I could do.

Only one thing I wanted to do.

Chapter 5

Piety

The resume in front of me wasn't coming together.

One of my clients at the shelter was trying to get a job. She had a place to stay as well as childcare, and if she could just get a job, we could make a case for her getting custody of her kid. I needed to get a resume together so we could practice her interview techniques. We were so close. Things would get better for her once the last block fell into place.

Normally, this was the part of my job that I loved. Carol had done the hard part, leaving her husband and asking for help. But I couldn't focus on this task to save my life.

I was distracted. By the dream slash memory, by Kaleb, by everything that had been going on in my life.

And I was miserable.

My heart hurt.

Throwing down my pen, I leaned back in my chair and shoved my hair from my face. "Focus," I told myself. "I've got to focus."

Getting up, I went to the coffee maker.

It had long since gone burnt. Disgusted, I dumped the dregs out and started a fresh pot. At the rate I was going, I wouldn't be done before midnight anyway, and I definitely didn't want to sleep.

If I slept, I'd dream about Kaleb again.

Once the coffee was done, I leaned against the counter, sipping the hot brew and coaxing my muddied brain into thinking. All the key info was *there*. I just had to get it down.

Outside, rain pounded against the window, and thunder crashed. It was a miserable night. Or a great one, depending on who you were with and what you were doing. Astra was out with a guy, probably snuggled up and doing something debauched.

And here I was alone and miserable. The storm was adding to my overall melancholy state, but I tried to block it out. Returning to my desk, I settled down and stared at the laptop.

Carol could do this. She had a solid work background.

She was trying to get hired at a daycare, and she had experience with kids.

She'd left the workplace when she had her daughter, but she'd done some volunteering since. This should write itself.

After a brief mental pep talk, I buckled down. And a half hour later, I was done. The resume wasn't perfect but it would do.

Now I had nothing left to occupy my time, and it didn't take long for my thoughts to drift back to Kaleb.

What was he doing?

Had things worked out with Camry?

The phone rang, and I grabbed it, hoping it was something else that might distract me. Right now, I'd even talk to my parents.

But it was just Carlos, the nighttime doorman for the

building.

"Hello, Miss Piety. Lovely weather we're having, yes?"

I eyed the storm and smiled. "Absolutely, if you like floods. Do you like floods?"

"I like the rain. Are you having a good night?"

"Good enough," I lied. "And you?"

"Of course. Ma'am…there's a young man here to see you. I believe he stayed with you and Miss Astra a few nights last week. His name is Kaleb…"

I didn't even hear the rest of the sentence.

* * * * *

In my rush down to the lobby, I neglected to think about the fact that I was wearing the oversized t-shirt I slept in. The cool air blowing in through the vents had me shivering, but I wasn't about to go back upstairs.

When the elevator doors slid open, and I caught sight of him, my heart lurched.

For one moment, everything stopped.

It just stopped.

I stumbled to a halt, my fingers curling into fists so I didn't reach for him. But I wanted to so fucking bad. He was soaking wet, broad shoulders slumped, head hanging low. And all I wanted to do was wrap my arms around him.

"Kaleb."

At the sound of my voice, he looked up, and I found myself lost in those pale blue eyes.

"Piety," he said, his voice raw.

"Hi." I sounded breathless, like I'd run every flight from the loft down here to the lobby. I felt like it too.

"Can we...?" He looked around. "Can we talk?"

"Of course." I didn't know what else to say, and I lifted a hand. "Come upstairs."

He stared at my hand for a moment, and I didn't realize what he was looking at so intently until the light bounced off the ring. My wedding ring. The one I still hadn't been able to take off. Slowly, he accepted my hand, and I turned, knees shaking and heart racing.

Giving Carlos a weak smile, I tugged Kaleb into the elevator behind me and pushed the button for the loft. Barely daring to breathe, I closed my eyes.

He still held my hand.

His skin was hot.

Hot and damp from the rain, and I could smell him. Fuck, he smelled good.

I wanted to peel the clothes away and touch him, kiss him...do all the things I thought I'd never get to do again.

On the top floor, the elevator stopped, and the doors slid open.

We still hadn't spoken.

We still held hands.

Moving into the loft, I slowly tugged my hand free and tried to breathe a little deeper. Talk. Right. That's what we were going to do. Rain crashed into the windows, and the electricity from the lightning seemed to be gathering inside my loft as well. Tension hummed between us, so charged and erratic, I thought I'd come out of my skin.

I grabbed a towel and handed it to him without meeting his eyes. "Here, why don't you dry off? You're soaked to the bone."

"Yeah." He gave a cursory rub of his hair and

shoulders, then stood there, twisting the towel around his big hands. "I'm sorry, Piety."

Okay, that wasn't a bad start. "For which part?"

He looked up then, met my eyes. "I've made a mess of things, and I needed to tell you that."

There was hell in his eyes. Still, as he stood there, watching me, all I could think was…*a mess? You call this a mess?*

He'd blackmailed my parents, left me without a word…and he wanted to just call it a mess?

I didn't know what to say, so I just nodded.

He rubbed the towel over his face, then folded it neatly and held it back out to me. I took it, feeling out of place in my own home. Everything felt out of place.

It wasn't okay.

His sorry wasn't enough.

But what was I supposed to do?

He gave me a tight smile. "This was a mistake. I shouldn't have come. I'll go."

Without thinking anything beyond the fact that I couldn't watch him walk out that door, I threw the towel down and moved between him and the door. He stopped, his expression wary. Reaching up, I touched his cheek and he froze.

"Don't," he said roughly. He closed his hand around my wrist, the heat from him searing me through. "Just…don't."

"Don't what?" I asked. "Don't want you? Don't think about you? Don't ask you to stay?"

A muscle pulsed in his cheek.

"I don't want you to go." Pushing up on my toes, I pressed my mouth to the corner of his lips. "Don't go, Kaleb."

I would have leaned against him, but he caught my

upper arms in his hands and held me back.

"I'm soaking wet. We…this isn't smart."

"I don't care. I'm tired of being smart and thinking…I'm tired of wanting you and you not being there." I put my hands on the back of his neck and took a step toward him. "No matter what happened, I missed you, Kaleb."

I pressed my lips against his, and he groaned, his mouth opening as his tongue slide out to tease me. I felt his resistance melt, and then his hands were on my waist, pulling me tight against him.

I moaned at the taste of him, shuddered when he slid his hands down to my ass. His teeth scraped against my bottom lip, and I buried my fingers in his hair. I knew there were things we needed to discuss, issues to work through, and I didn't know what this would mean for the future, but all I was going to think about was this moment.

"Touch me." I could hear the pleading in my voice, but didn't care. "Please touch me, Kaleb."

His mouth took mine again, his kiss as possessive as his hands as they moved under my shirt, leaving a blazing trail of heat on my skin.

And froze for a moment before groaning. "Fuck, Piety, are you telling me you've been naked under this the whole time?"

His hands slid up my back, then around to brush his thumbs across my already-hard nipples. My eyelids fluttered at the zing of pleasure that went through me. Nothing compared to his touch, to the sounds he made. To the hard press of his cock against my hip.

I opened my eyes to see his pale irises blazing.

"You came downstairs naked. We've been standing here talking, and you're naked. I just can't…"

He dropped to his knees, and I bit my lip, bracing myself with my hands on his shoulders. He gripped my calf, pulling my leg over his shoulder. My entire body was pulsing with anticipation and when he slid his tongue between my folds, I dug my nails into his shoulders and swore, pleasure ripping through me.

His hand splayed across the small of my back, holding me in place as he moved his tongue over my clit. Perfect pressure combined with hot, wet friction had me rocketing toward orgasm, and the sight of his head between my legs pushed me even faster.

"Come for me, Piety." His voice was demanding, leaving no room for argument.

Not that I wanted to argue. Hell no. I wanted to come.

I gasped as he pushed two fingers into my pussy. His thumb moved over my clit as his fingers twisted inside me, knuckles rubbing against my g-spot. I was so close that every nerve felt stretched to the point of snapping. All the stress that had built since he'd walked out of my life coiled tight, ready to explode.

"Come for me, sweetheart."

My vision went white and my muscles tensed. I couldn't move, could barely breathe, as pleasure threatened to overwhelm me. I was still processing when his arm slid around my waist to hold me up as he stood. I whimpered when his fingers slid out of me, but then I realized he was tugging at his jeans.

I reached out and wrapped my hand around his thick shaft even as he freed it. He groaned as my fingers curled around him, hips moving into my touch. When I ran my hand down to the base, then back up to the tip, he reached up and braced one hand on the door by my head, his biceps bulging. He closed his other hand around mine, tightening my grip and pumping into my hand, hard and fast.

"Watching you come is one of the hottest things I've ever seen," he said, his voice rough. "But this...I could fucking come all over you."

The image sent a shiver through me. "Do it."

His eyes were wild as they met mine. He kissed me quick and hard, then let go of my hand.

"I'd rather come in you."

He lifted me without warning, and I wrapped my legs around his waist automatically, my hands clinging to his broad shoulders. I gasped as he filled me, deep and fast, pleasure riding the edge of pain. One arm held my hips, and he caught my wrist with his free hand. When he stretched my arm over my head, I raised my other so he could hold both wrists, leaving my weight balanced on his cock and hips.

"I've never wanted anybody the way I want you. You're like a drug." Kaleb shuddered as he skimmed his lips across my cheekbone. "My drug."

"You're mine." I tugged against his hold, but all he did was stroke his thumb across my wrist as he thrust into me. I felt completely surrounded, completely filled by him. He stretched me and filled me over and over, until *finally*, that horrible emptiness began to fade away. "Don't leave me again, okay?"

He bit down on the side of my throat. "I won't."

Each stroke had him dragging back and forth against my clitoris, pressing against the oversensitive bundle of nerves until each pass was almost as intense as an orgasm on its own. The soft cotton of my shirt dragged back and forth over my nipples, taunting me. Everything became about pleasure and pain and where the two of us came together.

Kaleb caught my lower lip between his teeth, drawing it out before letting it go to kiss me again. My mouth throbbed, lips swollen, but I never wanted him to stop kissing me, to stop fucking me. I just wanted *him*. In me, with me.

Always.

I pulled against his hold, and he finally released my hands so I could cling to him. He boosted me higher, changing the angle of my hips and then it was too much. I came hard and fast, but just when I thought it was over, he started to come, and the feel of him pulsing, emptying inside me, set me off all over again.

It was unending.

It was amazing.

It was stupid.

Chapter 6

Kaleb

We lay on the couch. Piety was warm against me, and I rubbed my chin against her hair. It was soft as the silk underthings she wore. I knew more about silk after a few days with her than I'd learned in my entire life., but I still preferred the feel of her skin against mine.

Speaking of...

"Is Astra going to walk in here and find me laying naked on her couch?" I asked.

We had a throw covering us, or mostly. But I really didn't want her best friend finding us like this. Especially since I had a feeling Astra would want to kick my ass for leaving Piety. Hell, *I* wanted to kick my ass for that.

"Not a chance. She's with a guy." Piety stretched against me, and the feel of her sleek body rubbing against me had my cock stirring. I was tempted to roll her over and take her again, but things had to be said first.

Before I could lose my nerve, I shifted around on the couch and pushed up onto my elbow. Her eyes were big and sleepy, her face still flushed from sex.

My heart clenched, just looking at her, and I wished we could just stay here like this forever, not have to deal with the rest of the world. But real life was out there, whether we liked it or not.

"We should talk."

Her smile was soft, sadness clinging to it. "That's what we've been doing. You came up here to talk."

"No." Stroking my thumb over her lower lip, I sighed. "I'm serious. There's...more. Stuff I should have told you before."

Her eyes cooled slightly, and I braced myself for the rejection I suspected was coming.

"If this is about my parents," she said, voice level, almost...gentle. "I already know. I mean, did you think I wouldn't find out? That they wouldn't tell me what you did?"

"What *I* did?" I asked, frowning.

Well, that answered a lot of questions. I'd spent the past week wondering what they told her. Her calls had gone from worried to agitated and then to...careful. There had been no emotion in the last message she had left for me and that careful lack of any feeling had managed to convey quite a bit.

I might not have known the specifics, but I could see now that she hadn't been told the whole truth. I should have known her parents would've put a spin on it that made me out to be the bad guy. Her father was a politician, for fuck's sake.

"Come off it, Kaleb." She eased away from me and sat up. "I understand why you did it. I really do. I was trying to get things together to help you out anyway, and if I had been upfront and honest, you wouldn't have been so desperate. But don't try to make this into anything other than what it was."

She'd been what...?

I pushed that aside, climbing off the couch and grabbing my jeans. They were still wet, but I pulled them on anyway. I didn't want to have this discussion naked.

Piety had smoothed her shirt down and now sat studying me with studied casualness. "We can get past it. We really can. But, just…don't try to justify how it happened. I don't want to think about it."

Some of the frustration I was feeling dissolved.

She'd let it go, I realized. She would let it all go even though it was clear that whatever she'd been told had hurt her.

I leaned down and cupped her face. "I'm losing a little bit more of myself to you all the time."

My lips brushed against hers and I thought about staying quiet, just keeping it all inside. Her parents may have treated her poorly, but she still loved them, and I knew how much learning the truth would hurt her. It might even be enough for her to turn on me, and I'd lose her forever.

A small selfish part of me thought I should just accept it, enjoy what time I had, while I could.

But she'd never been anything but honest with me.

I could do no less with her.

I straightened with a sigh. "I don't know what they told you I did, but your parents paid me to leave town, Piety. They said if I signed the annulment papers and left, agreed not to talk to you, they'd give me money – cash. It was everything I needed to take care of Camry."

Shock danced across her features.

Here it comes…now she'll push me away…

"What?" The question came out flat.

"Their lawyer came here to see me," I said, that familiar feeling of exhaustion bearing down on me again.

I paced over to the window. The storm had blown over, but it was still raining, the sort of summer storm that blotted everything out.

I continued without looking at her, "You and Astra were gone and this lawyer showed up...Stuart Rushmore."

Even his name disgusted me, but I kept my voice even.

"He came here and told me that he wanted to talk to me, said he could help me." Turning back to her, I shrugged. "He said he was a friend of yours. It wasn't until I'd already let him in that he clarified and said he was actually your parents' lawyer. Then he laid out the deal." Shame flooded me. "And I...took it."

"That's why you haven't returned my calls." She swallowed, her gaze falling to the floor.

"I'd given my word. It means something to me. I don't have much, but that's one of the few things I do have." I looked around her loft, evidence of how little my word had meant in the end. "Or had. I'm here now."

"And why are you here now?" Her tone was careful, cautious, and I hated that what I'd done made her feel that way about me.

"Because. There's nothing left. I spent the last of the money to buy a ticket back here." I realized how that sounded as soon as I said it, so I hurried to explain.

I told her everything, what had happened with Stefano, and how Camry had come to my room high, how she'd completely blown me off. Piety listened without saying a word, her expression guarded until my voice broke as I told her about Camry walking away. Piety came to me then, wrapping her arms around me, and I hugged her back, not even trying to disguise how desperately I needed her.

"Everything was completely fucked up, but all I could think about is you and how much I miss you and how much I wish I hadn't left." I let the words pour out of

219

me. "So I came back, praying you'd understand, forgive me. I know all this sounds terribly selfish, and I suppose it is, because I know I messed up more than I can say. But you're too important for me to let go without a fight. I need you, Piety. And I don't need anyone." My hands flexed against her back. "I don't know what I'm going to do if I can't have you."

She eased back, looking up at me with the sort of searching expression I felt all the way to my very soul.

Then, slowly, she kissed my forehead. Each of my cheeks. My chin.

"I'm sorry," she said finally. "I've been so angry at you these past few weeks, and it wasn't totally your fault. It was my parents manipulating you like they've tried to do to me my whole life. I should have known."

"Don't apologize to me. It was my fault." I stroked my hand up her back, my fingers passing over each bump of her spine, memorizing each nuance of her body. "I made the fucked up decision to take the deal and leave when I should have talked to you."

"We all make mistakes. They're in the past now." She sighed and tucked her body against mine. After a moment, she asked, "What are you going to do about Camry?"

"I don't know. I don't think I can do anything." Misery settled inside, but anger and hurt were useless, I knew. Giving in to them solved nothing. "I've given up everything for her, sacrificed most of my life to take care of her. And now this…" I shook my head, unable to put into words the sheer helplessness I felt.

"We're going to find a way."

Piety sounded so certain that I dared to feel a flicker of hope. Hope that maybe, just maybe, I could be happy.

Chapter 7

Piety

"I got the job."

Carol stood in front of my desk, twisting her fingers, looking stunned.

"Congratulations!"

I came out from behind the desk and hugged her, keeping it light and easy so she could break away. She was doing so much better than when she first came here, but I knew physical touch was still hard for her. Like so many others in her situation, she'd gone from an abusive father to an abusive husband, and relearning physical contact was never easy.

She nodded nervously, her dark eyes bouncing all over the place. "I got the job, Ms. Van Allan. They hired me."

"I know," I smiled at her. "Congratulations."

Carol pushed her hair back from her face with shaking hands, then went back to twisting them in front of her, staring at them instead of looking at me. "I just don't understand. Why would they hire me? I haven't worked in years."

"Apparently, they saw something in you that they

liked. Now it's time for you to look in the mirror and see the same thing they saw." I gestured for her to sit down, then settled in the chair next to hers and took her nervous hands, squeezed gently. "It's the same thing I see when you're with your daughter or talking to the other women here. It's the same thing that gave you the courage to leave your husband. You're tougher than you think. You're going to do fine."

She nodded, sniffling, and I knew she was going to be okay. Things wouldn't be easy, but I meant what I said. She could do it.

A few minutes later, I walked into the small break room and a wave of clapping broke out from the other workers. I gave a small bow, and then laughed as they continued.

"Stop it. Or go applaud for Carol. She did the hard part."

The applause faded, but the positive energy in the room remained. It was always important to celebrate the victories like this. After all, this was why we did the work in the first place.

One of the girls who handled the new intakes opened the microwave, pulling out her usual lunch – a microwave burrito. The smell of it hit me hard, even as I wondered how she could eat them. She was talking to one of the other women, something about a case she was working on, but nothing more than the first few words really connected because as that smell grew stronger, my stomach rebelled.

Oh, shit.

Lurching toward the bathroom, I almost bowled over the woman coming out. I dropped to my knees in front of the nearest toilet, emptying out my stomach with near violence while my heart hammered in my ears.

"Oh, honey…are you okay?"

That was when I realized I had an audience.

Another wave of nausea hit me and I groaned before gagging. A few more seconds passed before I thought it might finally be over.

"Oh for the love of my great aunt Bessie," a familiar voice boomed. "Somebody might think you'd never seen a woman get sick before. You people, give her some *room*."

I cringed at the sound of that voice. It was Felicia Winke, my boss. The last person I wanted to be sick in front of. Sometimes, having a famous father or coming from a well-to-do family had its disadvantages. Like having to prove to people like Felicia that I was willing and able to work hard.

Her words sent people scurrying, and before long, I was alone in the bathroom with just her. I thought maybe I was done.

Maybe.

She stared at me hard. "How long have you been sick?"

I passed my hand over the back of my mouth. "Just this once."

"Unlike some people, I know that throwing up can come from a variety of reasons. Do you think you're contagious?" Her words were blunt, but I knew that was just Felicia. She didn't believe in sugarcoating anything.

I shook my head, my stomach settling however uneasily. "I don't think so. Probably something I ate just didn't settle well."

She narrowed her eyes before nodding. "Okay. If it gets worse, go home. We don't need an epidemic. And try toast and ginger ale. We always keep some around."

I started to refuse, but a ginger ale actually sounded

nice. I took it slow getting up, not wanting to overdo it. As I sat at the table a few minutes later sipping the cool drink, I took out my phone and read through my emails. I hated feeling like I was slacking, even if I had thrown up.

"Are you feeling better?" Felicia sat down across from me, eyeing me again.

"Yeah." I shrugged. "I think I just needed to get whatever it was out of my system."

She looked at her nails, then glanced back up at me. "Are you seeing anybody?"

There was a deliberate casualness behind the question that worried me. Especially since Felicia rarely asked personal questions.

I hadn't wanted to tell anyone about the marriage and the subsequent annulment, so I'd taken to wearing my wedding ring on my right hand when I was at work. Nobody here knew about Kaleb, and since it wasn't likely they'd ever meet anybody in my family, explanations weren't necessary.

"Why?" I asked.

"I'm just wondering." She tapped her nails on the top of the table. "It's kind of funny, don't you think, that those nasty microwave burritos have never bothered you before, but today, you turn green and puke your guts out right after. Then five minutes later, you're right as rain."

I didn't like where this conversation was heading. "What are you trying to say?"

Felicia gave me a sympathetic look. "Piety, I've had those sort of 'stomach issue' three times myself. The last time was about a decade ago."

I stared at her, her meaning beginning to sink in as I remembered her youngest kid was around ten years-old.

"Oh, shit," I breathed. A cold sweat broke out on the back of my neck.

"So…it's possible?" she asked.

I covered my face with my hands, unable to even answer her. My head was spinning and I thought I might throw up again.

She moved over next to me, and patted my shoulder. "Honey, it's okay. You just need to find out for sure."

I thought about the wine I'd drunk last night. The sip of scotch I'd had the other day. Hell yes, I needed to find out. If I was pregnant…I groaned. Could I be?

We hadn't been using condoms this whole time, but I was on the pill.

Except I remembered a girl I'd gone to high school with who'd been on the pill and gotten pregnant. It was really rare unless a dose was skipped or antibiotics were taken, but it could happen.

"Oh, man."

Felicia smiled at me. "Well, you've gone from oh shit to oh man. I'd say this might not be such a bad thing."

I dropped my head down onto the table. I needed to go to the store. I needed to…I didn't even know what I needed to do. I couldn't think straight.

"Take a few more minutes." She got up and headed out of the room. "But on your way home tonight, you might want to think about buying a pregnancy test."

I took the extra minutes she'd advised and sent Astra a text. Astra's response came back a couple minutes later, but those minutes felt like hours.

What's going on?

I just threw up. I responded. *And I don't think it's the flu.*

Her response was an emoji, one with the guy and a giant open mouth. Yeah, that's about as surprised as I felt.

Chapter 8

Piety

I hadn't had time to go to the store last night. Or rather, I'd been too afraid to. I was still trying to convince myself that I'd just eaten something that hadn't settled well. That had to be more common than getting pregnant while I was on the pill. Right?

I'd have to do it eventually. I knew that, but maybe it was just a stomach bug. I'd already thrown up two other times, again aggravated by some awful smell.

Felicia brought in crackers and more ginger ale, so the second and third time, a sleeve of saltines were waiting for me.

She'd also given me a questioning look, and I'd just given her a weak smile in her return. When she shook her head, I knew exactly what she was thinking. I needed to man up and take a test so I could figure out how I was going to handle this latest curveball. If that's what it was.

Now, stressed out and drained, I sat on the couch, curled up against Kaleb as I rubbed the inside of my wedding ring with my thumb.

"Are you feeling alright?" he asked.

I was about ready to blurt it all out, to let him freak

out with me, when a fist pounded on the door. I scowled, wondering who it was. But I already had a bad, bad feeling. There were only so many people it could be.

"Piety," my father said through the door.

Shit.

He knocked again, harder. "Open up. I know you're there. Carlos told me you were here. Your mother and I need to talk with you and...Kaleb."

The distaste in his voice got me up off the couch. Furious, I stormed over to the door and threw it open.

He opened his mouth to start one of his patented politician's speeches, but I wasn't in the mood.

"Yes, Dad. We do need to talk. Who in the hell do you think you are?" I demanded. "You paid my *husband* to leave and never say a word to me? What kind of man does that to his own daughter?"

He glared at me, but said nothing as he and my mother came inside. I hadn't asked them to, but they did what they wanted regardless of how anyone else felt. Which was exactly how we'd gotten to this point.

"And you lied to me."

"I didn't lie," Dad countered automatically. "I haven't said a word to you since the reunion."

"Nice political maneuvering, Dad. Fine, you had your little lapdog lie." I rolled my eyes. "It amounts to the same thing. Stuart's your mouthpiece and does all the dirty work for you anyway."

"Piety, can we close the door? The neighbors..." My mother placed herself halfway between my father and me.

Right the neighbors. I barely resisted the urge to roll my eyes again. That was my mother. Always worried about what other people might think.

"Fine," I said. I slammed the door and I went back to the couch but didn't sit down. I knew better. I was too

228

familiar with my father's intimidation tactics, and I wasn't going to play that game today.

I looked at Kaleb and held out my hand. He took it and placed himself at my side. He had risen the moment he heard my father's voice, and now he lifted his chin, meeting my father's gaze squarely.

"How can you stand there and look me in the eyes?" Dad demanded.

"It's not hard. I don't have any respect for you, so why should I have a hard time looking at you?" Kaleb said evenly.

A deep red flush began working its way up my father's neck. "When you take a man's money, you give him your word, and you want to talk about respect?"

Kaleb scowled. "I didn't wrong you. I wrong your daughter. I gave her my word long before you and I made any sort of agreement. Besides, I didn't make the agreement with you. I made the agreement with your... mouthpiece." Kaleb tilted his head. "If it makes you feel better, I can apologize to *him*."

"Stop it," I said, cutting between Kaleb and my father before it could escalate. I appreciated the support, but this needed to be about the truth. "Dad, you have no right to be angry at Kaleb. You're the one who went behind my back and manipulated not only him, but me too."

"You're angry with *me*?" My father managed to look indignant. "This no good con artist took our money, the money we paid to protect *you*, and you're mad at *me*?"

"We all know you didn't do it to protect me," I snapped. "And Kaleb isn't a con artist."

Dad scoffed. "He took my money easily enough."

"I took it for my sister," Kaleb said flatly.

My dad turned his head, giving Kaleb the sort of

disgusted look I'd seen him give when a neighbor's dog crapped on our lawn.

"Your sister?" he asked, the doubt thick in his voice.

"Yes."

"Let me guess, she's suffering from some sort of terrible disease, and you need the money because she'll die without it?" Scorn ripped from his words and he shook his head. "Do you even know anything about this man, Piety?"

I was about ready to scream from frustration, but Kaleb threw a bucket of cold water on the entire thing.

"Actually, my sister is a prostitute and a drug addict. I took the money to pay off her dealer. I was hoping to get her into rehab, but that didn't go over very well. She took what little money I had left and ran off with it."

Well, that was one way to get my parents to shut up for nearly a full minute. I tightened my grip on Kaleb's hand as I waited for the impending explosion.

Mom finally spoke, her face white as her fingers danced at the base of her throat. "Let me get this right. You're a *stripper*, and your sister is a *prostitute*? And you wonder why we didn't want you around our daughter?"

I took a sidestep closer to Kaleb. "Mom!"

"You're wrong," he said. "I've always known exactly why you didn't want me around Piety. I'm not good enough for her. I'm not an idiot. I know that. But then again, neither are you."

Dad's mouth fell open in shock. Mother's face went red. And I couldn't find my voice to say a single word. Not that I knew what I'd say to Kaleb's declaration.

He continued, "You see, she's got a heart that's bigger than anyone I've ever met. But you two are more concerned about appearances and how things might look. She worries about people and how things will affect them. I don't know how the two of you managed to combine your DNA and create this amazing woman." He turned from them and looked directly at me. "Frankly, she's the best person I've ever met. And you're right, I'm not good enough for her. But that doesn't mean I'm not going to work my ass off trying to be."

"You are unbelievable," my mother whispered.

My head was spinning from what he'd said, but I managed to get out two words. "Don't, Mom."

She ignored me and took a step toward Kaleb. "You have no idea who we are. How *dare* you judge us!"

"That's rich." Kaleb snorted. "You don't know anything about me either except for the fact that I stripped for money to try to help out my little sister."

"A sister who's a drug-addicted prostitute," my father said with a harsh laugh.

"A twenty-one-year-old girl who lost her mother and father when she was just a kid. Do you have any idea what that's like?" I asked, unable to stay out of the conversation any longer. "Kaleb's been raising her since he was a teenager. He gave up *everything* to take care of her."

Uncertainty flickered across their faces, but my parents didn't know how to admit they were wrong, and I knew this time wouldn't be any different.

"Just go," I said when my dad started to open his mouth. "We're not doing this. We're not."

"Piety…" Mom began, "we just–"

"No," I raised my voice over hers. "I care about him. You have no right to interfere. This is my life, and I'm going to live it. I'm not living it just to be some sort of paragon that you can put up on a pedestal and show off when it's election time. It's *my* life, and it's about damn time you accept that!"

231

I turned away until I heard the door shut. Kaleb came up behind me, his hands squeezing my shoulders. "I'm sorry."

I shook my head. "Don't be. This has been a long time coming."

"Still, I haven't helped."

I smiled up at him. "Actually, you have. This all needed to come out before it completely ate away my soul." I sighed. "You know what? We should just pack and go to Vegas. We need to figure out how to help your sister. I can get the next few days off from work."

After the past couple days, Felicia would understand.

Chapter 9

Kaleb

She was quiet.

She'd been quiet ever since last night, ever since her parents had left. The fight between them…

Closing my eyes, I wondered if the rift between them was so big it might never be repaired.

I hoped not.

They were overbearing assholes, but I could tell they loved her, and I knew she loved them.

I felt guilty for my part in all of this, and that part was huge, but at the same time, I was…amazed. Nobody had ever stood up for me like that, had ever fought for me. I was the one who went to bat for people. No one did it for me.

I knew my parents would have had my back if they'd lived, but they'd been gone a long time. The years I'd had with them felt like a different life.

For too long, it had just been me and my sister, and I'd always been the one carrying the weight. Now, I had someone who had stood next to me and stood up *for* me.

I didn't know how to handle it.

Finally, unable to deal with all the chaos inside me, I looked over at Piety. She was sipping from a glass of club soda, staring down at the book on her lap.

She hadn't turned the page in ten minutes.

I reached over and took her hand. She started, and the club soda sloshed over the rim.

"Lost in thought?" I asked, reaching for a napkin to clean up the spill.

"I guess." She smiled up at me.

"I…" Blowing out a breath, I tried to think of the right way to say what I needed to say. "I'm sorry for the problems I've caused between you and your parents."

"You didn't cause anything. The problems were already there. You just helped bring them to the surface." She sighed and put her book down, shifting around in the seat to face me. "My parents love me. I know that. But I have no doubt that their love comes with…" She bit her bottom lip and considered her words.

"Strings?" I offered.

Her smile was sad. "Yeah. Always conditional. And they don't understand me. They never have. And they've never stood up for me the way you have. You think I've got a big heart, but they think I'm an alien for just…*caring* about people."

She lifted my hand to her lips, kissed the back of it.

"You do have a big heart." I crooked a grin at her. "So big, I sometimes think you might *be* an alien."

"Stop it." She tipped her head back, laughing.

Some of the tension in the air dissolved, and I stroked my thumb over the inside of her wrist, feeling her pulse flutter under my touch. "I can't tell you how many times I wished my parents were still here, still around to deal with this mess with Camry. But then I look back and realize how lucky I was to have had them for as long as I did. They always had my back. They supported me. That's worth…a lot."

234

"More than gold, I think," Piety said, her voice sad.

"Yeah. I bet it is."

Her eyes met mine, the dark blue depths almost purple under the cabin lighting.

"I haven't had anybody stand by my side the way you did since they passed away. It means a lot. Thank you."

She squeezed my hand. "Nobody has ever stood by me like you have, other than Astra. So...same goes."

We lapsed into silence for a long time, then she laid her head against my shoulder and opened her book. As she read, I thought about how much things had changed since that morning when I'd woken up in her bed.

* * * * *

"The bed," I said against her mouth.

Piety laughed. "Who needs a bed?" She pushed my shirt up and scraped her nails down my sides.

I gasped and caught her hands. "No."

She giggled. "You're ticklish. I love it."

"Bed," I said again.

Instead, she twisted out of my grip and curled her arms around my neck, pressing her mouth to my chin, nipping at it with her teeth. "No. Too far. Way too far."

As she rubbed against me, I had to agree. She was right. That bed was too far away. The whole other side of the suite. In a different room entirely.

"Okay, you're right. Right here."

I boosted her up into my arms and carried her the few steps into the dining room, laid her out on the formal table. In my wildest dreams, I never would have imagined a hotel room with a formal dining area. Then again, in my wildest dreams, I never would have imagined Piety.

I caught the hem of her flirty little skirt and pushed it up to her hip, leaving her bare from the waist down. Hooking my fingers in the silken scrap of her scarlet panties, I slid them down her legs. I wet my bottom lip, my eyes fixed on the prize between her legs.

"I want to…"

"Then do it." She spread her legs wider. "Put your mouth on me."

I smiled at her, then knelt down to put myself at the perfect height for tasting her. She gasped, lashes fluttering down as I licked her, opening her folds with one hand while keeping the other on her belly to hold her in place.

Pressing my mouth to her cunt, I caught the nub of her clitoris between my lips and sucked on it, deep, hard pulls that made her curse and writhe. The taste of her was heady, and knowing that I was the one to bring her that much pleasure made my already hard cock throb painfully. I'd never had a problem with oral sex in the past, but Piety was the only woman who'd ever made me crave it.

Delving into her pussy with my tongue, I coaxed her higher and higher until I knew she was hovering on the edge. Usually, I'd use my fingers to take her over, but I wanted her to come on my mouth alone. I did everything I knew would make her moan and sigh, those little sounds I loved to hear, and then she was crying out my name as she came.

I softened the passes of my tongue to short, sweet licks that made her gasp and squirm as they drew out her climax. When her body finally went limp, I stood, freeing myself from my jeans.

"I don't even remember what it's like not to want you," I confessed as I wrapped my hand around my dick. "And I don't want to."

"Come here," she said, the words both a plea and a demand.

I did, spreading her thighs and settling between them. It felt like coming home. Without using my fingers to prepare her, I knew she was going to be even tighter than usual, and I forced myself to take a few deep breaths. I teased the head of my cock across her clit and she scowled up at me.

"Stop teasing me."

I grinned at her as I reached for the front of her dress with my free hand. "But it's so much fun."

I managed to flick open a couple of buttons, baring her silk-clad breasts. Her nipples were visible through the fabric, hard little nubs that I wanted in my mouth.

"Keep that up, and I'll go without panties for the next two days, and you won't get to so much as *touch* me." She gave me a wicked smile, drawing my attention from her breasts.

They'd have to wait. I needed to take her *now*.

"That's just mean." I positioned myself at her entrance, and when I thrust inside, both of us shuddered.

She was almost too tight, her grip nearly painful. My cock throbbed inside her even as her muscles quivered around it. I wasn't going to last long, but we had all night.

"I need this," she said. "All the time."

I needed *her* – all the time. I was starting to wonder how I'd even existed without her. As I pulled back, my eyes met hers and I could see my own desire reflected back at me. I filled her again with one smooth stroke, letting the pace build naturally until she was begging me to fuck her harder, and I could do nothing but comply.

I pulled her up against me, needing her closer, and the change of angle sent her plummeting over the edge. I drove up into her twice more, and then her teeth were on my shoulder and I was done.

Her name was on my lips as I came, and I knew I was lost.

Chapter 10

Piety

Light filtered in through the curtains. We hadn't gotten around to pulling the blackouts before we'd fallen asleep the night before, tangled around each other.

The light wasn't what woke me though.

It was the incessant, annoying chimes from my phone.

Only one person would be *that* persistent.

I groaned, throwing my forearm over my eyes. If I grabbed a pillow, buried my face in it, and tried really hard, I might be able to block her out.

A grunt next to me made me realize that wasn't going to happen. Astra wasn't just being a nuisance to me. She was annoying Kaleb too.

Sighing, I grabbed the phone and squinted at it, my eyes struggling to adjust to the light. It was too early for conversations.

It didn't matter that it was ten o'clock back home and my body was still on that time. My body *wanted* it to be midnight, making it totally acceptable to still be asleep.

But logic and want never seemed to align.

Swiping a finger across the phone before I could

follow that thought through, I muted the notifications, then went into my messages just as the next one came in. Without bothering to read any of them, I sent her a quick greeting.

You are such a pest sometimes. I was sleeping!

Her answer was a smiley face and *LOL*.

Yeah, she could laugh.

Scrolling back up, I read her messages.

With a grimace, I propped myself up. Somebody had told her that my parents had been to the loft.

Yeah, it wasn't fun. Kaleb told them about his sister. You'd think he'd confessed to being a serial killer.

Astra texted back with another emoticon, but this was a sad face, followed by an angry one.

That pretty much sums up how I feel. I didn't want to deal with their drama so we just came back out to Vegas. We have to figure out how to help his sister anyway.

I eyed Kaleb next to me, and then slid out of bed.

Astra texted me twice more, but I ignored her as I went into the bathroom and took care of some necessary business. Once that was done, I moved into the main area of the suite and curled up on the couch, going back to our conversation.

She wanted to know why and how things had changed with Kaleb. It was too long to go into detail about that in text, and I wasn't ready to have that talk with her, so I summarized.

My parents lied. They had Stuart pay Kaleb off so he would leave. He didn't go to them. They went to him. It still sucks that he just disappeared, but he was feeling desperate. His sister is in serious trouble.

As I waited for her to receive and read, I stared at the door.

Her answer took a few moments, and when I read it,

I saw why.

It was…long.

So let me get this straight…your parents had their dipshit lawyer claim Kaleb had blackmailed them. Am I right there? And you've spent the past few weeks feeling like a piece of shit thinking you put them in that position. Or that's how you felt. But it turns out that THEY set the whole thing up and were the ones who went to him? What sort of shit were they smoking?

There were several more expletives following the last statement and I started to laugh, muffling the sound behind my hand. But just as I went to respond, another text popped up.

And why the hell didn't he get in touch with you and talk to you sooner? I don't want to hear this shit that he felt like he shouldn't. You were busting your ass to help him. Doesn't he know that?

He didn't though. I texted her back.

He doesn't have what we have, A. I've always had you. You've always had me. Ever since his parents died, it's just been him and his sister. She was a kid, always relying on him. I don't think he knows how to rely on somebody.

This time, the little emoticon she chose to represent her mood was one sticking out his tongue. I could almost hear the raspberry.

I stuck my tongue out at the phone.

"Astra?" A deep voice came from across the room.

Startled, I almost dropped my phone.

Jerking my head up, I eyed Kaleb, who was standing in the doorway, wearing a pair of low-slung jeans, and looking sleepy-eyed and completely beautiful. "Yeah. She…um…she spent the night with a friend last night. Got my note, wanted to see what was going on."

241

My gaze strayed to his chest where my nails had left their mark at some point during our sex marathon night. When I looked up, he was grinning at me.

"We've got things to do today." My mouth was dry, but I knew if I wasn't careful, the two of us would end up naked and all over each other – again – so my gaze went back to the phone and the message that had just come through.

He seems to know how to rely or at least TRUST you. So whatever you're doing, keep it up. And keep me posted. Later, PS!

I texted *bye* to her and then tucked my phone into my lap, watching as Kaleb made his way over to the coffee pot, a giant yawn cracking his jaw.

"What do you need to do today?" I asked softly.

He shrugged restlessly. "I've texted Camry again. I texted her last night when we got in, but I haven't heard back from her. Who knows if I even will."

He turned and met my eyes, staring at me solemnly. "I don't know how this will go, Piety. My work visa is only for a few more months and once that time comes, then what?"

Yeah. I'd worried about that myself.

Maybe Camry wasn't worried about immigration and violating a bunch of laws – considering her student visa had been revoked when she'd dropped out of school and she hadn't done anything about it – but I knew her brother was a different creature altogether.

"Fuck," he muttered, tipping his head back and staring at the ceiling. "If it expires, and I have to go back while she's still tangled up with Stefano, then what do I do?"

I wanted to tell him about the deal with the DA but without Camry to testify against Stefano, they couldn't do

242

shit. But hopefully we'd figure it out. We had to. Right?

But I had other, selfish reasons for wanting to tell him we'd be in this together. Reasons that had to do with needing him here with *me*. I had an important purchase to make soon. But I bit my lip, holding everything I was thinking back. This was about him and his sister right now. Everything else could wait a little while longer.

Getting up from the couch, I went over and hugged him. "We'll work it out."

Leaning against him, I focused on the sound of his heart beating and closed my eyes.

He loosely looped his arms around me and rested his chin on top of my head. "I'm glad you're here, Piety."

"Right back at you."

I just wished I knew how long I'd have him.

* * * * *

The sound of his phone ringing was like a death knell.

It was almost noon, and all the things I thought we needed to get done had just never quite come together.

Camry hadn't called him.

The calls I'd put in to Astra's cousin, Samuel, had yet to be returned.

But now, as Kaleb's phone rang, the two of us stared at it, and I knew we both felt a strange kind of dread.

He finally answered it right before it would have kicked over to voice mail.

I knew from the expression on his face that the call was going to be…problematic.

I listened to his side of the conversation, mostly monosyllabic, and his voice never changed inflection even once.

When he finally disconnected, he moved over to the window and stared outside. "That was Camry," he said tightly.

"You don't sound overly happy."

He laughed, but it was bitter and...broken. "It was just typical Camry. I'm meeting her in a little while."

I wanted to tell him it wasn't a good idea, but I didn't think there was any point in arguing with him. He had to do what he had to do. We'd come out here for this anyway. And with so much undecided between us, it wasn't my place.

"Any chance she's decided to leave Stefano and come back with you?"

"Fat fucking chance." Kaleb gave me a grim look, then went back to staring outside. "I...ah...she asked me to come alone. I should probably get going. It's on the other side of town, and I'll have to take a cab."

"I..." My throat was dry. I didn't like the sound of this. Not at all.

Panic began to chatter and screech inside me.

I didn't want him to see his sister alone. I didn't want him leaving me *period*.

What if...?

My mouth went dry.

I needed tell him.

It was possible – not necessarily *probable* – but *possible* that I was pregnant. He wouldn't take off alone to deal with his sister when we had something going on here. What if something happened? He wouldn't take that chance...would he?

"Are you sure it's a good idea to go alone?" I asked,

uneasy at the idea.

"Yeah." Kaleb looked away. "It'll be fine."

I *really* didn't like this. Heart hammering against my ribs, I turned away and shoved my hands through my hair.

"Okay." I nodded and made myself say it again. "Okay."

If I said it enough times, everything *would* be okay.

That was how it worked, right?

"Are you all right?" Kaleb sounded closer, and I spun to meet his gaze.

"I'm fine. Just…on edge. I need to um…I want to meet with a lawyer that Astra's cousin, Samuel, suggested anyway. Samuel? You remember talking to him back in Philly?"

"Of course." His eyes studied my face.

Searching for the lie. For the fear.

But I hid it, locked down deep. If he could do this, so could I.

"What's this about the lawyer?" he asked. His eyes continued to study mine, probing, and I knew he'd seen my uneasiness.

Okay, so what? He knew I didn't like the idea of him meeting up with Camry again – and the fact that she'd told him to come alone? Yeah, that was even more worrisome.

"Piety?"

"Oh. Yeah. Well, Samuel knows somebody here in Vegas who specializes in immigration, and I want to see if she can help you and Camry out." I did need to talk to the lawyer. Samuel had recommended we all speak with Liushi Testudo while we were here, and I *did* plan on doing that. I just needed to make sure he got me in to see her.

I offered Kaleb a smile and reached out, tugging him closer to kiss him. His mouth was warm, and I wanted to stay there forever.

Really…forever.

I couldn't imagine not being with him, not having him in my life.

And what if I *was* pregnant? He couldn't possibly leave the US now.

Chapter 11

Kaleb

The house was empty.

I'd been waiting there for too long already, and Camry was either ignoring me on purpose, or she was so strung out she didn't know I'd been texting her.

Of course, it was possible she was passed out.

Drunk.

Or maybe she'd overdosed...

"Stupid bastard, just stop it already." I groaned and rubbed my hands up and down my face, as if it would scrub the images from my brain. I couldn't do that though.

I'd been dealing with these nightmarish thoughts ever since I realized just how bad Camry's drug problem was. Sooner or later, she would either be forced to get clean, or she would end up dead. These things never ended well, a fact I'd been adjusting to for longer than I liked to admit.

Shit, what if she was inside there and she was strung out...or worse?

"Camry!" I practically threw myself at the door, banging on it so hard, it was a wonder it didn't rattle on its hinges.

There was no answer though.

Spinning away, I paced down to the window and stared inside, hands cupped around my face to block out the light. It didn't do any good. I couldn't see a damn thing thanks to the layer of dirt coating the window.

I slammed a fist into the wall. A faint pain shot through my hand, but I ignored it as I turned around and braced my back against the building.

A car came rolling by, thick black smoke blowing out the back, and I could feel the eyes of the occupants roaming over me, sizing me up. Like any big city, Las Vegas had its fair share of bad neighborhoods. This was definitely one of them.

I stared back, waiting until the driver took a right and disappeared. Then I shoved away from the house and jumped over the mostly broken porch, walking around the house, looking for some sign that Camry was here, or recently had been. The house was a boarded-up wreck, and if anybody *had* lived here in recent memory, they probably needed to be tested for shit like tetanus and anthrax...and who knew what. There was no way anybody could live in a dump like this and not get sick.

Of course, Camry hadn't told me she *lived* here.

She'd said to meet her here.

And that had been – I checked the time – over an hour ago.

What the hell was I doing still waiting around here?

"I'm fucking done."

I'd had it.

I gave another look around the house. I'd give her one more call and maybe another to that ass Stefano, then I was going back to the hotel.

"Where are you?" I demanded when her voicemail

came on. It wasn't her, of course, and that just made me even angrier. "I'm done with your bullshit and tricks. This is enough, Camry. I'm done."

Then I tried calling Stefano. I gave him a similar version of the message I left Camry, although I was a lot less polite.

Then, without bothering to give the hellhole behind me another look, I headed for the sidewalk. I was going to find a bus stop and get back to the hotel.

* * * * *

By the time I reached my destination, I was hotter than hell, frustrated and tired.

But I was ready to see Piety. I *needed* to see her. Hold her. Touch her.

Except...when I let myself into the room, she was gone.

The room was quiet, and judging from the looks of things, housekeeping had come and gone. I moved through the suite in silence, hoping she was resting or something. She'd seemed tired the past few days, but no. I was alone.

Pulling out my phone, I sent her a text, then flung myself down on the couch and threw my arm over my eyes. I was trying to work up the energy to take a shower, then maybe scrounge and see what sort of food was here. There had to be something, although I doubted the cheese, fruit, and crackers would fill the hole in my gut.

I could order room service, but I never felt right doing that without Piety being here.

Just as I went to sit up and drag my tired ass off to the shower, the phone rang.

I grabbed it, thinking it was Piety. Or maybe Camry. A few hours too late. But Samuel Westmore's name flashed across the screen. I blew out a breath and pinched the bridge of my nose. I wasn't in the right frame of mind to talk to Astra's cousin, but I'd have to get over that.

There was a second ring, then a third.

"Hello."

"Kaleb, Samuel Westmore here. How are you doing?"

"I'm doing alright," I said, lying through my teeth.

And he heard it. "You sure about that?"

"Well, if you want the truth..." I paused, then decided against it. "I could tell you how I really am, but you don't have all night, and I was just starting to mellow out. What can I do for you, Mr. Westmore?"

But he wasn't ready to let it drop. "You sure you don't want to talk about it? Might help. Not to mention, it's all confidential."

"Shit. What the hell." I sighed and gave him a quick rundown of what happened with my sister, leaving out the more personal details between Piety and me.

"You know she's sick." Samuel's voice was gentle and understanding.

I didn't want any of it.

"Yeah, I got that memo. She's sick. And I know she did this to herself. I know she's an addict, but she chose this life, and I'm tired of being understanding. Tired of trying to help her turn her life around when all she wants to do is fuck over me and anybody else who cares about her." The anger in my voice caught me off-guard but I couldn't undo it, couldn't stop it. Didn't want to. "I'm just tired of it."

"I bet you are. I can't imagine how hard this is." He was quiet a moment, then added softly, "Maybe you need to talk to somebody about it."

I scoffed, but he cut me off.

"I'm serious. The families of addicts have a harder time than a lot of people realize. You had an even harder time because you've been trying to be a parent to her as well as dealing with your own shit. You never had a chance to finish growing up yourself, Kaleb."

The words made me uncomfortable, and I chose to focus on something else. "Tell me something, Mr. Westmore. Is it typical for an attorney to tell his clients to get counseling?"

"More common than you know," he said easily. "Sometimes I feel like a teacher, a bouncer, and a playground monitor all rolled into one – *and* a counselor." He laughed. "We do what we have to, Kaleb. But listen, none of this is why I called. I assume you know about the annulment papers."

Those few simple words soured my mood even further.

Samuel didn't wait for my response.

"Piety signed them also. At the time, I believe she thought it was what you wanted. The annulment was finalized today."

"I understand." She was under the impression I'd gone and blackmailed her parents, so of course, she'd thought it was what I wanted. But it wasn't. I was tempted to shout that into the receiver, to yell at him, convince him, somebody, anybody...*Piety*...that I didn't want the fucking annulment.

I wanted her.

But, how could I?

It was too late anyway now.

Besides, the whole thing had been a joke, a jab at her parents and a job for me. There was no way anybody, especially us, could take it seriously.

So what if it felt serious?

So what if it felt more real than anything I've ever felt?

It didn't matter...did it?

Yes...

A small, sly voice in the back of my mind whispered to me.

It felt very real, and it mattered very much.

But I kept all of that trapped inside me, locked away.

Samuel must have picked up on some of my tension, and an awkward silence stretched out over the next few seconds.

He cleared his throat. "I do have other news. I think we might have a solution for the situation with your sister and her abuse problem. It would entail you both moving to Philadelphia so we can do what we need to in order to help her. Would that present much of a problem for you?"

"Move to Philadelphia," I murmured. Walking to the window, I looked out at the city. Even now, with evening approaching, the unrelenting heat was pounding down, and I could see little heat mirages off in the distance. Beyond the buildings, the earth was scorched, dried and brown. Leave Vegas?

No problem.

Be closer to Piety?

Hell. Yes.

"No. No, sir. Nothing here would present a problem."

Then I thought about my sister.

She might present one, but if I had to, I'd just knock her out and drag her ass back east with me, whether she wanted to go or not.

Chapter 12

Piety

"Well, here's an interesting fact…"

Liushi Testado leaned forward, her long hair pulled into a knot that left her elegant face unframed. She had high cheekbones and dark eyes, and she was, in a word, beautiful. She smiled at me, clearly enjoying something about whatever *interesting fact* she was holding back.

"This Stefano character has been under investigation for a while."

It was a sign of how tired I was that my brain took a few seconds to remember just who Stefano was, but once I had, I leaned back in my chair. "I know. I talked to Samuel about it. The DA want some help."

"Yes. They've tried to bring him in more than once, but nothing ever sticks." She shrugged. "Now, this isn't my area of law, but I know people. I could make some calls. If your friend Camry was willing to testify against Stefano, if would make it an easy case to get her approved for a green card."

I laughed, shaking my head. "First, she's not my friend. Second…right now, I think Kaleb is having a hard time even getting his sister *away* from Stefano."

"But that's the plan, right? Get her away from him?"

Liushi cocked her head. "If not…well, maybe it would be best for her if she were deported back to Australia. It would take having somebody tip off Immigration. It's not like she's abiding by the agreement set forth when she came here to study. If she was removed from this man's influence…"

My stomach knotted at the very thought of it. If Camry left, then so would Kaleb. He'd never let her go back to Australia alone. Maybe not even if he knew...

"There are other ways to get her away from his influence. Once we do that, maybe she'll straighten up and see how damaging all of this is."

"True." Liushi lifted a shoulder, the elegant cut of her red suit highlighting her every subtle curve. "Of course, you have to get her away from him, convince her how damaging all of this is, and then we'll still try to find the right way to keep her in the country. Like I said, testifying against him would be an almost sure win."

I made a face, because while it made sense to me in theory, I knew too much about how girls like Camry behaved. Stefano was probably as much a drug to her as the chemicals he was feeding her. He gave her something. Made her feel something. Wanted, maybe? I couldn't know.

I checked my phone, wondering if Kaleb had texted. If he'd gotten through to her, that would at least be something.

But there was no message from him, and I was left with nothing to do but nod at Liushi and thank her.

She gave me a card and told me to stay in touch.

Once the card was tucked away, I left her office and headed back out in the late afternoon sun.

* * * * *

My stomach was upset, so I found a place that served mostly soup. Over a bowl of chicken noodle, I tried to tell myself that it could be any number of things making me feel sick.

I didn't know why I was so determined to convince myself that it was anything other than what I suspected it was.

Part of me was even excited. Almost giddy about it.

But everything in my life was in complete upheaval.

Did I really need a change like...*this*?

And what about Kaleb?

I'd signed the annulment papers. It would be finalized any day now.

This wasn't the time for any of this.

When is it ever the time? a small voice in the back of my head spoke up. *You act like life is supposed to be something you've figured out, and nobody ever has it all figured out. Not even your parents. Not even you.*

Slowing to a halt on the sidewalk, I let that roll through my head as I considered it.

Because it was true.

When did anybody ever have it all figured out?

I needed to talk to him.

About *everything*.

Changing directions, I headed back to the hotel. Another quick look at my watch had me thinking he might already be there. The meeting had been over an hour ago. He could be done. He could already be back, waiting for me.

We needed to talk. And we should talk.

The sight of a drugstore sign caught my eye, and I

slowed my steps, studying it.

We should talk, I thought again. And I should know for sure before we do. Kaleb should know. He deserved to know.

I went inside, but nerves overtook me, and instead of going straight to the section I needed, I swung by the pantry area and picked up a box of crackers. It wasn't like I wouldn't need them. Then I forced my feet to walk in the direction of the right aisle, and I stopped.

Heart pounding, I studied the boxes.

So many different ones.

They all blurred in front of me, and I finally grabbed one at random, reading it.

Digital readout.

Two weeks sooner.

Ninety-eight percent accurate.

Good enough.

My hands shook as I paid for the purchases, and I wondered if the cashier noticed, but she seemed completely oblivious. Nervous twenty-somethings coming in to buy pregnancy tests were probably run of the mill around here.

I headed for the door, feeling more settled somehow.

I was going to stop wondering.

I was going to get an answer.

But then I swung left and saw her.

She was leaning against the light post, arms wrapped around her middle, looking scared and nervous and cold, even in the burning heat.

As I slowed to a stop, she lifted one hand to her mouth and started to bite at her nails. She swung a look down the block away from me, then pushed off the light post and started to pace. When she turned in my direction, she faltered.

The tears in her eyes had my heart aching.

"Camry," I whispered.

"Um." She looked behind me, then behind her, so jumpy, it was like she expected the shadows to come to life and steal her away. "Hi. It's Piety, right?"

"Yes. Is...where's Kaleb?" Compassion welled inside me, and I took a step forward. "Honey, are you okay?"

"I...shit. Fuck. I can't talk about this..." She went left, ducking into the narrow alley between two buildings. "I shouldn't have come here."

"Camry, wait. What's wrong?"

But she shook her head and continued to walk.

Feeling helpless, I went after her, my little plastic bag slapping against my leg.

"Talk to me, Camry. Where is Kaleb?"

She stopped when I put my hand on her shoulder and turned slowly, facing me.

Her eyes were still open too wide, and now that I was closer, I could see the oversized ring of her pupil. She was high, but she seemed steady enough. Probably so used to being strung out, it was her normal. Shaking her head, she said, "You shouldn't be here."

"Don't be silly."

Camry just shook her head. Then, slowly, her gaze flicked past me, her tongue snaking out to wet cracked, dry lips.

I heard it then.

It was quiet, so quiet, I couldn't have heard it over the sound of my voice a moment ago.

But I heard it now and spun around, ready to face whoever it was.

I had a good idea who it was too.

I never made the full circle.

I saw something swinging down at me, and I lifted my arm.

Then everything went dark.

Chapter 13

Kaleb

Night had fallen over the strip.

The only time Vegas was even remotely appealing was when the sun had set, and the lights were all ablaze.

Or maybe if I was out past the city, in the desert. I didn't mind the desert.

Standing in the elegant suite of the Bellagio, I stared outside and brooded.

I hadn't heard from Piety all day. Not so much as a phone call.

It was past nine now, and I'd been here for a few hours by myself. I'd given in and called down to room service for a pizza, although it sat like a stone in my belly and every passing minute made it worse.

"Where are you?" I muttered.

I pulled out my phone to call her again, only to stop and put it away.

She hadn't responded when I called five minutes ago. I'd sent any number of texts and messages, so she knew I was waiting to hear from her. Calling every few minutes wasn't going to help.

I figured I could hold off for five more minutes.

I paced and ended up by the bar, pulling out a bottle of whiskey, studying it before putting it away.

A few more circuits around the room had me back by the window and staring outside.

"This is getting ridiculous."

I didn't know what I should do.

Call Samuel?

The police?

Would they even do anything? It hadn't even been ten hours, and they wouldn't do shit the first twenty-four hours.

Although maybe if they knew who she was...

I eyed the phone again and wondered if I should have Samuel get in touch with Piety's father.

That would suck for me, but if it would get people moving...

"Fine," I muttered. I'd do it. I could deal with the devil for Piety.

But just as I went to punch the number, the phone lit up, signaling a message. Relief punched through me.

It faded fast though, followed on the heels by confusion, fear, then anger.

Hello, Kaleb! Sorry I wasn't at the house to meet you, brother. I ran into a friend of yours...Piety! Wow. You really did get married, huh? I'm truly happy for you. Now...if you'll just do me a favor, you can have your wife and be on your way. You know the money I needed before? I now need ten times that. In cash. Be a good brother and get it for me – today.

I read it through once, twice, three more times, trying to make it make sense.

There was a date and time at the bottom. Hours away – just hours. What the fuck was my sister thinking? If she really had Piety...I couldn't...I swore, and my hands started to shake.

Then, another text came through, and I dropped my phone, the screen going blank.

But not before I'd registered what I was staring at.

A picture of Piety. But not just a picture of Piety.

There was a pregnancy test in it too.

And the test was...*positive*.

Another message came through.

Looks like you're gonna be a daddy! Let's get all this tediousness out of the way so you can get started with your new little family, hmm?

I grabbed the phone, spun, ready to hurl it into the wall.

But I stopped myself.

Think, I said silently. Going to my knees, I braced my hands on the floor and flexed them.

Think...

Chapter 14

Piety

I'd feigned sleep for as long as I could, trying to get a grasp on what was going on, and now that I'd opened my eyes, I'd managed to get a decent handle on the situation – I hoped.

Camry was too strung out and nervous to be quiet or subtle. Stefano was too arrogant.

They'd sat around talking about their plans with no regard to me, so I'd taken it all in. Now that I was awake, my biggest challenge was trying not to let on that I'd heard them talking.

"Come on, Piety," Stefano said, waving the pregnancy test in front of my face. "It's been almost an hour since you woke up. It's time to go and take a tinkle."

The hair stood up on my arms, and I wracked my brain for an excuse to delay doing what he wanted.

"You're going to be suffering from blood loss – extreme blood loss – if you don't take this test." Stefano tossed the box from one hand to the other. "Camry, why don't you get her a soda or something? It might make things a little easier."

"I'm not thirsty." Shit, if they made me drink

something, I'd pee my pants. And if the test was positive they would have something else to threaten Kaleb with. I couldn't let that happen. But if I was pregnant, I couldn't risk *not* knowing.

Fuck.

"Sure you are. You took a nice long nap. Gotta be feeling a little dry." Stefano sat straddling a chair, facing me. I was in a twin of the same chair, but I wasn't quite so casual – hard to be when I was tied to the damn thing.

"No, I'm not feeling *dry*. I'm feeling *nauseated*. If I drink anything, I'll throw it up." There.

"Oh…maybe she *is* pregnant." Stefano laughed and edged closer. "Come on. Let's just get the test done so we can get in touch with your hubby and get this whole mess behind us."

"I've got a better idea…let me *go,* and I'll get a hold of Kaleb." I smiled sweetly at him. "He can come pick me up, and we'll just forget this whole thing ever happened."

"Not going to happen that way. See, Kaleb gave me a lot of trouble. I figure he owes me something extra for it." Stefano winked at me. "This way, I don't have to worry about him trying to jerk me around again."

"He doesn't owe you shit." Maybe I shouldn't have said that.

Stefano just laughed at me and shoved off the chair. "You wouldn't understand, angel. Come on. You're getting out of that chair and going with Camry here into the bathroom. You're going to be a good little girl and piss on that damn test."

He knelt in front of me and started untying the ropes. I glared at him.

"And if I don't?"

Something ugly lit his eyes. "You don't want to

know the answer to that, Piety. See, I've been nice so far. Don't make me change that. Or maybe you'd rather have me follow you in there. I always get a kick out of watching a pretty girl like you take a piss."

His entire persona changed, and it sent a shiver down my spine.

He reached up and stroked a hand down my hair. "Now…are you ready to go with Camry and use the fucking toilet?"

"Sure." I bared my teeth at him, refusing to show how afraid I was. "But only if you say please."

"Oh…I like you. You've got balls." He leaned in, pressed his lips to my ear. I didn't let myself cringe away as he murmured, "Pretty please, Piety. Go piss on that damn stick. I want to get the show on the road."

* * * * *

A few hours ago, I'd been giddy, almost eagerly awaiting this moment, but now, I was hoping and praying the test would be negative.

If it was negative, that was one less thing they could use against him.

One less thing *I* had to worry about.

They hadn't tied me back up, but I wasn't fooled into believing it meant anything. After Camry watched me pee on the damn stick, she'd grabbed it from my hand. Now, Stefano was pacing back and forth, holding onto the test as he watched it reveal my future.

I wanted to vomit. That he was here, watching something so personal taking place, made me sick – and

265

furious. I wanted to hurl the chair at him, but he had something else in his other hand.

A gun.

I didn't doubt his ability to use it either.

"Well, well, well..."

I had no doubt what the smile on his face meant.

I'd been counting down the seconds in my head, and when he looked up at me, I already knew.

"Yes?" I said, feigning boredom.

"Congratulations. You're going to have a bouncing bundle of joy in a few more months, precious." Stefano came closer and showed me the test before gesturing to the chair with his gun hand. "Sit back down. Camry, tie her up."

Numb inside, I sat down.

I didn't even move as she strapped my wrists down, jerking the rope tight. Her mouth was pressed, eyes jumping all around. I recognized the signs. She was coming off whatever drugs she'd been on.

It wasn't until Stefano came forward and tucked the pregnancy test in the vee of my shirt that the numbness cracked, then disappeared entirely. "Get off me," I shouted.

But he continued to fuss with it, twisting it around until he was satisfied.

Then he took the box and placed it in my lap, facing out. "That way, he knows what we're telling him. He's pretty enough to look at, but he's kind of...well...dumb." Stefano tsked under his breath.

"That's funny, coming from an asshole like yourself," I snarled.

His smile faded. "Be nice, Piety. You be nice, and I'll be nice."

"This doesn't feel very nice," I said, jerking against

the ropes.

But he turned away, moving a few feet before he turned back to me.

I sat stiffly as he took a few pictures with my phone, then started texting. "And here we go."

"You asshole," I said, shaking my head.

I couldn't believe this was happening. All because I – *we* – tried to help Camry.

Stefano was texting away on my phone, and I shifted my attention to Camry. "He gave up *everything* to help you, and this is how you repay him?"

She flicked a look at me. "You don't know anything about it, princess. So shut up."

"I know this baby is *his* – that means you'll be an aunt."

Her mouth dropped open for a second, then she shook her head. "Shut up."

This was really happening.

Distantly, I heard the little *whoosh* indicating the text had been sent.

And…silence.

Seconds passed, then a minute.

I counted a full two minutes off in my head before there was any response, and I closed my eyes.

"Fuck yeah!" Stefano said. "The ball's rolling now."

"He won't be able to get you any more money. *I* gave it to him last time. And I'm stuck right *here*. I can't exactly go to the bank when I'm tied to a chair."

My belly heaved, and I hoped I wouldn't throw up. Somehow, I didn't think Stefano would let me get cleaned up if that happened.

Stefano shrugged. "He'll figure something out. I've done some digging on you. You're a rich little bitch, aren't you? He can call Mommy and Daddy, talk to them."

"Oh, man. And you have the balls to call *him* stupid?" I laughed, but the sound held a hysterical note. "If you think my parents will give him a dime, you really are an idiot. They despise him."

"He'll figure out something." Stefano shrugged and slid the gun away. He yawned and glanced at Camry. "I'm going to lay down. Watch her."

Once he was gone, Camry came over and took the pregnancy test out from between my breasts, then put it in the box. "It will all be over soon."

Her voice was soft, hesitant now. Maybe it was because Stefano wasn't there. She didn't look as certain as before.

"You don't really think my parents will give him money, do you? They think he used me all this time. They won't believe anything he says."

"Kaleb doesn't use people. He'll get them to understand." She shrugged.

"My parents don't *get* people like Kaleb. They won't believe him, I tell you." I jerked at the ropes on my wrists, panic getting louder and louder in my brain. "You're risking the baby's life, Camry. Your brother's *child*. How can you do this?"

"Stop." She turned away, moving to the couch. After she dropped down onto it, she shot me a dark glare. "You wouldn't understand, okay? You're beautiful, you're rich, you've got your parents – *and* you've got Kaleb now too. Your life has been so fucking easy."

"You've *always* had Kaleb," I fired back, my temper giving me the strength I needed to push her. "And you never appreciated him. And for the record? You're not the pregnant woman tied to a fucking chair all because you were trying to help some drug-addicted drama queen."

She jerked as if I'd slapped her, and I could have kicked myself. I'd gone too far. Pissing her off wasn't exactly helping my situation here.

"Just…" Camry looked away, pushing her hair back with shaking hands. "Be quiet, okay? And stop trying to piss Stefano off. You won't like how it goes. You won't."

* * * * *

The phone went off, signaling another text from Kaleb.

Camry smirked at me. "He's working on it, honey. Thought you said he couldn't get the money."

I narrowed my eyes at her. "Thought your boyfriend said Kaleb wasn't all that smart."

She twitched, but it wasn't from anything I said. She needed another hit, and it showed.

I tried a different tactic. "What are you going to do if something happens to your niece or nephew?"

"Nothing's going to happen!" she shouted, getting off the couch to pace. "Shit, will you shut up? All he has to do is pay and everything will be fine!"

"And when this is over…?" I laughed, feeling more and more desperate. "I just go about my merry way? You think Stefano is just going to let me and this baby *go*?"

"He gets the money, that's all that matters."

"Bullshit. He's in so much trouble with the cops, he won't take the chance of something coming along that might *actually* stick. And this could fuck him over. Kidnapping. That's a lot of hard time." I shot a look at the door, hoping I wasn't saying too much. "Do you know who my father is? A senator. Do you know what a jury will do to a guy who kidnapped a senator's pregnant daughter?"

"He's…stop it, okay?" Her hands were shaking now. "You ain't going to say anything because you're smart. So it's all good."

"It's not!" I struggled against the ropes, moaning a little as the fear threatened to swell out of control. "How can you do this? What in the hell would your parents think if they could see you? If they knew you were threatening your brother's baby?"

She went pale, the blood draining out of her face. "That's not…I'm not…"

"They hell you're not!" I glared at her. "Fool yourself all you want but don't expect me to buy it. If Kaleb doesn't pay, I'm the one who's fucked – me *and* his baby, and you know it. And you're *helping*!"

"Shut up."

The cold, flat order came from the door, and I whipped my head around just in time to see Stefano come out of the bedroom. His eyes were heavy, hair mussed. He'd been sleeping, I could tell. But he was wide awake now and was focused on Camry.

She rubbed at her arms.

"You need something, baby?" he asked in a tone far more gentle than what he'd use with me.

"Yeah." She nodded jerkily. "I'm hurting…hurting bad. And she won't shut up."

"She's going to shut up, or I'll gag her."

"I'm already about to throw up," I said nastily. "Gag me and watch me choke on it. Then how am I supposed to help you get money?"

His eyes narrowed. "Be quiet, bitch."

270

"Don't, Stefano," Camry said. She touched his cheek. "We can't gag her. If she does get sick…"

"Okay, okay. But she needs to shut her trap." He gave me a threatening look, then reached into his coat, pulling out a small metal box. "Here. Find something you like."

I swallowed as I watched her cradle the cigar case sized box to her chest and carry it over to the table.

He came to me then, dragging the chair he'd used earlier closer. As he sat down, I sighed and tipped my head back, staring upward.

"You really are a ballsy bitch, you know that?"

"Your point?"

"My point is this…I don't give a rat's ass about a baby." He lowered his voice and leaned in, voice low. "If you keep this shit up, I'm going to punch you in the gut, good and hard, not once, not twice, but as many times as I feel like. What do you think will happen to that fucker's baby then?"

My blood went to ice.

He held my gaze, a cruel smile twisting his lips. "You understand me now?"

I knew I could say only one thing. "Yes."

"Good." He got up, shoving the chair carelessly off to the side before going over to Camry. She was bent over the table, her hair fisted in one hand as she snorted something through a small tube. "Oh, baby…you found the good stuff."

She hummed happily, and I swallowed back the bile as he went to his knees next to her, then tugged her around to face him. "Give me a kiss."

I was screwed.

I was so seriously screwed.

Chapter 15

Piety

The world kept dancing in and out of focus.

My head fell forward, eyes closing.

I slept.

I don't know how long but something clattered, and I jerked my head up, startled awake. My neck was killing me.

It was dark, and for a moment, I had no idea what was going on.

I tried to move, and everything came to me, the world snapping back into sharp focus. I wanted it to go back to the way it had been just a few minutes before.

Man, how could this be happening?

I was tied to a chair.

My head was pounding, my mouth was dry, and I hurt in ways I didn't think it was possible to hurt. Stefano hadn't even laid a hand on me. Neither had Camry. I'd just been forced into this unnaturally still position, unable to move for hours on end.

And they were waiting for Kaleb to show up with money he didn't have.

And I was pregnant.

Maybe not, I tried to tell myself. That test had boasted it was ninety-eight percent accurate. What about the two percent? Were they false positives or false negatives? I tried to remember my classes in biology, but nothing was coming to me. The tests were based on the human growth hormone that kicked on in pregnancy, right? So…could there be a false positive? Or was a false negative more likely?

I didn't know.

Fear was a sticky, metallic taste in the back of my mouth.

I was most likely pregnant and trapped in a building with a man who cared more about money than anything else. Sadly, it was a mindset I understood. There were too many people in *my* life who cared more about the almighty dollar than anything else.

How could this be happening?

Tears burned my eyes, but I forced them back. Crying wouldn't help anything and would probably make that bastard happy. No way was I going to give Stefano that satisfaction.

I managed to fight them down and get myself under control, and I was happy with it. It was a small victory, but in these circumstances, every damn victory counted.

I felt somebody watching me, and I searched the dim room with my eyes, trying not to move any more than I had to.

"Your boyfriend isn't helping things out much here, sugar," a low voice drawled.

I managed to control the flinch, and I swallowed, trying to unstick my tongue from the roof of my mouth. "Can I get some water?"

"I look like a fucking maid to you?"

"It's probably escaped your notice, but I'm not

273

exactly able to do it myself. If you were to untie me–"

"Fat chance. Just be quiet, okay?" He sounded far less cocky now, and I wondered if I'd missed something during the brief patches when I'd dozed off.

I set my jaw, looking away, but to my surprise, Camry came over.

"Hey," Stefano snapped.

"She's pregnant, okay?" She held a can in her hand and lifted it to my lips. "It's ginger ale. Might be better for your stomach. I don't know if you're feeling sick or not, but just in case."

I didn't want her being nice. I wanted to be able to hate her.

But the ginger ale settled on my stomach far easier than water would. A little bit of it ran down my chin, and she used her sleeve to wipe it off.

"Better?" she asked.

Her eyes were heavy, and when I looked at her, she averted her gaze.

"Oh, I'm just peachy," I said sourly.

She gave me a jerky nod, and I could see the guilt in how she held herself, how she was moving.

"He ain't responding to my texts anymore, sweetie. Why do you think that is?" Stefano demanded.

"I don't know. Maybe his phone died." I was so tired I couldn't think of anything better.

From the corner of my eye, I saw Camry sit down and Stefano hold out the metal box from earlier. She licked her lips, eying it nervously. Her gaze came to me, but she wouldn't look directly at me.

"Come on, sugar. Been a while. You gotta be needing something," he said in a tone far more gentle than even before. "Try this. It'll make you feel unlike anything you've ever felt."

"Yeah, yeah, alright." She accepted the tube he offered and snorted the white powder.

My belly heaved, and I willed down the nausea through sheer determination. I was being held hostage, and she was shooting up.

But in a way, he's holding her hostage too, a soft voice murmured.

I ignored it. I didn't want to feel pity for her. Not now. Maybe not ever.

I didn't know if I ever want to feel sympathy or compassion for anyone again and that utterly infuriated me. It was like they'd broken something vital inside me.

Stefano continued to glare at me, the insolence returning to his eyes and I thought he knew exactly what I was thinking. Camry's lashes fluttered down, and a smile drifted over her face.

"Oh, that's better," she murmured. "That's so nice."

"Why don't you come here, baby? Gotta be tired." He guided her close, and she laid down. He rubbed her shoulder and before long, she was asleep. Must be nice, being able to get lost in herself.

Exhaustion pressed in on me, and I could feel my own eyes growing heavy again, but just as my head started to droop, Stefano said, "You know, if I don't hear something soon, it ain't gonna go well for you. I don't give a fuck whose kid you are."

"You don't think you can do something to me and just get away with it, do you?" I glared at him, so tired of this whole mess that I could feel the grip I'd held on my temper and my fear sliding away from my grasp.

"Ah, I'm just gonna…disappear. See, if he don't show up, you're dead." He mimed making a gun with his hand and pointed it at me. "And you can't tell them shit. And my girl here…?"

He laughed and nodded his chin toward the box. "I got all sorts of goodies for her. She won't ever wake up. I made it look like she's the one who's been sending the texts, see? And I've got a hundred people who'll vouch that I was anywhere but here."

"You're a bastard."

"Be nice." His eyes glittered with malice, face mostly lost to shadow. "Be nice, honey, and maybe you won't suffer too much."

I opened my mouth – and nothing *nice* was going to come out – but was saved from my own stupidity by a heavy knock on the door.

I whipped my head around, fear skittering through me. The tense muscles in my neck screamed out at me, but I ignored it as I watched with trepidation Stefano get up and make his way to the door.

"Who is it?" he shouted, still several feet away.

"Kaleb."

My heart lurched into my throat.

"I've got your fucking money, so open the damn door."

"Alright, alright…" A bright, sharp smile split his face and Stefano turned to look at me. "You just sit tight, sweetie."

I panted, blood draining out of my head and leaving everything looking fuzzy.

Stefano had the gun in his hand, didn't he?

I thought he did. I was almost positive.

"Kaleb! He has a gun!" I called out.

"Be quiet, bitch." A moment later, I felt the gun press against the back of my head. "You be quiet, or I'll just put a bullet through the door *and* him. You got me?"

The words were delivered in a lethal, deadly voice. I swallowed, slowly nodding and hoping he didn't pull the trigger when I moved.

Be careful, I thought. *Please be careful, please, please, please...*

A moment later, Stefano knelt beside me, jerking at the ropes. "You get your wish, princess. I'm untying you. I'm going to let you open the door so you can tell your boytoy to come in. Then we'll get down to business. If you as much as flinch, I'll put a fucking bullet through your little pretty head, you understand?"

"Yes."

He jerked me up, and I stumbled.

"Stop playing around," he yelled.

"I've been tied up for hours," I snapped before I could stop it. "My legs are asleep, and nothing wants to move, dumbass!"

I froze instantly, wishing I could yank the words back.

To my surprise, though, Stefano grinned at me. Man, he was crazy. Still grinning, he reached up with both hands and framed my face. I could feel the cold metal of the gun digging into my skin. "You're one tough piece of ass, you know that? I almost wish I could keep you. Show you a real good time."

Before I could respond, he let me go and spun me around. "Move."

I stumbled again but steadied myself. I did *not* want him touching me.

Each step had more sensation returning to my legs, and it was like a thousand pins and needles were stabbing into me, but I gritted my teeth and ignored it.

The door was ten feet away, then five, then two...

"Open the door. Just a little. Stay behind it."

The gun's muzzle was pressed tight against the back of my ear, making it clear that arguing would be a little

277

bit stupid. So I did exactly what he said.

Kaleb slipped in through the narrow opening, carrying a duffel bag.

The sight of him hit me hard in the chest, and this time, no matter how hard I fought, I couldn't hold back the tears.

"Kaleb," I whispered.

His eyes came straight to me, and he started to take a step in my direction, only to stop as he realized a gun was pressed to my head.

"Let her go," Kaleb said roughly.

"In a bit, in a bit." Stefano kicked the door shut and locked it then jutted his chin toward the table. "Let's sit down and get to business. Don't try any bullshit or your pretty little wife here will get a third eye."

"There's no business left. I'm taking Piety, and my sister, and getting out of here."

His eyes flicked to me, and he stared at me for a lingering moment before looking back at Stefano.

"Well, see…your little sister is taking a nap." Stefano laughed and gestured toward the couch. "Tell you what…you can take *one* of them, after we're done doing business. Your choice."

"Asshole," I muttered.

He ignored me and gestured to the table again. "Come on. Let's sit. I want to check the money."

"It's all there," Kaleb said. "Let Piety go now."

"Sit," Stefano said again, an edge to his voice.

Kaleb sat.

But when I went to take a step closer, Stefano pointed the gun in my direction. "Keep a few feet away, sweetie. I want to check my money."

"It's all there," Kaleb said again.

"Yeah, yeah. Put the bag on the table. Unzip it."

Kaleb sighed and did so, his eyes searching the room. I knew the moment he noticed his sister. His mouth went tight.

Then he looked at me, and again, our gazes caught and lingered. His gaze tracked to the front door, then back to me.

What? I wondered. *What are you trying to tell me?* I couldn't think clearly enough to figure it out, and tears burned my eyes. I was going to get us all killed. Kaleb and our baby.

"Man, I knew you'd come through," Stefano said, that sly smirk firmly back in place as he looked at us. "I should have upped the dollar amount. You made this look easy."

"Yeah, it was a real walk in the park. Are we good now?" Kaleb asked and rose from the table, sounding bored.

"Hmmm." Stefano slowly zipped the bag, shaking his head. "What are you looking so smug about?" Stefano asked. He studied Kaleb with narrowed eyes, a look on his face that I didn't like at all.

But the question made me wonder. Kaleb did look really, really calm.

Swallowing the knot of nerves in my throat, I tried to move to where I could watch both, but the room was only so big, and every time I moved, Stefano shifted his attention – and the gun – toward me.

"I'm not smug." Kaleb lifted one shoulder, his face composed, entire body relaxed.

"Well, you look pretty damn chill about all of this." Stefano looked even more suspicious.

"I don't have any reason not to be chill." Kaleb snorted, then slid me another one of those piercing looks, before glancing at his sister. "I'm getting what I want.

279

I'm getting Piety, I'm getting my sister, and we're getting out of here, all three of us."

"Yeah, well, I don't think your sister is going anywhere." Stefano looked please with himself as he gestured toward Camry's unconscious body. She lay sprawled on the couch, one arm and leg half on the floor, her face turned in our direction.

I didn't know if it was my own fear, or something more, but she seemed unnaturally pale, and I stared at her chest, searching for signs that it was still moving.

It did, but that didn't make me feel any better.

"Don't worry, I think I can carry her just fine," Kaleb said, his voice dry.

"And if I tell you that I'm not letting her leave unless that's what she wants?" Stefano's brows beetled together over his eyes, an ugly snarl twisting his face as he took a few steps closer to Kaleb.

"You don't want to do that." Kaleb just looked at him, looking unconcerned.

"Yeah?" Stefano brandished the gun, holding it sideways, gangster style. I would have rolled my eyes if I hadn't been so afraid.

Kaleb shot me another look, that intense gaze piercing straight through me. That silent unspoken message was still there, but I still couldn't get it.

"You ain't taking her anywhere she don't want to go. That wasn't the deal." Stefano sounded bored, then his eyes brightened, and he snapped his fingers, like he'd just come up with a great idea. "I know. Why don't you try to wake her up? If you can, she's all yours."

The confidence in his voice, the cocksure tone of it made me worry. He had already planned on killing me and pawning this off on her if things went bad. Was there something wrong with her? Was *that* why she was so pale? So still?

Had he given her some bad drugs? Or too much?

I knew way too many women and kids who'd gotten a bad mix. I had horror stories I could tell, and I wouldn't put it past him either.

But I couldn't voice any of those fears right now, could I? Not with him staring me down, almost daring me.

"Here's the thing." Kaleb's face took on a menacing expression, and he took a step toward the other man.

Stefano's gun came up, and he leveled it at Kaleb's chest.

Fear exploded inside me, and I said, "Stop it, okay? Stefano, you got your money."

"Be quiet, bitch," he said, not even looking at me.

Kaleb held up a hand in my direction. I don't know if he was trying to calm me or quiet me, and I wanted to rip out my hair.

"I'm taking both Piety and Camry, and we're leaving. You got your damn money, so we're going. If you don't like it, you go ahead and shoot me." A bit of a smirk twisted his lips, even as I felt that fear expand and explode like it was going to eat me alive. "But I can guarantee you that won't go well."

Stefano laughed. "What, you think you're Superman? You think bullets will bounce off you?"

They were close now. So close.

Not even two feet separated them, and the gun was only inches from Kaleb's chest.

I tried to say Kaleb's name, but I couldn't even make my damn jaw move. I'd never felt fear like this, had never understood what it was like to be petrified by it.

What happened next was so mind-boggling, I still can't completely understand it.

Stefano nudged Kaleb's chest with the muzzle of the gun. "Come on, pretty boy. Do something."

And Kaleb did. He shot out a hand, twisted and moved. There was a sickening loud noise, and I clapped a hand over my mouth to silence a shriek. *Gun*, I thought. It was the gun.

But it wasn't loud enough to be a gun shot.

My brain knew the sound of a weapon. Dad owned a whole room full of firearms, and I'd learned how to handle them young.

It wasn't a gun.

But in the quiet of the room, it sounded terribly loud.

A split second after that thick, wet, cracking sound, a scream erupted and Stefano just...collapsed. He went inward, going to his knees while Kaleb twisted and moved, all but jerking the man around by his arm, an awkward marionette and his puppet master.

His wrist, I realized. Kaleb had broken the man's wrist. That horrendous crack I'd heard was the sound of a bone breaking, not a bullet.

Stefano was shouting, voice ragged and hoarse, now on his knees in front of Kaleb.

I had no idea how Kaleb had *done* that. I'd taken several courses in self-defense, and the fluidity of his movements bespoke of the ease some of the martial arts instructors had used.

"Wow. I think you really are Superman," I said, completely aware that I sounded like an idiot, but my brain was struggling to keep up too much for me to care.

Suddenly, Stefano roared and surged back to his feet, fumbling at his back with his one good hand. A moment later, there was another gun, but instead of trying to disarm Stefano again, Kaleb lunged for me.

"TIME!" Kaleb shouted.

It was a huge bellow and within a split second I was pinned under him.

Feet pounded.

Wood crashed.

Voices raged.

Through it all, Kaleb held me pinned to the floor, protecting me with his body. He murmured reassuringly, "Be still, baby. Just...be still."

At least that's what I thought he said through the cacophony that followed.

There was more crashing, shouting, and above it all, authoritative voices bellowing out, "Drop the gun!"

That command came from multiple directions, and I could hear more than one speaker.

As I shivered and shook, Kaleb murmured to me, "Be still. Don't move...you'll be alright."

I didn't have any choice. I was so stunned, I don't think I could've moved if my life depended on it.

"Be still...you're safe, baby. You're safe."

* * * * *

"Your blood pressure is fine. Your pulse is strong and steady. Unfortunately, there's nothing I can do to check on the baby, but if you're just barely pregnant, everything should be fine. But it would be a good idea to go to the hospital and get checked out." The paramedic gave me a solemn smile and held out a lollipop. "Want some candy? Always helped my wife when she was upset while she was carrying our first." He looked thoughtful for a moment and then added, "And our second. And our third."

"How many kids do you have?" I asked, shooting out a hand to take the sucker. It didn't matter that it was just a cherry flavored lollipop.

"Three." He grinned at me and added, "I'm trying to talk her into a fourth, but she says this third one will be the ruler of the universe, so I'm not sure if I can do it."

Kaleb sat next to me, rubbing my back. He was listening, sort of. But his eyes were on his sister, and so was most of his attention.

I understood.

Once the paramedic had assured him I was okay, he had focused on her, and to be honest, so had I.

She was still just as pale, just as still as she had been in the house. She hadn't moved once, hadn't made a sound.

I'd heard talk that was a little too familiar. The antidote to the overdose they suspected she'd been given wasn't working.

Her heartbeat was too slow, her blood pressure as well.

The paramedics were worried about her, and they were loading her into the back of an ambulance. They were already prepping a second treatment, and I closed my eyes, resting my head against Kaleb's shoulder.

Don't let it end like this, I thought. Not now that Stefano was out of the picture.

I hadn't told anybody what Stefano had threatened. Not yet. I would, but the cops hadn't even gotten around to taking my statement yet. They were too busy focusing on Stefano and Camry and gathering precious evidence, but I knew they'd get to me.

He was wailing for a lawyer from the back of a squad car, but the detectives were ignoring him. One told him

284

he could get his phone call once they got to the station.

I had a feeling he wasn't going to get out of this quite so easy.

Kaleb and the cops had actually been outside for over an hour, he told me, waiting for the right movement. They'd had microwaves up, the kind you'd think would exist in spy movies, and they'd caught the better part of the conversation from the past hour.

The cops probably already knew about his threat to kill me and frame Camry for it. Since he'd decided to go and kidnap somebody this time, it seemed to me he'd have a harder time sidestepping things. And I knew my dad would throw his weight into prosecuting the man too.

For once, I didn't mind at all knowing that being his daughter was going to make a big difference here. Stefano needed to be taken off the streets for decades, no matter what it took.

"Are you okay?" Kaleb murmured against my temple after the paramedic left.

I laughed weakly. "Okay?"

"Shit. What a stupid question. How can you be okay?" He hugged me tighter and whispered, "I'm so sorry, so fucking sorry you got caught up in this."

"Don't." I turned my face into his neck. "You're not responsible for this, so don't apologize." Then I tipped my head back and smiled at him. "And it could have been so much worse."

I shook my head, still baffled by everything he told me. I had no idea how he'd done all of this. Saving me. Shifting around, I wrapped my arms around his neck and cuddled close. The tears wanted to come out, but I didn't want to cry right now. Not here.

Later, maybe. When we were alone.

He nuzzled me, murmuring nonsensical words under

his breath. None of them made sense, but they did their job, soothing me when nothing should have been able to. I took a deep breath, and for the first time in hours, let some of the fear inside me drain away.

"Hey, Kaleb?" A watery laugh escaped me. "I think I'm pregnant."

He laughed too. The sound was strangled and raw. "Really? Huh. Maybe we should have a talk."

"Yeah, but not yet. I want to stay like this."

Chapter 16

Kaleb

"She's awake."

The doctor's words hit me like a leaden fist, heavy and bruising, and I stumbled back against the wall.

"What?" I asked.

"She's awake," he said again, gently smiling at me as if he understood. He came further into the waiting room where the nurse had asked me to wait. Camry was being examined when I came to check on her, so they hadn't let me in. I'd been about to leave and go back to Piety's side when the doctor appeared around the corner.

I'd been here before, waiting in a hospital to hear news about my family, and I'd prepared myself for the worst. And now he was telling me...

"She's awake." I swallowed, the words foreign and strange in my mouth. "Are there...?"

She had another treatment in the ambulance, and they'd told me her heart was dangerously slow. I hadn't understood any of the medical mumbo jumbo, save for that – dangerously slow.

I made myself finish the question. "Are there complications?"

"I think, after a few days of observation, she'll be fine. She's very malnourished, which isn't uncommon for addicts, so I'd like to keep her here and monitor her for a few days while we push fluids and try to stabilize her on that front." He glanced around and then nodded to one of the chairs. "Why don't we sit?"

I all but collapsed into the chair, the fear and adrenaline draining out of me, leaving me weak.

"Your sister…" He offered me a kind smile. "Camry has struggled with her addiction for some time, hasn't she?"

"I don't know if struggle is the right word. She's had quite a bit of fun with it lately, seems like." I felt bad saying it, but I was so tired of making excuses for her. I loved her, but she could have cost me something precious tonight – today. Fuck, I didn't even know what time it was. Anger tried to take root in me once more, but I didn't have the energy for it. Not right now.

"Well, I doubt we could call it fun. Your sister is quite depressed." The doctor settled back in the chair, studying me. "I understand you lost your parents young, and you had to raise her."

I could already feel the defensiveness rising, but I struggled to keep it at bay. "Yes. I know I wasn't able to give her everything–"

"This isn't your fault." He raised a hand. "I didn't mean to imply that. Your sister was old enough to understand what she was doing when she first started using. I've talked with her to some degree. She said you explained to her growing up, about drugs, sex…you had to be a brother and a parent. That couldn't have been easy."

I could feel the blood staining my cheeks, but I didn't look away. "Who else was going to?"

"And that's just the thing. You did everything you could, and she made the wrong choices. She chose. And you've tried to be there for her as much as you could. She understands that. She's…angry with herself more than anything, and that's the root of much of her depression, more than likely."

I narrowed my eyes. "Are you an ER doc or a shrink?"

He chuckled. "I started out in psych before I realized it was a lot easier to fix the body than the mind." His pale eyes became intense. "I think she wants help. Every addict hits rock bottom, Kaleb. And every loved one of an addict eventually hits a point when they don't want to reach out anymore. Sometimes that needs to happen before a person's ready to change, but I don't believe that's the case with your sister. This isn't the time to walk away from her."

Something tangled and twisted welled up in me. It was guilt, a feeling I knew too well. Throat tight and burning, I said, "Is it that obvious?"

"Well, I overheard the police talking. I can't imagine how angry you must be – and rightfully so." He inclined his head. "If you were to walk away from her now, you'd be completely entitled. Nobody could blame you at all."

"I would blame myself." I got up and moved to the door, staring out the block of glass toward her room. "I can do it…one more time."

But that was it. If she messed up again…

"I think one more time is all she needs."

* * * * *

289

A trim Asian woman was walking out of Camry's room just as I approached the door.

She paused and met my eyes. "You must be Kaleb."

"Ah, yeah." I racked my brain, trying to figure out who she was, but I came up empty.

"I'm Liushi Testudo, a friend of Samuel Westmore's." She smiled. "I've been trying to help him work on a way to keep you and your sister stateside. Assuming that's what you want, of course."

It was what I wanted...wasn't it?

A hard breath exploded out of me, and I shot a look at the room, where I could see Camry lying in her bed. She was curled up on her side, facing away from me. "What were you...ah...she needs an attorney, doesn't she?"

Medical bills. Lawyer bills.

How was I going to pay for any of this? Forget staying in the US. I'd be lucky not to be run out of the country.

"Yes," Liushi said. "She does. But that's not the kind of lawyer I am. I was testing the waters, so to speak, on behalf of a friend at the district attorney's office. Samuel gave me a head's up on what's been going on, and I called the DA and asked if he'd mind if I spoke with Camry. I had a feeling she might be willing to help us."

"And just what were you testing the waters for?" I had to fight not to throw in the word *sharks*.

This woman looked kind enough, but this was my baby sister. My fucked-up baby sister who could have gotten herself and Piety – and our baby – killed. She and I might have issues that needed to be dealt with, but I'd be damned if I threw her to the wolves.

"To see if Camry be willing to make a deal with the

290

DA and testify against Stefano Fuentas. I don't think you realize just how hard the police here in Vegas have been trying to put him away." She smiled again. "Her testimony could corroborate nearly every other piece of evidence the DA has against Fuentas, and her knowledge of his activities could lead them to even more. They want to make sure they have enough to put a nail in that snake's coffin, and she's agreed to help them do that." Liushi rested a hand on my arm for a moment. "Be gentle with her. She's fragile."

I stared at the narrow back of my sister and wanted to laugh, wanted to punch something.

Fragile.

She looked damn fragile, alright. Like she needed someone to take care of her. Except I'd been trying to help her for years, and had gotten shit for it.

But, I reminded myself, I'd told the doctor I'd give it one more try.

Thinking of my parents, they would've wanted that too.

One more try and if I didn't see a real effort, I'd wash my hands of her.

Slowly, I entered the room. Camry flinched at the sound of my footsteps, quiet as they were, but she turned toward me, her head down, face hidden.

"Hey," I said and stopped at the foot of the bed, feeling out of place and awkward. I hated it.

When had the two of us gone from being family to near strangers? The first few years after our parents had died, we'd been good together. I couldn't put my finger on when things had changed, but they had, and it made me sick. "Camry."

"What do you want?" she asked in a small, tired voice.

"What do I...?" I lashed down the anger that tried to come spiraling out. I had to make this last effort a valid one. "Camry, I was scared sick you wouldn't wake up. What do you think I want? I wanted to make sure you were okay. I needed to see you."

Finally, her eyes flicked my way through the heavy tangle of her hair.

It was dull and lank, and I remembered how it had once been her pride and joy. Was it the drugs? The malnutrition? I didn't know.

Somehow, the sight of her lying in the bed looking so broken managed to crack the hard shell of apathy and I sat on the edge of the bed.

Camry squeezed her eyes closed. "Why do you even want to be around me?"

"Because you're my baby sister," I said, brushing her hair back. "And I love you."

"Why? After everything I've done? After what could have happened?"

"Cam–"

Abruptly, she sat up, flinging my hand away. Color flooded into her cheeks, washing away some of the pallor and her eyes glistened. "You don't *get* it! Stefano made it all seem like it would be a big joke, and I *let* him talk me into it, but I knew it wasn't. I knew that he did horrible, awful things, and that he'd do them to her. But it didn't matter because he promised to give me money, and money meant *drugs*. Nothing else mattered. Not your cute girlfriend, not you. Not even..."

Her voice cracked.

"Not even the baby," I finished for her.

"Yeah." She lifted a fist to her mouth, gnawing on her reddened knuckles, worrying skin that was already sore and cracked. "Now I keep thinking about what might have happened, and I feel *sick*. But what's worse...I'm coming down off a high, and it's..."

She held out her hands and showed me how they were shaking. I took one of them in mine.

"And you're scared."

She nodded and her tears spilled over. "I was willing to do anything to get a fix, and I'm almost there again. So...yeah...why are you here, Kaleb? I'm a pathetic, weak mess. I can't do this. Not on my own."

I put an arm around her. "I guess that's why I'm here. You've never admitted any of that before, and I think that means you're ready to accept help. Let me be strong for you, Camry. Let me help you."

* * * * *

I left her sleeping, moving as quickly as I could through the hospital to the floor where Piety was being held for overnight observation.

They had Camry on a suicide watch. I didn't know if it was something she'd said or done, or if it was typical because of the drug abuse, but she was on the far side of the hospital from Piety, and I felt pulled in two, wanting to be there for them both.

Piety was lying on her side, a mirror of the way I'd found Camry, but instead of facing away and locking the world out, she was facing the door, eyes wide and expectant.

Waiting for me.

A smile curved her lips as I approached, and the ragged, aching mess in my chest faded away.

Just like that.

I snagged a chair as I went to her side, dropped it by the head of the bed, and sat down. I wanted to sit next to her, hold her, but I wasn't taking any chances. Not with her, not with our baby.

"I thought I might lose you," I said bluntly. "I've never been so scared in my life."

She reached up, cupping my face, and I turned my head to kiss her palm.

"I thought the same about you." She tugged me closer.

I never needed encouragement to kiss her, so I went gladly.

But she didn't kiss me.

She bit my lower lip – hard.

And fuck if it didn't send blood rushing straight to my dick.

"If you *ever* stand in front of a man with a loaded weapon like that again, I'll kill you myself," she said, her fingers tangling in my hair as she held me in place. "You understand?"

"I...yeah." My lip throbbed, but I didn't care. "I understand completely."

I leaned down and bit her lower lip, not as hard, just a slow, light pressure of my teeth on the plump curve, tugging it out before releasing it all together. I rested my forehead against hers.

"And don't you ever...hell. Don't ever leave my sight again. Okay?"

She laughed weakly. "That might be hard. And awkward. Like now. I have to pee. You don't need to come in."

"I should inspect the loo, just to make sure it's safe." I nuzzled her neck then stood, watching as she eased

294

upright.

A fist grabbed me by the throat, and I wanted to pull her into my arms, hold her while promising that nothing bad would ever happen to her again.

Instead, I helped her stand, and then stood guard while she went to the toilet. We were in a hospital and a ton of cops were still roaming the halls, but I didn't care. *Nothing* was going to get to her again.

When she came out, I caught her in my arms and tucked her head against my shoulder. The only time I could breathe was when I was with her, and I didn't know if I could ever let her go.

"Like this," she mumbled.

"Hmmm?"

"I want to stay like this for a thousand years."

I chuckled, rubbing my chin on top of her head. "We may need to pause from time to time to eat."

"Eat. Go to the bathroom..." She backed up and looked at me from under her lashes. "Ah...have a baby."

I blinked, suddenly feeling nervous. Right. "Um, yeah. Commercials for those tests say they're accurate really early, but it still seems too—"

"They're running a blood test. We'll know soon. The blood tests always hit the mark, Kaleb." She reached up and put her hand on my cheek, her expression serious. "If you...I mean, neither of us were planning this, so I understand if you—"

"I want to be with you." I cut her off and pressed my mouth to hers.

She sighed against my lips. "Kaleb?"

"It's insane, and I know it doesn't make sense, but I want to be with you. And if there's a baby, then I want the baby."

"Really?" She laughed, the sound bright and happy,

flooding the room. "Oh, man. Yes. Me too. Yes."

I lowered my head to kiss her – really kiss her – but there was a knock at the door.

We turned as one.

A man in a white lab coat stood there, and he nodded at us. "I know it's early yet, but you have some visitors, Ms. Van Allen. Their plane just landed."

My stomach dropped out, and Piety stiffened.

"Your parents," I murmured under my breath. "I'll go—"

But it was too late.

Piety's mother just barely beat her father through the door. She was, incongruously – at least I thought so – dressed in blue jeans and a blouse, her hair pulled back from her face.

"Piety," she said, her voice trembling.

The moment I released Piety, her mother was there, folding her into her arms. I edged back, even as Piety tried to catch my eye.

Looking at the doctor, I nodded at him. "I'll be in the waiting room."

"Kaleb." Silas Van Allan was standing in front of me.

Shit.

He held out his hand and I stared at it for what felt like an eternity before I shook it. "Mr. Van Allen."

He had dark circles under his eyes, and his gaze flicked past me to linger on his wife and daughter before re-focusing on me.

"Kaleb, please. I owe you the deepest of apologies," he said, his voice shaking for a moment before it firmed. "I misjudged you terribly, and I can never make up for that. You risked your own life to save my daughter. Please...will you...?"

He looked away, emotions warring on his face. Unsure how to handle this reversal of events, I reached out and took his hand again. He tightened his grip, eyes coming back to mine.

I waited for the cameraman to jump out and yell something like, *Joke's on you, mate!*

But the only thing that happened was Silas jerking me up against him in one of those back-slapping hugs that left me feeling like he might have jarred a few teeth loose.

Then he let me go and went to his daughter, and I was caught up in an embrace from Piety's mother, one that smelled of a soft perfume. Oddly, it reminded me of my own mother's scent, and my throat went tight.

"Please forgive us," she said, pulling back and staring at me solemnly, her eyes so much like her daughter's that it was surprising I hadn't noticed it before. "We were unkind, but we've only ever wanted what's best for her."

"It's…I understand."

"I don't see how." She offered me a wobbly smile, then looked over at her daughter. "We would like to…make a gesture, if you would. We heard that your sister is going to be helping put away that awful man, and we understand that she will be needing some...care for a while. Silas and I want to help. And we'll do everything we can to make sure the two of you can stay here in the US."

Chapter 17

Piety

Kaleb slid his mouth down my neck, teeth and tongue burning every place they touched. I wanted to grab him and rip his clothes away, but he wasn't having any of it.

I'd spent the night at the hospital, plus half the next day, waiting for the doctor to look me over so he could discharge me. Now, we were on our way to a hotel. We'd fly home tomorrow, but for tonight, the Bellagio would do.

Kaleb ran his hand up and down my thigh on the drive over, and the need to *touch*, to *connect,* was overwhelming. I wasn't sure how either of us could manage to hold on until we were through the door.

Finally, inside our hotel suite, his hands slid up my back, dragging my shirt with it, I unbuttoned his, with far more speed and far less grace than he showed. I needed to see him, touch him. I'd spent too much time recently thinking that I'd never get to do this again.

"Naked," I said. "I want you naked."

"Yes," he said breathlessly. "I want to see and touch every inch of you. That's the only way I'll be sure you're okay."

His tongue flicked the corner of my mouth, and my knees went weak.

"These past few days have been hell," he said.

"Absolutely," I agreed.

He ran his fingers through my hair and tugged my head back, but the desperate, dark kiss I'd been anticipating – *craving* – didn't happen.

Instead, he kissed me soft and slow, his lips gentle, tongue caressing mine. Instead of an explosion of passion, this was a slow burn, sparks being coaxed into flame. My heart swelled and tears burned in my eyes as he trailed a path down my chin, then my neck.

"Hold on to me," he murmured, boosting me up.

He didn't have to tell me twice. I'd hold onto him forever.

I wrapped my legs around his waist, arms around his neck, and he held me close as he carried me to the bedroom. Without a word, he laid me down and slowly stripped away every article of clothing I wore, letting his fingers trail over my skin. When I was finally, deliciously, bare, he pressed his lips to my belly.

Before he could move his mouth lower, I tugged on his shoulders. As much as I loved having his mouth on me, the ache inside me needed more.

"Take me." I could hear the desperation in my voice. "Please."

I *needed* it, needed to feel him deep inside, moving against me, and I needed to see his face as he made love to me. Everything that had happened in the past few days made me realize just how much he meant to me, and I knew this moment between us was going to be pivotal.

He nodded, as if he understood exactly what I meant.

Maybe he did.

We were almost…careful with each other. It wasn't something I could explain, the gentle way he touched me or the slow, almost teasing way he entered me.

By the time he filled me, we were both holding our breath, and it was almost painful to have him withdraw – we were part of each other.

But I needed more.

So did he.

He moved, finding a rhythm that kept him from being gone from me for too long, while I clung to him, my heels hooked over his ass, tightening every time he was too far away.

"Don't let go," he said, just as I started to come.

I wanted to tell him I wouldn't, not ever.

But I didn't have the breath.

So I just clung to him instead.

Epilogue

Piety

"Wow."

That voice, hesitant and soft, was now almost as familiar to me as Astra's and Kaleb's.

I looked up, met Camry's gaze in the mirror, and smiled at her. She smiled back, still hesitant and shy.

Things between us were…odd.

We were developing a friendship, but it was slow, and I was fine with that. I'd rather it be slow, real and enduring, than either of us faking it just because we were sisters-in-law.

I was wearing my wedding dress, and not some sexy little party dress like the one I'd worn when I'd married Kaleb just to piss my parents off.

In less than fifteen minutes, we were getting married…again, but this time in an official ceremony.

Something fluttered in my belly, and I gasped, pressing a hand to the round bump beneath my dress.

"Wow." Now, I was the one to say it.

"Nervous?" Camry offered a quick smile as she tucked her hair behind her ear.

She looked good. Much better than she had when I'd

301

first met her. It'd been nearly three months, but she was clean now, and working on outpatient therapy as she made good on her deal with the Las Vegas DA.

"Um…well, yeah, but I think the baby just moved."

Her eyes widened. "Whoa. Cool."

I grinned at her, echoing her statement.

Astra came sailing in, wearing a dress of dusky gold, reminiscent of the glamorous twenties. She even had a band around her head, one that did nothing to restrain her curls.

She caught sight of me and caught my face in her hands, then kissed me. "Checking – gotta make sure the lipstick is kiss-proof, PS."

I batted her hands away. "The baby kicked," I said, grinning.

"Really?" Her eyes popped wide, and she went to put her hand on my belly, but I smacked her away.

"No. Daddy gets to feel it first."

"Oh, fine. Spoilsport." Then she did a quick circle around me before turning to look at Camry.

Astra was nothing if not fiercely loyal, and she'd been upset when I'd told her Camry would be released from her mandatory rehab in time for the wedding.

But, the first thing Camry had said to Astra when they met yesterday was, "If you want to punch me, I'm fine with that."

Astra had huffed, saying, "I'd probably break you in half with a small swat."

That'd established a tentative truce between them, and I trusted it would hold.

My mother knocked before slipping inside, checking to make sure I was ready before opening the door for my father.

"Are you ready?" he asked.

I barely recognized the warm, loving man he'd become over the past few months. Nearly losing me, and then finding out about the baby, had changed everything. There were still times when they frustrated the hell out of me, but I no longer felt like every choice I made disappointed them. Now, I had a family I was happy to bring a child into.

"I'm ready," I said, smiling up at Dad as I wrapped my arm around his.

Kaleb was out there in the church, and I didn't intend to make him wait for me any longer.

Acknowledgement

First, we would like to thank all of our readers. Without you, our books would not exist. We truly appreciate each and every one of you.

A big "thanks" goes out to all the Facebook fans, street team, beta readers, and advanced reviewers. You are a HUGE part of the success of the series.

We have to thank our PA, Shannon Hunt. Without you our lives would be a complete and utter mess. Also a big thank you goes out to our editor Lynette and our wonderful cover designer, Sinisa. You make our ideas and writing look so good.

About the Authors
MS Parker

M. S. Parker is a USA Today Bestselling author and the author of the Erotic Romance series, Club Privè and Chasing Perfection.

Living in Southern California, she enjoys sitting by the pool with her laptop writing on her next spicy romance.

Growing up all she wanted to be was a dancer, actor or author. So far only the latter has come true but M. S. Parker hasn't retired her dancing shoes just yet. She is still waiting for the call for her to appear on Dancing With The Stars.

When M. S. isn't writing, she can usually be found reading– oops, scratch that! She is always writing.

Cassie Wild

Cassie Wild loves romance. Every since she was eight years old she's been reading every romance novel she could get her hands on, always dreaming of writing her own romance novels.

When MS Parker approached her in the spring about co-authoring the Serving HIM series, it didn't take Cassie many seconds to say a big yes, and the rest is history.

Printed in Great Britain
by Amazon

15863642R00180